'How dared you humiliate me before your mistress?' Her eyes flashed green fire. 'Why did you drag me in front of them as if I were some kind of prize?'

'My mistress once, but never since I first saw you,' he muttered hoarsely. He took two strides towards her, a nerve pulsing in his throat. 'My only thought was to see you and speak to you again when I saw you with the boy. You looked so beautiful with your hair blown by the wind and that wonderful, sleepy look in your eyes. I did not mean to humiliate you. I have thirsted for the mere sight of you these many days.'

'W-What do you mean?' she whispered. 'What are you saying?'

'Don't you know? How can you not feel it?' he whispered. 'It burns inside me like the fires of hell. I want—I need you so badly. Yet if I take what I desire, I am forever damned.'

She saw the tenseness in him and shivered. 'Why should you be damned?' she whispered, a little frightened by the intensity of his gaze. What terrible thing was in his mind that he should stare at her like that? She made an involuntary move towards him, as if wanting to ease his torment.

'Annelise, no,' he groaned. 'Do not tempt me so...'

Anne Herries was born in Wiltshire but spent much of her early life at Hastings, to which she attributes her love of the sea. She now lives in Cambridge but spends most of the winter in Spain, where she and her husband stay in a pleasant complex of villas and apartments nestled in the hills that run from Malaga to Gibraltar. She likes to swim, walk and lie in the sun weaving her stories of love, passion and intrigue. She writes for pleasure and to give pleasure, owing much of her inspiration to her appreciation of the beauty of nature. If she can bring a smile or perhaps a tear to the eye of her reader, she has achieved her ambition . . .

Anne Herries has written ten other Masquerade Historical Romances, including *The Flame and the Sword*, *The Sleeping Demon*, and *The Devil's Mercenary*.

# FOR LOVE
# AND LIBERTY

## Anne Herries

**MILLS & BOON LIMITED**
ETON HOUSE    18-24 PARADISE ROAD
RICHMOND    SURREY    TW9 1SR

First published in Great Britain 1988
by Mills & Boon Limited

© Anne Herries 1988

Australian copyright 1988
Philippine copyright 1988
This edition 1988

ISBN 0 263 76182 7

Set in Times Roman 10 on 11½ pt.
04-8810-77303 C

Made and printed in Great Britain

# CHAPTER ONE

'I THINK I shall sit here and rest for a while,' Lady Sophia Redstone said with a sigh, sinking on to the stone bench in the little arbour. 'You and Henry go on and explore the gardens, Annelise.'

The girl to whom she had been speaking looked at her in concern. 'Are you feeling ill, Sophia?'

'No, just a little tired. I expect it is the heat.' Lady Sophia was a lady of advancing years, to which she made little if any concession. She was dressed in the height of fashion, her grey curls peeping from beneath a fetching straw hat. 'Go on, my love,' she insisted. 'I know how much you are longing to explore. I shall be perfectly safe by myself for an hour or so.'

Annelise Pembleton hesitated as she looked at the woman she had come to love almost as dearly as her late mother. She was anxious about her, but there was also another reason why she would have preferred to stay with Lady Sophia: a reason she could not possibly put into words.

'Oh, come,' Henry Greenway said, speaking for the first time. 'There's no need to worry. Grandmama will be better left to herself for a while—and you've been saying how much you wanted to visit Fontainebleau.'

Annelise frowned, knowing that she could not make a fuss. 'We shall not be too long, dearest Sophia,' she said. 'If you're sure I can't do anything for you?'

'Go on.' Lady Sophia waved her away with a smile. 'I like young people to enjoy themselves.'

Reluctantly Annelise started down the path with her employer's grandson at her side. Lady Sophia treated her more as a daughter than as an employee, and she was very grateful to her for taking her in after the terrible tragedy that had killed both her parents. Mr Pembleton's carriage had gone over a cliff edge in the mist, killing him instantly and injuring his wife. Mrs Pembleton had lingered on a few days, dying in her own bed.

It would be impossible to tell such a generous woman as Sophia that her grandson was not a gentleman. Almost as impossible as it was to keep the impetuous young man at bay without provoking a serious quarrel. Annelise had already had to fend off his advances on several occasions, and a solitary walk in secluded gardens was the last thing she would have chosen. Her situation was, however, precarious.

After her father's death, she had discovered that she was practically penniless. She had always known that her mother had difficulty in keeping up appearances, since her father's gambling had almost prevented them from living decently. Mrs Pembleton had secretly sold most of her jewels to clothe herself and her only child properly, and until her death she had managed to live like a gentlewoman, keeping the full extent of her difficulties from Annelise.

When Annelise discovered that her father had lost their house at the gaming tables during his last visit to London, she was almost glad that her mother had died without ever knowing the truth. After being informed by lawyers that she no longer had the right to live in her own home, she sought the advice of her neighbour, hoping that Lady Sophia might recommend her as a companion to one of her wealthy friends in London.

'Indeed I shall not,' Lady Sophia had cried indignantly. 'You will come to me, my dear child. If anyone has a need of a companion, it is I.'

Annelise had accepted her offer gratefully. It meant that she could stay on in the small community that had been home to her all her life. There had been no mention of payment for her services, but Lady Sophia was always generous to her, ordering mourning gowns for them both and passing on little gifts from her own extensive wardrobe. Annelise's small store of money had soon gone and she was now totally dependent on her friend, who provided her with food, lodging and travelling expenses. In the circumstances, she felt unable to mention Henry's behaviour. Lady Sophia would have been upset and shocked if she learned that he had tried to force his kisses on her at least three times in the past month. He said that he was in love with her, but Annelise did not believe him, nor did she encourage his affections. She would have been much happier if he had returned to his usual haunts in London instead of accompanying them to France.

Annelise slowed her steps as she saw the direction they were taking. Lost in her own thoughts, she had not realised that the formal gardens had given way to a wood.

'I think we should turn back now, Henry,' she said. 'If we go any further this way it might take us hours to find the path back to Sophia.'

'Come on, Annelise,' Henry coaxed. 'I thought you liked walking? We've only just started to explore.'

'No. You may go on if you wish, but I shall return to your grandmother.' All Annelise's instincts warned her against penetrating further into the woods with Henry as her only companion.

As she turned away, he grasped her arm, swinging her round to face him. 'Don't be a little prude, Annelise,' he said, clearly annoyed. 'I've been wanting to be alone with you for ages.'

'Well, I have no wish to be alone with you!' Annelise told him. 'Why will you persist in this, Henry? I am not prepared to...'

Before she could say any more, he had pulled her into his arms and was forcing a kiss on her. She struggled violently, and when he tried to grab her again, she lashed out, striking him across the face. He recoiled in surprise: it was the first time that she had ever retaliated so fiercely.

Annelise regretted the blow immediately. 'I'm sorry, Henry. You left me little choice.'

'Vixen!' he cried. 'Go back if you want to—I'm going on.'

'Henry!' she called after him as he strode away. 'What shall I tell Sophia?'

'Tell her what you like,' he muttered, without turning round.

Sighing, the girl began to retrace her steps to the little arbour where they had left Lady Sophia. She would have to invent some story to explain Henry's absence.

It was the graceful way she moved that first drew Gérard's attention, that and the fact that she was walking alone in the gardens of Fontainebleau. She was not one of the court, of that he was instinctively certain, though she had a simple elegance that made every other woman he had seen that morning look suddenly overdressed. Her full-skirted gown of grey silk had a square-cut neckline that was modestly covered by a frilled white fichu. Hair the colour of chestnuts in sunlight was piled up in a sleek chignon that allowed two shining ringlets to fall delicately over one shoulder. Yet it was not until she paused for one moment, glancing his way, that he realised how beautiful she was.

'*Mon Dieu,*' he said, moved to speak aloud without being aware of it. 'A man might kill for those eyes...'

He heard a soft chuckle behind him, and turned to see the mocking smile on André Beaumarchais' lips. 'So the little English miss takes your eye, my friend? You are wasting your time. Brienne says she is made of ice.'

'Brienne!' Gérard's mouth curled scornfully, a flash of anger in his expressive dark eyes. 'A woman wise enough to refuse the attentions of that depraved swine deserves only respect.'

Gérard went on studying the girl. She seemed to be in some distress, and he toyed with the idea of going to her assistance.

'We all know how much you love the Marquis,' André said, a hint of amusement in his eyes now. He regarded the finely chiselled features of his friend's face with affection. The Comte de Montpellier was not the most popular man at court, but he knew him for a loyal comrade. Outspoken and hot-tempered, he had made several enemies, but none quite as dangerous as Pierre de Brienne. 'Your tongue is sharper than many a man's sword, Gérard, but be careful of Brienne. He never forgives an insult.'

'He has only to name his friends. I would willingly rid France of him—and his kind. They are parasites living on the blood of the people!'

André nodded, agreeing with the sentiment if not the manner in which it was spoken. 'Ah, the people...' He gave Gérard a quizzical smile. 'Your concern does you honour, monsieur, but it makes you few friends at court—especially in these days.'

'They are blind fools,' Gérard muttered hoarsely. 'Can none of them see which way the wind is blowing? Every attempt to raise money from those best able to afford it is strangled at birth. Yet they expect the people to pay without complaint. How long can it go on, André? How long before the oppressed rise up to sweep Brienne and his ilk into the pit of hell?'

'Rebellion?' André's brows rose. 'I do not believe it will come to that. His Majesty has said publicly that something must be done.'

'Words are easy!' Gérard scoffed impatiently, then checked as he saw André's eyes. His friend was a staunch royalist, and he did not wish to quarrel with him. 'I do not doubt that Louis means well, but he is ill served. Make no mistake, André, I do not wish to see rebellion in France. I fear it. There is a deep-seated anger in the hearts of our people, an anger that has been allowed to ferment for many years. If it should once be let loose...'

André's hand clasped his shoulder. 'I know you, my friend. I do not doubt your loyalty, but there are those who would carry tales against you to the King.'

'Let them! I say what I believe, and no man shall make me say otherwise.'

Seeing the stubborn set of his mouth, André laughed and changed the subject. 'She is leaving, Gérard. You have lost your opportunity, and it is my fault for distracting you with talk of politics.'

Gérard had already seen the girl hesitate and then turn aside. He wondered if she had lost her way, and was tempted to go after her. For one moment her eyes had met his, and he had felt disturbed by something in her look. He had seldom seen so lovely a face, and the mere sight had made his blood run hot. She was a stranger, he did not even know her name, and yet his inclination was to snatch her up and carry her to some secret hiding-place where they could be completely alone. Already he could taste the sweetness of those lips and feel the softness of that creamy skin against his own.

'Perhaps it is as well you claimed my attention,' he replied, with a smile of self-mockery. 'If she is as cold as Brienne claims, I might have made a fool of myself. A man could lose his head over such a woman.'

'Brienne is an ageing, foul-breathed roué,' André said with a grimace. 'I'll wager you could breach that citadel if you had a mind to it.'

'I do not even know her name.' Gérard shook his head, knowing that it would be foolish to become embroiled in such an affair. That girl was not a sophisticated woman of the court; she would expect too much from him. There was no room in his life for a woman like that. 'At another time I might have accepted your challenge for the sport of it, but there is more important work to be done.'

'Yet there must also be a time for play.' André's blue eyes danced with mischief, his thin, intelligent face breaking into a grin. 'Her name is Annelise Pembleton. She had a French grandmother. Her parents were killed in an accident last year, and she is Lady Sophia Redstone's companion. I should imagine she cannot enjoy the change in her circumstances. I'll wager my horse against yours that she will be yours within the month—if you apply yourself to it.'

'You would hazard Pegasus?' Gérard stared at him. 'You almost tempt me to it. I would pay a fortune for him—but it is not fair. I cannot lose either way. I win the girl and your horse.'

A burst of merry laughter broke from André's lips. 'He is yours only if the fair ice maiden becomes your mistress within the month. Come, the odds are fair— how can you refuse?'

Remembering their carefree days together at the Sorbonne, and the wild nights, Gérard knew that his friend was trying to lift his spirits, to recapture a happier time before the tragedy that had turned him into the man he was today. It was not possible to turn back the clock, and yet it would be pleasant to flirt a little with the lovely girl he had glimpsed so briefly. After all, he had nothing to lose but a horse!

'I do not know where to find her...'

'Lady Sophia was talking of going to Paris and then Versailles.' André's grin was reminiscent of a wolf cub at play, at once both evil and innocent. 'Did you not tell me that you had some business of your own in Paris?'

Amused at his friend's conniving, but not yet convinced, Gérard arched his brow at him. 'Did the little English rose prick you with her thorns? Is that why you want me to seduce her—to ease your hurt vanity?'

'You have forgotten Marielle,' André said with a shake of his head. 'I wish Mademoiselle Pembleton no harm. A companion with no fortune and no prospects might count herself fortunate to have you as her protector. Knowing you as I do, I am sure she would not suffer by it. No, Gérard, I dare not even attempt the citadel. You know my heart is entirely Marielle's. Even a glance at another woman would seal my fate. She would never speak to me again!'

Marielle was one of Queen Marie-Antoinette's ladies, and though beautiful, Gérard thought her proud and cold. He did not believe that his friend stood much chance of making her either his mistress or his wife. André was comfortably provided for, but not rich. Mademoiselle Marielle Dubonnet had her eyes set on more promising pastures, yet he could not hurt his friend by voicing his opinion bluntly. In this case, he believed discretion more valuable than frankness.

'My apologies. I had forgotten the delectable Marielle,' he said. 'Very well, the wager is set—but I shall hazard a thousand livres against Pegasus. My horse is not his equal.'

'The court is to remove to Versailles,' André said. 'His Majesty wishes to go hunting. Instead of going with Marielle, I shall come with you. It may make her realise my worth if I am not forever at her beck and call.'

'You believe absence makes a woman's heart warmer?' Gérard nodded. 'At least it will serve to test your own feelings—and I shall be glad of your company...'

Annelise glanced out of the coach window. They had left behind the wild beauty of the forest and she could no longer smell the scent of pine or see the majesty of ancient oak trees. Leaning back in her seat, she smothered a sigh as she looked at Henry's sulky face. He had still not recovered from his tantrum in the wood, and she had no doubt that he would find some way to make her suffer for it. This trip to France would have been so much better without him.

When Lady Sophia had announced her intention of travelling to France, all her friends had warned her against it. General opinion was, first, that Sophia was too old to stand the journey, and second, that it was a bad time to travel in that country.

'Nonsense!' Lady Sophia refuted all the well-meaning advice offered her. 'I may be past the first flush of youth, but I'm a long way from the grave yet,' she declared. 'And as for the rest...' She screwed up her mouth in disbelief. 'The French peasants have always been poor. They were starving when my father took me to Versailles as a girl, and I remember talk of unrest. It came to nothing then and it will come to nothing now.'

Since they had been in France, Annelise had begun to wonder. She had noticed the sullen look on the faces of men gaunt from hunger, and the way they stared at her as she rode by in her friend's carriage. It was almost as if they were calculating the price of the clothes she was wearing in terms of how much food the money would buy. Thin, with greasy hair and ragged clothes, they made her very aware of how fortunate she was, but it was the plight of the children that touched her heart, making her throat tighten. Little pinched faces with bright hopeful eyes stared at her from the side of the road as if silently begging her to help, and how often had she longed for a few coins of her own to give them! Suggesting it once to Lady Sophia, she had been crushed by Henry's sarcastic response.

'If Grandmama is foolish enough to do as you suggest, it would start a riot,' he said, looking at her as if she were a fool. 'These people are savage brutes; they would as soon slit your throat as look at you. Give them a crumb, and they will take everything you have.'

'I'm afraid Henry is right, my dear,' Lady Sophia had agreed regretfully. 'My father forbade me to offer them money when I was a girl. He said that they made themselves out to be poorer than they are to play on the consciences of their betters.'

Henry nodded his approval. 'Quite right. One shouldn't encourage them to beg. There is work enough for the honest man.'

Disgusted at his attitude, Annelise wondered if he knew how pompous he sounded. His boots would probably cost more than these men could earn all year. Not that he had earned the money to pay for them himself! Sensing his smouldering gaze on her even as she looked out of the carriage windows, she ignored it. He was the kind of man she particularly disliked and whom she was forever meeting in both English and French society, who was selfish and careless of everything save his own pleasure.

A sigh escaped her as she remembered his unpardonable behaviour in the woods. Were all men as selfish as Henry? Her father had frittered his fortune away without a thought for their comfort, and she was relieved that she could not now be expected to marry. Having no dowry, it was unlikely that she would receive an offer from a man of her own class. The sons of country landowners looked for the daughters of wealthy men to consolidate their fortunes. Most of her friends had little say in their own futures, seemingly content to exchange their single status for a comfortable home, children and servants to wait on them. Apart from a slight regret that she would not have children of her own, she was inclined to think that a spinster's life might suit her. She was an independent girl with a temper that was slow to rise but formidable when in full force. For the moment, she was content to be Lady Sophia's companion and could have been completely happy, if it were not for Henry...

Suddenly Annelise found herself thinking of a man she had noticed in the gardens at Fontainebleau. She had been aware of him because he had been staring at her so intently. For that moment when their eyes met and held, she had felt mesmerised. It was as if she had been running for a long time, and her chest felt tight. She had thought he meant to approach her, an odd sensation that was half relief, half regret running through her as he turned away to speak to another man.

It was ridiculous, of course. The man was a stranger and they would never meet again—so why should she have felt that they had met before? He had been very striking, though, his lean face finely drawn with high

cheekbones and an aristocratic nose; his mouth full and
sensuous. He had been wearing court dress, his satin
coat moulding to his shoulders—shoulders so broad that
they needed no padding to show them off. Large boned
and tall, there was not an ounce of excess flesh on him.
He had been wearing his dark hair long, drawn back
from his face and tied with a bow: a black satin bow.
A delicate blush touched her cheeks as she realised that
she had noticed this tiny detail. She must have been
staring at him almost as intently as he had at her. How
very embarrassing! He would think her very bold.

'Did you enjoy your visit to Fontainebleau?' Lady
Sophia asked, hiding a yawn behind her gloved hand.
'The château was not as impressive as Versailles, I
thought, but it is steeped in history. Diane de Poitiers
lived there until Catherine de' Medici took it from her
after King Henry died. That was pure spite, of course.
She couldn't bear that her husband's mistress should
have such a lovely house to remind her of the happy
times spent there. Did you know they say Catherine had
spy-holes bored in the floors of her palaces so that she
could watch her husband with his mistress?'

Annelise smiled to herself. Lady Sophia adored gossip,
and collected stories about the French kings and their
mistresses. Sometimes she wondered how the old lady
managed to discover the most intimate details.

'The gardens were beautiful,' she said. 'Were they not
laid out by Le Nôtre?'

'Yes, I'm sure you are right,' Lady Sophia began.
'Oh!'

Her cry of alarm was caused by a sudden lurch of the
coach. There was a sharp cracking sound and she was
flung forward as the carriage tipped drunkenly to one
side, swaying sickeningly for a moment before settling
at an awkward angle.

'What's happening?' she whimpered, clutching at the padded side of the vehicle and looking very shocked.

'We've broken the leading pole,' Henry announced with a curse as he stuck his head out of the open window. 'It's these damnable roads—and we're in the middle of nowhere.'

He opened the door and jumped out, beginning a fierce argument with the unfortunate coachman and Lady Sophia's groom. The men unharnessed the horses, leading them to the side of the road before gathering round the offending pole, which was seen to be badly shattered. Henry came back to the window.

'You'll have to get out. We need to drag the coach off the road.'

Lady Sophia was pale and trembling. She pressed a scented kerchief to her lips, feeling the odd pain in her breast. It had happened once or twice lately, but she had dismissed it as indigestion. This time, though, it was really rather unpleasant and she was reluctant to move, but Henry was holding out his hand impatiently. She was shaking as she gave him hers. He half lifted her to the ground, a look of unusual concern in his eyes as he saw how shaken she was.

'Are you ill?' he asked. 'Annelise, look to your mistress. The shock has been too much for her.'

Shaken herself, Annelise had already made a brief enquiry about her friend's well-being, but now the note of alarm in Henry's voice made her take more notice. It was unlike him to notice his grandmother's condition. Seeing how grey her friend's face looked, Annelise hurried to join her on the grassy verge.

'Were you hurt just now?' she asked. 'Perhaps it would be best if you sat down for a while. The grass is quite dry.'

'Yes, I think I will.' Lady Sophia gave her an apologetic look. 'Would you fetch my vinaigrette, my love? I left my reticule in the coach.'

'Of course,' Annelise said, feeling anxious. It had been a nasty shock for all of them, but Lady Sophia was not a young woman. She climbed back inside the coach, snatching up the velvet purse, from which she took a small silver box and handed it to Sophia.

Opening the top, Sophia waved it under her nose and inhaled. The little sponge inside was soaked with a restorative substance that made her cough. She clicked the lid down and declared herself much recovered. Indeed, her heart had ceased to behave so stupidly and the pain was easing.

'Well, this is a nuisance,' she said with an attempt at normality. 'The coach cannot be repaired tonight and we must be still some distance from Paris.'

'The coachman must walk to the nearest inn and fetch help,' Annelise replied. 'Do not distress yourself. I am sure that...' She broke off as she heard hoofbeats approaching fast. Along the road they had just travelled, a coach was coming towards them at speed, and she caught her breath. Would the driver see the obstruction in his path in time? There was a startled yell and a shrill scream from the horses as he tugged at the reins, halting them bare seconds from disaster. 'Thank God! I thought there must be a collision.'

'What the devil!' A head was poked through the window of the second coach, and a tirade of abuse poured from the man's painted lips. Seeing at last that cursing would not help, he got out of the coach, twitching the stiff skirts of his satin coat angrily as he minced towards them on high-heeled shoes. Annelise's heart sank as she saw who it was. Why, oh why, did it have to be he? 'Your vehicle is blocking the road, madame,' he announced unnecessarily. 'Please have it removed at once.'

'We are trying to do so, Monsieur de Brienne,' Annelise said quietly, moving in front of her friend to protect her from his wrath. 'Perhaps, if your servants could assist ours, it might be done sooner?'

He glared at her as if he were about to launch into another tide of abuse, then turned and gestured impatiently to his groom. 'You were almost the cause of an accident, Mademoiselle Pembleton. Only my driver's skill prevented it.'

It was on the tip of her tongue to reply that it was his coachman's reckless driving that had almost resulted in disaster, but she checked herself. 'I apologise, monsieur. Lady Sophia is unwell. Can you tell us if there is an inn nearby? Our vehicle is in need of repair.'

'You will find one a few leagues further on,' he said crossly. Then his eyes narrowed as he looked at her, noting the delicate blush on her cheeks and the sweet curve of her mouth. She was beautiful enough to whet his jaded appetite, something fewer and fewer women could do these days. At their last meeting he had found her unapproachable, her eyes cutting him with disdain when he had paid her a magnificent compliment. He was not used to being treated so coldly and it had made him angry, but now she was behaving with proper modesty, showing the respect he felt due to his importance. It was an interesting situation, and one that might turn out to his own advantage. 'Perhaps I could offer you and Lady Sophia the comfort of my carriage? It would be no trouble to me to take you as far as the inn.'

Annelise disliked the way he was eyeing her, rather as he might a filly he was preparing to purchase, but she knew her friend was in desperate need of rest. Lady Sophia could not walk to the inn, and she ought not to be sitting in the fierce heat of the afternoon sun. Controlling a surge of revulsion, she forced herself to smile at him. 'You are very kind, monsieur.'

The servants had combined to push Lady Sophia's coach to the side of the road. Henry was red-faced and sweating as he came up, having been unwise enough to help them. 'There's an inn not far from here,' he said. 'I'll take one of the horses and go for help.'

'The Marquis has kindly offered to take us in his carriage,' Lady Sophia said. 'Please help me up, Henry. Then you may tell Jarvis to stay here with the baggage until arrangements can be made to convey it to the inn.'

Henry looked disgruntled as he realised that the ladies were to travel in comfort, but he thought it would make him look foolish if he changed his mind and asked to ride in the coach. Besides, he was a little out of his depth with sophisticated courtiers like Brienne, feeling that they thought him a country oaf and rather stupid. He had never been a brilliant scholar, and his French was stilted and spoken with a very English accent. Unlike Annelise and his grandmother, who were both fluent in the language, he felt ill at ease in the company of such men. Not that he respected them. He thought their manners so nice as to be almost pompous and their clothes too pretty by half. He was damned if Brienne was not wearing perfume and rouge! It was typical of these Frenchies. Any man worth his salt smelt of horses and sweat—and was proud of it!

'Very well, I shall see you later,' he said, turning away. 'I'll go on ahead to see that rooms are prepared for you.'

'Come, madame, give me your hand.' The Marquis was a model of polite concern as he helped Lady Sophia into the coach. Having seen her comfortably settled, he turned to Annelise with a gleam in his eyes. 'Mademoiselle...'

She could have entered the coach without his help but felt obliged to give him her hand. His fingers clasped hers possessively in a moist, warm grip that made her want to pull free at once. Controlling the shiver of revulsion that went through her, she managed to give him a smile that was polite but had no warmth.

'Thank you, monsieur.'

Brienne inclined his head, giving an order to his servants before climbing in. He sat as close to her as he could, his leg pressing against hers intimately as the coach began to move forward. Annelise held her breath, waiting for one second before leaning across to enquire after her friend's comfort. Under this pretext, she was able to move away from him without making it too obvious, though as he made no further attempt to touch her, she believed he had understood her motive.

It was but a short journey to the inn, though it seemed an eternity to Annelise. She was painfully aware of the man at her side, feeling his nearness a threat even though she knew she was safe enough while Lady Sophia was there. Thankfully, the inn proved to be a respectable house where they could comfortably stay for the night. The host hurried out to greet them, obviously pleased to have so many distinguished guests. He conducted Lady Sophia up a short flight of stairs, ushering her into a bedchamber that was both clean and adequately furnished. Assuring them of his undivided attention, he bowed his way out, leaving the ladies to themselves.

'Thank goodness the Marquis came when he did, my dear,' Lady Sophia said, sinking on to the bed with a sigh. 'Such foolishness! I am better now, of course, but I think I should like to rest.'

'May I do anything for you?' Annelise asked.

'No. I shall be perfectly well in a little while. You rest yourself, my dear.'

'If you are sure you do not need me, I think I might go for a walk. There was a small stream a short distance back, and it looked very pleasant. You know I like to walk when I can.'

'If only I had your energy.' Lady Sophia sighed. 'When I was your age, I spent every night dancing and was always ready to go riding in the morning. What it is to be young! Well, you must do as you please.'

After first making sure that Sophia had everything she might need to hand, Annelise went to the room the innkeeper had allocated to her, tidying herself quickly before going out into the hall and down the stairs. It was not a large house, and she could hear voices downstairs as she paused for a moment to get her bearings. Glimpsing Henry in the parlour refreshing himself with a glass of wine, she hurried past, making her escape into the sunshine.

# CHAPTER TWO

How GOOD it felt to be alone for a while! Annelise was very grateful to Lady Sophia for taking her in, but it was heaven just to slip away now and then. She walked swiftly, skirting the back of the stables so as not to be noticed, wanting to be quite certain that she had managed to avoid Henry's eagle eye. If she could tell Sophia of his advances, her ordeal would be at an end, but she knew it would upset her and she did not want to cause an unpleasant scene. If only her mother had not had to sell all her jewels. With just a little money of her own, she would have felt so much more independent. Really she ought to ask Sophia for a small wage, but she could not bring herself to do it.

All her troubled thoughts fled as she came to the stream. Catching sight of it earlier through the trees, she had not realised quite how beautiful it was. The sparkling water rushed busily over large boulders, its sound like music to her ears. There were daisies growing thickly along the bank, purple vetch and pink willowherb. Tiny jewel-coloured birds swooped to kiss the surface with their breasts before soaring to the sky. It was very warm, but the tinkling of the water had a refreshing effect. She found herself a patch of dry grass beneath a tree and sat down, content to observe the beauty around her. One day, when she had leisure, she would try to capture this scene on canvas.

There had been warm summer days in the little Sussex village where she had grown up. She had spent hours walking, observing the peculiar shape of a tree or the way the river changed colour with the seasons. Later, when she was able, she had begun to sketch and then paint her impressions, discovering a talent for expressing her love of nature. Sometimes her mother had scolded her for wasting her time, but she had never neglected her household tasks.

Those happy days were gone forever, and she knew she had to provide for herself. She had been more than fortunate to be given an opportunity to travel with her friend. It must improve her education, and that would be a help when... Her reverie was interrupted by the sound of a twig snapping beneath someone's foot. She looked up, expecting to see Henry. Instead, the Marquis de Brienne was standing a short distance away, and she was immediately aware of the danger of the situation, seeing the wolfish expression on his face. Getting to her feet at once, she stared at him uncertainly. The Marquis was infinitely more dangerous than Henry!

'I have disturbed you,' he said, a gleam of satisfaction in his eyes. This was more than he had hoped for. It was just by chance that he had glanced out of his carriage window and seen the girl slipping away. 'Forgive me, mademoiselle. You looked so charming that I only wished to observe you from a distance. To worship at the shrine of innocent beauty.'

He was lying to soothe her anxiety, thinking to lull her into a state of unawareness, but she had seen that look in his eyes, and knew he must have followed her from the inn. Men like Pierre de Brienne did not follow women for the pleasure of watching them from a distance. Alone in this isolated spot, she was at a disadvantage. It had been foolish to seize this chance of a solitary walk, for this was not a quiet English village where everyone knew and respected her family. This was

France, and the Marquis, if rumour were true, had little respect for anyone or anything.

'Excuse me, monsieur,' she said. 'I must return to my friends.'

'Stay for one moment,' he murmured silkily, a slight movement of his eyelids reflecting his excitement. It would be amusing to tame the English bitch! 'It is so peaceful here, and I would relish the opportunity to be alone with you for a while. Do you not think we could find a pleasant way to pass the time? You must be aware of the very warm feelings I have towards you . . .'

She felt her heart jerk as he moved deliberately to block her path, but fought for calm. She must not show fear; he would enjoy that too much. Her deep emerald green eyes glinted with annoyance as she looked at him. No gentleman would take such an advantage, and she was tired of being pestered by men with no manners. Twice in one day was definitely too much!

'Please allow me to pass, monsieur.' The ice in her tone allowed little doubt of her feelings.

Brienne's eyes narrowed menacingly. 'What, have you no gratitude for my kindness earlier? You might be sitting by the road yet had I not picked you up.'

'I am grateful for that,' Annelise said, her cheeks pink. 'I have thanked you already, as has Lady Sophia. What more do you expect?'

It was the wrong thing to have asked. She realised it as she watched his mouth curve into a sneer of triumph, and guessed what was in his mind. Instinctively she moved backwards as he reached for her.

'How dare you?' she cried indignantly, a surge of disgust running through her as she saw undisguised lust in his face. The man was depraved! 'Have you forgot your manners?'

'I believe my generosity deserves some reward. Come, mademoiselle, your coldness does not deceive me. I am certain there is passion in you. Do not play the innocent, for I am in no mood to be thwarted by a mere companion! You should think yourself fortunate that I deigned to look on you with favour.'

'What are you suggesting?' Annelise stared at him in horror. Henry's clumsy attempts at seduction had never frightened her, but there was something chilling in the way that this man looked at her; something predatory that made her feel like a victim. 'You cannot mean... You cannot...' She backed away from him in disbelief. Nothing she had yet experienced in the twenty years of her life had prepared her for this. She realised that the rumours about him must be true. Rumours of rape, brutality—and even, it was whispered, murder. Lady Sophia had tended to discount them, but she too was an innocent, having lived quietly in the country away from the intrigues and scandals of court life for so many years. Panic suddenly swept through her and she put out a hand to ward him off. 'Don't you dare to touch me!'

He laughed, an ugly leer curving his mouth as he lunged at her again. Fear spurred her to such desperate action that she kicked his shin as hard as she could and ran, gathering her full skirts above her ankles. She had neat, slender ankles and shapely legs, and in her haste to avoid capture, she was unaware of just how much was revealed by her undignified flight through the meadows, or of the picture she made as she scrambled up the grassy bank that led to the high road, her petticoats frothing about her knees. Her one thought was to outdistance the man chasing her. Fortunately she was young and had a healthy constitution; her pursuer had never really stood a chance and his pace had already slowed to a walk.

Thus it was that the two riders did not at first see him. The sight of Annelise appearing over the bank with her petticoats flying and her straw hat slipping on its ribbons halfway down her back was so astounding that both men reined to a halt, staring with obvious surprise at her and then with amusement at each other. She paused momentarily as she saw them, her eyes opening wide as though in shock or embarrassment, then she set off down the road, running as if all the demons in hell were after her.

'I must be seeing things,' André said. 'I could have sworn that was your modest little English rose.'

'Yes—and look yonder.' The smile on Gérard's face was replaced by a frown. 'There is the reason for her flight.'

André turned his startled gaze in the direction indicated. Seeing a very disgruntled-looking Marquis limp up the bank and stare after the fleeing girl with obvious frustration, he grinned. 'Methinks the lady declined,' he said, loudly enough for Brienne to hear. 'And none too gently, by the looks of it.'

The Marquis glared at him but made no reply. He had been made to look a fool, and a dignified retreat was clearly called for. However, Annelise had kicked him hard on a particularly tender spot and it was becoming painful for him to walk. Contenting himself with a promise of revenge if ever he got the opportunity, he turned and limped away, preferring to take the alternative route to the inn and his waiting coach. The sooner he was on his way, the better. That cold bitch was not worth the effort he had wasted on her!

Gérard watched him for a moment, his dark eyes brooding. The outcome of whatever had taken place a few minutes earlier was plain—but what had the girl been thinking of to meet the Marquis in such an isolated place?

It was an ideal spot for seduction. No sensible woman would risk being alone with a man like Pierre de Brienne unless she was willing to accept the consequences. She must have agreed to meet him, so what had Brienne done to make her change her mind? She had surely not believed that the Marquis would be satisfied with a mere flirtation?

'You say nothing?' André glanced at him curiously.

'Since I do not know what took place, I can make no judgement.' Gérard shrugged, seemingly unconcerned, though the glitter in his eyes told his friend the true story. 'My throat is dry. We'll stop for wine at the inn.'

Sensing the anger in him, André was silent. Gérard could not imagine that the English girl had been keeping a tryst with Brienne? He personally had met Annelise only once, but that was enough to convince him that she would never encourage the attentions of such a man. Besides, he had heard a tale circulating at court about her coldness towards the Marquis at a masquerade party she and her friends had attended a few days previously. The girl had been nicknamed 'the Ice Maiden' by the thwarted Marquis, and the ladies had laughed about it behind their fans. How naïve this English girl was not to know how to refuse an amorous advance without making her admirer angry! Love affairs, flirtations and discreet assignations were the lifeblood of the court, and it was a simple thing to encourage or discourage by a look or a flick of a fan. It was obvious that Annelise was an innocent—a country girl! André knew that many of the sly whispers were born out of jealousy. Her fresh complexion had made half the women die of envy, and her natural elegance put their studied sophistication to shame. Wearing simple gowns and hardly any jewellery, she outshone them all—Marielle Dubonnet excepted, of course—and they hated her for it. Yet even if she had been keeping a rendezvous with Brienne, why should Gérard be angry? When André had suggested the wager to him it had been in an attempt to turn his mind from... Well, he had been jesting, not expecting his friend to take him seriously. Now he wondered if the Comte had been more affected by the girl than he had at first realised. If so, it would be little less than a miracle!

'We can cancel the wager if you wish,' he said suddenly.

'Why?' The dark eyes had an unusual hardness in them. 'Are you afraid that I shall succeed?'

'Damn you, Gérard! I've never defaulted on a wager yet.'

'Nor I.' The Comte de Montpellier turned his gaze on his friend. 'Win or lose, it will be worth the effort, I think...'

Looking at his face, André wondered.

Reaching her own room, Annelise locked the door and leaned against it, her breast heaving as she fought to recover her breath. She was no longer afraid of being caught by the Marquis, realising that he had given up the chase almost at once, but her thoughts were in confusion, her cheeks hot, mostly because of the look of what she had thought was scorn in *his* eyes. It had shocked her to see *him* like that; the man from the gardens of Fontainebleau, as she had named him. In his riding-coat of dark blue cloth, his appearance seemed somehow sterner. The laughter she had glimpsed about his mouth earlier had disappeared completely, leaving it hard and cold. Or perhaps that was only her imagination? Because she had felt such a fool for appearing like that over the bank with her clothes in disarray?

Taking off her hat, she went to the wash-stand in the corner and poured water from a porcelain jug into the bowl, splashing her face and neck. The cooling sensation was very welcome, helping to restore her composure. It was foolish to imagine that she had seen censure in the stranger's eyes. At most, he could only have been surprised by her odd behaviour. Why should he be angry? It could be nothing to him. Yet she had thought there had been a glint of anger there, or perhaps it was merely a natural disgust at such unladylike behaviour? She knew that the French were strict about matters of etiquette, though from her recent experience with the Marquis, their morals left much to be desired! No, she would not condemn them all because of that man, she decided. She was a fair-minded girl, and until today she had met with nothing but kindness from the gentlemen of France—if not from some of the ladies. Aware of jealousy in certain quarters, she had done her best to ignore it. Was it her fault if their husbands paid her pretty compliments? She had certainly done nothing to encourage them.

Without being vain, Annelise knew that she had been blessed with an exceptionally pretty face. Before her parents had died there had been talk of finding her a rich husband in London, but she did not wish to marry for money, she was determined to marry only if she found a man whom she could truly love and respect. Now, of course, this was no longer a problem. She would probably end her days as a lady's maid. No, as a governess, she decided. That would suit her very much better. It had troubled her conscience to be dependent on Lady Sophia's generosity, and now she had made up her mind. She would say nothing for the moment, but when they returned to England and her friend had no more need of a companion, she would look for a position in a large household—a house full of children. As an only child, she had felt the lack of kindred spirits, but at least her loneliness had taught her to be self-reliant.

A little smile tipped the corners of her mouth as she recalled the startled look in the Marquis's eyes when she kicked him. Had he really imagined that she would swoon in his arms? She had put every bit of her strength into that kick, and she knew it had hurt. Glancing over her shoulder just once, she had seen him limping. It served him right, she thought with satisfaction. She had given him no reason to think she would welcome his advances—but then, a man like that needed none. It was unfortunate that it was his carriage that had come along when Lady Sophia was in such need.

Remembering the grey look about her friend's face after the accident, she forgot her own problems. The journey might be proving too much for Lady Sophia, after all. It was time she went to see how she was, and she knocked softly at the door, not wanting to wake her if she was sleeping, but Lady Sophia called out at once that she might enter. Annelise's eyes went anxiously to the gentle, lined face, relief flooding through her as she saw an improvement.

'You are feeling better, I can tell.'

'Yes, much better, my love.' Sophia's faded blue eyes twinkled at her. 'Such a foolish thing to happen. It was just the shock, I expect.'

Annelise felt a rush of affection. A post as governess would have to wait until she was quite sure that Sophia did not need her. 'Would you like me to help you to dress?'

'If it is no trouble. It was most inconsiderate of Bertha to fall ill the moment we went on board ship. I simply could not bear the thought of having a stranger to act as my personal maid.'

Since Bertha's illness had seemed serious, they had been obliged to leave her behind in Calais, and Annelise had taken on her duties without complaint—she had had little choice. It would only be until Bertha felt well enough to join them in Paris.

It took almost an hour to get Lady Sophia ready, by which time it was past five. Annelise hurried away to change her own gown, arranging to meet her in the dining-parlour. Henry would come to escort his grand-mother as usual, and as she liked to dine before six o'clock, there was not a second to be lost.

It wanted ten minutes to the hour when Annelise left her own room, immaculately dressed in a pale lilac gown. She was wearing a small gold watch, the bow set with diamonds, pinned to the dip of the bodice. Her father had bought it for her last birthday in a moment of un-usual generosity. She treasured it, and had refused to part with it, even though her last few coins had gone to pay the servants' wages. She was not sure why it meant so much to her, but the memory was something special and she was determined never to sell her father's gift.

Hurrying downstairs, she had almost reached the dining-parlour when she saw the two men standing in the hall. They seemed to be discussing whether to go in. As she hesitated, unable to avoid them but not wanting to push by, one of them came towards her and she re-called having met him before.

'Mademoiselle Pembleton—you remember we were introduced by Madame Dubonnet?'

'Monsieur Beaumarchais.' Annelise smiled, her eyes straying to the second man, despite herself. 'I am pleased to meet you again.'

'May I present my friend, mademoiselle?' André turned smoothly to draw Gérard into the conversation. 'Mademoiselle—the Comte de Montpellier.'

For a moment neither spoke as they gazed into each other's eyes, both aware of the charged atmosphere, then Gérard smiled. 'I am enchanted, mademoiselle. Tell me, how do the English ladies manage to keep their complexions while travelling in warmer climates?'

'With some difficulty,' Annelise quipped, feeling startled. It was an unexpected remark—a compliment, yet not a compliment. She usually found the extravagant praise of her beauty that some men heaped on her embarrassing, but the look in the Comte's eyes was having an odd effect on her breathing. 'Lady Sophia will never venture out without her hat and her parasol,' she managed to add.

'Yet I would have said that your skin was ever fairer than hers?'

Immediately, she knew that he was hinting at her mad flight through the meadows. He *had* been looking at her with censure! She thought she sensed a certain coldness beneath the charming smile and wondered at it, but then he was speaking again.

'The innkeeper tells us we must all share his parlour this evening. Do you think your companions will resent the intrusion? I believe you had requested a private room.'

'I am sure Lady Sophia could have no objection,' Annelise said, her face serious now. She was not sure how to take him; his manner was outwardly charming, but what was in his mind? 'Excuse me, please, I must join her.'

They stood aside to allow her to pass, and she went into the low-ceilinged parlour. It was a small but pleasant room with oaken beams and an inglenook fireplace, flanked by heavy dressers that were set with a variety of pewter platters and tankards. There were also several dishes containing joints of cold beef, ham, cheeses and

freshly-baked bread. The innkeeper's wife, a comely
pink-cheeked woman, had set a tureen of fragrant soup
on the table where Lady Sophia and Henry were seated.
They glanced up as she hurried to join them.

'I am sorry to keep you waiting,' she apologised, re-
ceiving a dark look from Henry. 'I was delayed for a
few moments.'

'You know Grandmother cannot eat later than six if
she is to sleep at all,' he reproved her.

'Hush, my dear.' Lady Sophia smiled at Annelise. 'I
thought you would not mind if we started the soup, but
now you are here and we can be comfortable.'

'It is very good soup,' Annelise said, as she swallowed
a spoonful of the tasty broth. Her eyes strayed to the
door as the two men she had spoken to a moment ago
entered and were shown to their table.

'I bespoke a private room,' Henry growled, scowling.
'That fool of a landlord must have misunderstood me.'

'No, he has only the one dining-parlour,' Annelise
said. 'Those gentlemen are the Comte de Montpellier
and Monsieur Beaumarchais. The landlord could hardly
turn them away...' She stopped speaking as the Comte
came towards them. He halted in front of Lady Sophia,
bowing his head in greeting.

'Madame, forgive this intrusion. It should have been
your private room. I trust we do not disturb you?'

'Not all all, monsieur.' Lady Sophia's eyes twinkled
as she looked up at him. He was handsome, and his
manners were those of a true gentleman. 'Perhaps you
will join us for some wine when you have supped?'

Gérard's smile softened as he looked into her face.
'We should be delighted, madame. Perhaps you would
allow me to order the wine? I believe our host has a
special vintage that all travellers are not privileged to
share.'

'You mean he would not waste it on the ignorant English?' Lady Sophia laughed good-naturedly. 'Well, young man, I shall try your wine—and you will find that my knowledge is not inconsiderable.'

'I am sure that you are as wise as you are beautiful, madame,' Gérard said, chuckling as she gave him her hand to kiss. The wicked twinkle in her eye told him that she had been quite a charmer in her day. 'Pray continue with your meal; we shall talk later.'

'What a pleasant man,' Lady Sophia whispered as the Comte returned to his table. 'I have scarcely met with such exquisite manners at court. Do you not think him very handsome, my love?' She looked innocently at the girl sitting silently beside her.

'Yes, he is charming,' Annelise agreed, her eyes following him until he sat down, but sliding away as his gaze turned towards her. 'I believe he liked you.'

She had liked the way he smiled at the old lady: there had been genuine warmth in him then, and kindness. It was as if he had instinctively known that Lady Sophia was not as well as she pretended to be, and had treated her gently. It was only when he looked at Annelise that the hard glitter came into his eyes. What have I done to make him distrust me? she wondered.

Turning her attention back to her soup, she tried to put all thought of him out of her mind, her task made harder by the knowledge that he was watching her. As their eyes met, he smiled, and her heart jerked. When he looked at her like that, she could hardly breathe, let alone eat, and averted her eyes again quickly.

The streets were thronged with people and carriages. From the coach window, Annelise was impressed by the buildings on either side of the tree-lined avenue. She had already glimpsed the great cathedral of Notre-Dame from the banks of the Seine, the Louvre and the Palais-Royal, and she was looking forward to exploring some of the crooked little streets that veered off at a crazy tangent from the main squares and avenues. She had not particularly wanted to come to Paris, but now that she was here, the atmosphere excited her. They had lost but one day of their journey, since the Comte de Montpellier had arranged for the swift repair of Lady Sophia's carriage.

Annelise could not deny that she was intrigued by the Comte. He and Monsieur Beaumarchais had proved to be entertaining companions, and she knew that Lady Sophia was delighted to have made their acquaintance. The Comte had said openly that he hoped to see them in Paris, his eyes seeking Annelise's as he did so, as if to convey that it was her in particular whom he wished to meet. He had even gone so far as to ask where they planned to stay and then recommended another hotel that he believed would suit them better, being in a quieter, more select part of the city.

'Ah, here we are—the Hôtel de Boussier.' Lady Sophia's announcement brought Annelise's wandering thoughts to a halt. 'It looks every bit as comfortable as the dear Comte promised.' She beamed at the girl. 'Was it not kind of him to trouble himself about our welfare? Now we must hope that rooms can be found for us all.'

Annelise merely smiled and nodded. She was not unaware of her friend's coy looks, but she was not prepared to be drawn on the subject of the Comte. Henry was looking disgruntled as he helped his grandmother from the coach, and she believed it was because Lady Sophia had refused to give him the money he had lost playing cards the previous evening with some English gentlemen he had met at the inn. He had preferred their company to that of his grandmother and the Frenchmen, but his pockets were sadly emptied by the experience.

'No, Henry,' Sophia had said gently but firmly when he applied to her for a further loan. 'I am sorry if it means you will not be able to gamble for a while, but you really must learn to live on your allowance. I have given you so much extra lately that I am short of funds myself. You must wait until I can make arrangements to have more money sent out from England.'

Henry had had no choice but to accept her refusal, but it had annoyed him, and he relieved his feelings by snubbing Annelise whenever he got the chance. His attitude had worsened towards her these last few days, and had he had cause for it, she would have said that he was jealous. Yet she had given him no reason to believe that she enjoyed the company of their new friends, even though she was more than a little attracted to one of them. It was difficult not to be when the Comte singled her out so often. He was constantly asking her opinion and deferring to her taste. If she had not sensed the anger beneath his smile that first evening, she might have thought that he was courting her. Whether it was the Comte's attentions or his grandmother's stubbornness over the gambling debt, Henry had made his feelings plain. He demonstrated them again now by leaving Annelise to disembark without assistance. She did so easily enough, following him and Lady Sophia into the hotel in time to hear the manager say,

'But of course your rooms are ready, madame. The Comte de Montpellier made the arrangements himself. He was most particular about them, Lady Sophia. I am sure you will find that everything is to your satisfaction.'

Annelise was startled by the announcement. Why should a man they had met casually at an inn go to so much trouble on their behalf? It was true that he had been very attentive to her and Lady Sophia, but this was more than she had expected. It seemed a little strange, and had the circumstances been different, she might have suspected his motives. Yet he had said nothing to her that was remotely out of place. He had not even tried to flirt with her, though sometimes there was a look in his eyes that made her knees tremble. It had been very kind of him to make the arrangements, so why should she have a vague uneasiness?

Lady Sophia could not stop singing his praises as they were shown up to their rooms. He was the most considerate man she had ever come across, she declared roundly. They were so fortunate to have met him!

It was obvious as soon as they were shown into their apartments that a special effort to please them had been made by the hotel staff. Not only were they the best rooms in the house, with views over the extensive gardens, but extra cushions had been placed on the sofas; flowers, baskets of fruit and wine were all laid out in readiness, and, in Annelise's room a book of Molière's plays. Picking up the leather and gilt bound volume, Annelise saw that it contained a play she had mentioned wanting particularly to read. How the manager had managed to find it at such short notice she could not think, but opening it and reading the inscription on the flyleaf, she realised that it was a gift from the Comte himself.

There was no corresponding book for Lady Sophia, and she could not fail to appreciate the compliment. It was the first time that he had shown Annelise such special consideration, and her friend seized on it with glee.

'I knew it,' she exclaimed. 'The Comte is taken with you, my love! What a triumph it would be if he should offer for you.'

'Sophia!' Annelise blushed. 'You must not say such things. He has shown no preference for my company. This was merely a—a kind thought.'

'Of course he has not tried to flirt with you.' The faded blue eyes twinkled with mischief. 'The Comte is no green youth, my dear. Do not expect anything too direct. He will make no improper suggestions at this stage, nor will he try to snatch a kiss in some hole and corner way. You are being courted by an expert. Each tiny advance will be so subtle that you scarcely notice it...'

A shiver ran down her spine. 'No, you are wrong! The Comte has merely been concerned for your comfort.'

'He did not give *me* a book of Molière's plays!' Lady Sophia clapped her hands in delight. 'Oh, how fortunate you are to be young and beautiful! I remember when I was a girl, a little younger than you are now... Well, suffice it to say that I had my moments at Versailles. It was a beautiful memory. One I have carried with me always.' She saw the surprise in the girl's face, and laughed. 'As a girl I was considered a beauty, and I was inclined to be reckless. When we returned to England, my father lost no time in finding me a husband, but he need not have been so anxious. The child I bore was my husband's.'

'You are not suggesting that I should have an affair with the Comte, are you?' Annelise stared at her in surprise.

'Marriage would of course be preferable, but he is so handsome, and the French are skilled in the art of love. These things must be managed with care, but...' She shook her head as Annelise blushed. 'We were not quite so nice in our ways when I was your age. Many a seven-month child was born to a lady of spotless reputation—and as many more bastards were smuggled out of the bedchamber in a warming-pan, to be brought up a goodwife in the country! But don't be shocked, my love. I only want you to be happy. I'm not suggesting that you should do anything you would not like.'

'He would never marry someone like me,' Annelise said, shaking her head. 'And anything else would be out of the question.'

'I thought you rather liked him?'

'I do...I mean, he's been very kind to us both. I—I feel a certain gratitude...'

'Stuff and nonsense!' Lady Sophia cried. 'I've seen the look in your eyes, my girl. I'll wager you are already halfway in love with him!'

'And you are a wicked tease,' Annelise said, laughing.

'I know, and it's well past my bedtime.' The old lady caught her hand. 'Forgive me, my love. It's just that I should like to see you well settled before I die. I'm very fond of you, and I want to see you happy. Sometimes it's as well to take your chances when they come; a memory can be sweet when one's husband prefers his club to his wife's bed.'

The odd note of pain in her voice made Annelise look at her sharply, but she said nothing. It was not the first time her friend had hinted at her unhappy marriage.

Having settled Lady Sophia comfortably for the night, Annelise kissed her cheek and went out, closing the door softly behind her. Her thoughts were troubled as she walked to her own room. Taking up the book again, she read the Comte's signature with a feeling of unease. Why had he given it to her? Was it possible that he was trying to break down her defences very subtly, in order to seduce her at the last? No, she did not believe it. She did not want to believe it! Besides, she was sure that he did not really like her. Yet, if he wanted to use her for his own pleasure, would that fact not make it easier for him? If he thought her unworthy of respect, it would make her fair game . . . But that made him less than a gentleman, and she had seen true kindness in him when he spoke to Lady Sophia. It was all so confusing.

Undressing, Annelise continued to think about the enlightening conversation with Lady Sophia. She smiled to herself, a glint of humour in her eyes. It seemed that her friend must have been a little wild as a girl. It was of course rather shocking, but also very amusing. Beginning to brush her long hair, she was startled by the knocking at her door. It was loud and insistent. Who could it be at this hour?

'Who is there?' she called, her heart pounding as she got to her feet and went to investigate. Surely it could not be the Comte? He would never disturb her so rudely.

'It's me, Annelise!' Henry's voice sobered her flight of fancy. 'Open your door. I want to speak to you.'

She hesitated with her hand on the latch. 'I am ready to retire, Henry. What do you want? Sophia isn't ill, is she?'

'I've just said I want to speak to you. It's important.'

Sighing, Annelise went to pick up a red velvet wrap that was lying across the bed. She slipped it on and fastened the buttons so that she was decently covered from throat to toe. Even so, she was uneasy as she opened her door just a fraction, peeping round the edge.

'What is so important that you must come knocking at my door at his hour?'

'This . . .' Henry put his shoulder to the door, thrusting it backwards and her with it. Before she could recover, he forced his way inside, making a grab at her and trying to kiss her. 'I want you, Annelise. You know I'm mad for you, so why do you deny me? I'll buy you anything you want . . .'

'You mean your grandmother will!' Annelise said scornfully, twisting away from his greedy mouth with a cry of disgust. 'You cannot live on your allowance now. Let me go this instant, Henry, or I'll tell her. If she knew you were always pestering me like this, she would be very angry.'

Henry drew back, his face sulky. 'She has already cut me off without a penny. Well, as good as.'

'No, her refusal to help you out was merely temporary.' Annelise looked at his flushed face. 'You've been drinking, haven't you?'

'What makes you say that?' He glared at her truculently. 'And what if I have? A man needs a drink before trying to melt an iceberg.'

He looked so much like a chastened schoolboy that she was tempted to laugh. Henry's attempts on her virtue had never frightened her: they were merely an annoyance. The odd thing was, she thought, he might really care for her underneath it all.

'I'm sorry, Henry,' she said. 'I can't help it if I don't love you. If you go now, I won't tell Sophia.'

'She wouldn't believe you,' he sneered, sensing her pity and feeling bitter.

'You know I could make her believe me, don't you?'

His lips curled back in a snarl. 'You're a cold bitch, Annelise! If it's the Comte you're after, he won't marry you. All he wants is . . .'

'Please leave, Henry.' She was suddenly furious. How dared he come here like this and insult her? She went to the door and opened it wide. 'Go now, or I shall start screaming.'

His face was ugly with spite as he looked at her. 'One day I'll make you sorry for this!'

She did not bother to answer, her face cold and proud, all inclination to laugh having left her. 'I'm already sorry that I opened my door to you. If you ever try this again, I shall . . .'

'I've learned my lesson. You're not worth the effort.'

She was left with nothing to say as Henry pushed past her and she found herself staring across the hall. A man had opened the door of his room and was standing on the threshold, apparently listening to their quarrel. As her eyes met those expressive dark ones, she experienced an odd, lancing pain in her breast. She could see contempt there: contempt for her. He believed that she had been entertaining Henry in her room. She could read it in his face.

As the swift anger swept over her, she slammed her door shut. How could he? How could he imagine that she would... But Henry had been in her room, and she was wearing her nightclothes. It must seem as if... She swallowed hard, her cheeks hot with chagrin. Why, oh why, had Henry come to her room tonight? It was almost as if he had done it purposely to shame her. Yet he could not have known how it would turn out. No, it was more likely that he had seen the Comte arrive and his jealousy had driven him to a desperate act.

The soft knocking at her door made her blood run cold. She tensed, shivering, as the voice called her name. 'Are you in difficulty, Mademoiselle Pembleton?' Gérard asked. 'Do you need help?'

She controlled her shaking and went to the door, standing close behind it. 'I am perfectly capable of looking after myself, monsieur. Please go away.'

There was an odd silence, then she heard the firm tread of his feet going back across the hall. She was trembling as she climbed into bed. It was foolish to allow the incident to upset her. What did it matter if the Comte believed she was a woman of easy virtue? His opinion meant nothing to her... But she did care what this man thought, though there was no reason why she should. No reason that she was prepared to accept. He could never be anything to her but a casual acquaintance. A chance meeting of eyes in the gardens of Fontainebleau and the sudden quickening of her pulses was not a sensible reason to throw all caution to the winds, nor was this stupid feeling she had of having known him all her life. Of having waited for this moment in time. He was a stranger, and, despite his charming manners, perhaps not a very nice stranger.

If he were planning to seduce her... Yet if that were all, why had he looked so angry just now? Why should it matter to him how many men shared her favours? Already he suspected her of encouraging the attentions of the Marquis de Brienne, and now Henry... Oh, he was not worth bothering her head over! He was just another man and it seemed that they were all the same, wanting only one thing from the women in their lives. She pummelled her pillow furiously, angry at herself for allowing him to disturb her peace. She was not interested in men—any men! She was never, never going to let a man make her miserable...

Tears slipped beneath her lashes and soaked her pillow as she drifted into a troubled sleep, but she was not crying because of the way the Comte had looked at her. Oh no, she was not that foolish! She was crying for her mother, and for Lady Sophia and all those unfortunate women who had let men spoil their lives... But never, never for herself!

# CHAPTER THREE

LIFE IN Paris was busy and exciting, every day filled with new sights and experiences—not the least of which was the slightly unnerving way in which the Comte de Montpellier sometimes looked at her, Annelise thought. She was still not sure what to make of him, though she enjoyed being the object of so much attention. What with visits to the theatre, horse-racing, watching the breath-taking beauty of a balloon ascent and attending countless receptions, two weeks had passed without her really knowing where the time had gone. The weather was very warm, and she worried that all this activity might be too wearing for Lady Sophia, but the old lady declared that she was feeling very well and would not be persuaded to rest.

'We came to Paris to enjoy ourselves, my love,' she asserted. 'If the Comte is kind enough to invite us everywhere, we should be not only foolish but rude to refuse his hospitality.'

Annelise remained silent, her thoughts confused. It was really very pleasant to be escorted everywhere by a man who seemed always to secure the best position at the races, and whose own box at the theatre was both comfortable and close to the stage so that one could see and hear everything; and if the Comte's hand occasionally held hers for a second longer than was necessary as he helped her from the coach, that was no reason to think it meant anything more than mere courtesy. That warmth in his eyes when he thought she was not aware of his look might be her imagination. The touch of his hand against her bare arm as he passed her a glass of wine at supper could be accidental, as was the caress of her shoulders as he helped her on with her cloak. Whether by design or accident, it was having an effect on her.

This morning they were to pay a visit to the Tuileries gardens, and afterwards to take a drive along the banks of the Seine so that she could see more of the fine buildings. The Comte had suggested the outing after Annelise had mentioned several places of interest that she would like to see.

'Why do we not all take a drive in my carriage?' he had asked, the previous evening. 'If you would allow me to be your guide, I should be only too pleased to explain anything that might not be known to you, mademoiselle.'

'You have already proved so knowledgeable that we cannot refuse,' Lady Sophia said at once. 'You must tell me the latest scandal, monsieur. I want to know it all!'

Gérard had chuckled, obviously finding the old lady's curiosity amusing, and obliging her by recounting a spicy tale about one of Louis XIV's many mistresses. Annelise was left with nothing to do but smile and look pleased. In fact her heart had raced as she caught the look in the Comte's eyes, knowing that it was just for her. Was he thinking that she would do very well as his mistress? she wondered.

She had found it difficult to sleep that night, pictures of his face coming continually into her head. She knew that she was a fool to let him command her thoughts this way, but she could not help herself. Going down to meet him as arranged the next morning, she found herself impatient to see him again, and it was with a feeling of disappointment that she found André Beaumarchais waiting for them.

'Gérard regrets that he is unable to keep his appointment,' he said, looking apologetic, 'but I have strict instructions to see that you are not neglected. If you will accept me, I shall be delighted to take his place.'

There was of course only one answer they could give, and Annelise managed to hide her disappointment behind a smile. 'It was kind of you to give up your day to us, monsieur.'

'I am happy to be of service—but the day may not be entirely wasted. Gérard will join us later if he can.'

'Oh...' Annelise could not hide the sudden leap of joy in her eyes. She blushed as she saw it had been noticed. 'It—it does not matter. I am sure that Lady Sophia will be content with you as her guide, monsieur.'

'Ah yes, but will you?' he said, so softly that she was not certain she had heard him correctly.

Henry had been disinclined to join them, and he waited only to see his grandmother safely in the coach before leaving on foot for an appointment of his own. He had spent less and less time with them this past week, and Annelise was sure he was sulking, though whether it was because of their quarrel or his grandmother's unusual stubbornness over money, she could not tell. With Monsieur Beaumarchais to see to their comfort, neither of the ladies missed the sullen Englishman. They spent an enjoyable morning in the Tuileries gardens, André finding a shady spot where they settled down to sample the hamper of delicious food provided by the Comte's servants. Cold chicken, wafer-thin slices of ham, pies, cheeses, fresh bread, fruit and wine were spread out on a white cloth, followed by nuts and candied pears. It was a feast indeed, and all it needed to complete Annelise's happiness was the man who had masterminded the whole.

He had not arrived when it was decided to leave the gardens to continue their drive. Hardly had they reached the carriage, however, when Lady Sophia complained of a headache. She looked at Annelise apologetically.

'I'm afraid we must cancel the drive, my love. I am sorry to be such a nuisance, but my head is very painful.'

'You are not a nuisance,' Annelise said at once, sprinkling a few drops of cologne on to a kerchief. 'Try this; it may help a little. You will feel better when you can lie down on your bed. I think the sun may have been too hot for you. It is very warm.'

'Thank you,' Lady Sophia said, sinking back against the squabs with a sigh. 'I really feel quite . . .'

What she meant to say was lost in the sudden noise from further down the street. A crowd of men and women had blocked the road; they were chanting something, waving sticks and shouting what sounded like abuse. André glanced out of the window, frowning as he saw what was going on.

'This is unfortunate,' he said. 'There seems to be a disturbance ahead. I would tell the coachman to turn and avoid it, but the road is too narrow.'

'What are they saying?' Annelise said, straining to catch the angry words. 'It sounds as if they are demanding bread. Yes, they say, "Food, give us food." I'm sure that's it.' She looked at him directly and he nodded, an odd expression in his eyes.

'The price of bread has soared this summer, partly because of the bad harvest last year. I—I am afraid that in some extreme cases the people *are* near to starving.' He looked slightly ashamed. 'No one seems to know what to do about it.'

'That's terrible!' Annelise exclaimed. 'Surely something can be done to help them? Has the King no granaries that could be opened to them? After all, it is an emergency.'

'Well, I'm sure His Majesty...' André faltered as her eyes accused him. 'You do not understand, mademoiselle. It would be impossible to feed them all. We are barely keeping the streets free of riots as it is...'

The crowd was close to the carriage now. The shouting was all around them, and Annelise could sense the hatred focused in their direction. Of course the peasants must resent those fortunate enough to ride in a carriage such as this when they could not afford the price of a loaf of bread. It was up to the King and the officials of his government to do something in an emergency like this, she thought, her sympathy all with the hungry people. Glancing out of the window, she saw gaunt-faced men and women, their dark eyes glinting with anger. A woman saw her and yelled a torrent of abuse, screaming that her child was dying of starvation. Then a stone hit the coach.

'What was that?' Lady Sophia cried, her face pale. 'Are they attacking us? What do they want?'

'They are begging for food,' Annelise said, looking at her in concern. 'Can we not give them some money? Perhaps they would take it and leave us alone.'

'I have only a few livres with me, but take it if you think... Oh!' Her cry of alarm came as the crowd began to rock the coach. 'Stop them! Someone stop them! My head, my head...'

André tried to open the coach door, calling out to the people that he wanted to speak with them, but he was held a prisoner by the wild-eyed men. They were too angry to listen to reason, acting mindlessly as one entity rather than as individuals. The rocking went on and on as the chanting grew louder and more menacing, and

the occupants were thrown together helplessly, Lady
Sophia screaming in fear.

'Give them money. Give them my jewels—anything!'

'It won't help,' André said, shaking his head at her.
'Calm yourself, madame; in a moment or two the patrols will come...'

As if in answer to his words there was a sharp crack
of musket-fire, and then several mounted men entered
the street, riding at a gallop towards the mob. The menacing chanting ceased and an odd silence fell over the
crowd as the patrol fired over their heads. They fell back,
huddling together, their eyes sullen with hatred as they
were forced away from the coach, waiting for the leader
to speak. In the unnatural silence, a voice could suddenly be heard.

'Disperse quietly, and no one will be punished.'

'Why should we?'

'Give us bread. Our children are dying!'

'Bread! Give us bread!'

'Your plight is the same as that of many others,' the
voice said, and Annelise recognised it as that of the
Comte de Montpellier. 'But you are not forgotten.
Everything that can be done will be done. A consignment of grain arrived from my own estate in
Normandy this very morning. Everyone who goes to the
warehouse at the corner of Montparnasse will be given
a share.'

'God bless you, monsieur.'

'Montparnasse? Did he say Montparnasse?'

'I know the warehouse. I'll lead the way. Follow me!'

The last speaker went off at a run and the others began
to follow, shouting to each other excitedly that a new
consignment of grain had arrived. Within seconds the
street had cleared, except for the soldiers who had
rescued the situation. André opened the coach door and

helped the ladies down, Annelise first. The Comte dismounted and came striding over to them.

'Thank God I came in time,' he said, looking at the girl's white face. 'You are not hurt?'

She started to shake her head, but before she could speak, he reached out and drew her into a crushing embrace. As his lips took possession of hers, she felt herself responding, her arms sliding up around his neck in a moment of abandon, too shaken by her recent fright to do anything but give in to her inner desires. For one wonderful moment she was swept away on a tide of sensation such as she had never before experienced. She clung to him, wanting the heady joy of this moment to go on for ever.

'Forgive me; I think Lady Sophia is ill.'

André's words reclaimed her senses. As the Comte instantly released her, she sprang away from him, her cheeks on fire as she realised what had happened. Staring at him in dismay for one second, she gave a little cry and turned away, her heart beating wildly. Then, seeing Lady Sophia lying limply in André's arms, she smothered her own emotions to hasten to her friend's side.

'What happened?' She felt a stab of fear as she saw the old lady's grey complexion. 'Has she fainted?'

'I was helping her down when she collapsed. I fear it is more than a fainting fit,' André said, looking concerned. 'I believe she is really ill.'

Annelise touched a limp hand and nodded. 'Her skin is clammy. I believe the shock was too much for her. She has not been well for some days. We must get her back to the hotel and send for a doctor.'

'André, take my horse and fetch Dr Vauban,' Gérard said authoritatively. 'Give Lady Sophia to me. Annelise, place a cushion under her head when I lay her down on the seat, and cover her with that blanket.'

They both moved to obey him without question. Within a few seconds, he had Lady Sophia comfortably settled and the coach was moving again, escorted by the patrol in case of further trouble. Gérard loosened the high neck of the sick woman's gown, taking her wrist to feel for a pulse. His face was grim as he turned to the anxious girl at his side.

'She is very weak. I have thought for some time that she was a sick woman. Has she mentioned anything to you? Any pain in the chest, for instance?'

'Yes...' Annelise made an effort to control her trembling limbs, feeling the prick of tears at the back of her eyes. 'She did mention a pain once or twice. She thought it was merely indigestion.'

'I think it may be her heart...' Annelise gave a cry of distress, and he frowned. 'I am sorry. I did not intend to upset you, but I think you must be prepared for the worst.'

'I know.' She shook her head, her eyes stinging from the tears she was trying to hold back. 'You—You have been so kind to us. She was so happy these past few...' Emotion caught in her throat and she could not go on.

'I have not been kind.' Gérard realised that he must be outspoken now for her own sake. It had amused him to flirt with her, but when she had clung to him earlier, he had realised that he could not go on deceiving her. 'Forgive me, Mademoiselle Pembleton; I have not been fair to you.'

'What do you mean?' She looked at him, her eyes wide at the unexpected statement.

'All I have done was for my own amusement. I intended to seduce you if I could. It was a cruel game.'

'I—I see.' She gripped the carriage seat so hard that her knuckles turned white, forcing herself to laugh carelessly. 'Is that all? Since I was aware of your—your little plot, monsieur, there is nothing to forgive. You saw me running from the Marquis, and—and you saw Henry leaving my room, so you thought me a woman of easy virtue, is that not so?'

'Perhaps.' He avoided her searching gaze, realising that he had hurt her. Yet he knew that it was better to be honest now than to let her go on hoping for something that could never be. 'So you were not deceived. Good! You are a sensible woman, and I am glad that no harm has been done.'

'None.' Except that her heart felt as if it were breaking. 'I knew it was merely a game. It was amusing for a while, but I am glad you have confessed it at last.'

'The charade is over,' he said. 'You have my promise. Will you try to forget it?'

'I shall do so. It was nothing.'

Annelise could not smile at him. The tightness in her chest was so painful that she thought she would die, and it was taking all her strength not to let him see how badly he had hurt her. How could he have kissed her in that way just now if she meant nothing to him? And she had clung to him like a fool! The shame of it twisted inside her, making her almost afraid to look at him. There was nothing she could do until they reached the hotel, but once Lady Sophia was safely in her bed, she would make sure that she had no further contact with him. If she had not felt so miserable, she would have been very angry. She knew the anger would come later, when she was no longer so worried about her friend...

Sitting by the old lady's bed throughout the night and for most of the next day, Annelise watched in vain for signs of a recovery. Lady Sophia lay unconscious, her breathing gradually becoming more difficult. The doctor came and examined her, shaking his head regretfully.

'I fear there is nothing I can do for her. You must prepare yourself, my dear young lady. The end is very near. I do not think that she will recover her senses.'

'No! Oh no,' Annelise sobbed, putting a trembling hand to her lips. 'She cannot be dying... She cannot...'

The physician patted her shoulder sympathetically and went away, leaving her to weep. She murmured a prayer, holding the frail hand in her own and pressing it to her lips. How could she bear to lose the only true friend she had in the world?

Henry came in once, standing to look down at his grandmother in silence for a moment before rounding on the girl angrily. 'It's your fault,' he said bitterly. 'If it had not been for you, she would have died in her own bed. She told me she came to France so that you should enjoy yourself. Now I shall have all the trouble of arranging to take her body back to England.'

'Don't! Please...' Annelise turned away, the tears cascading down her cheeks. 'I love her! Have you no pity?'

'Why should I pity you?' The spite in his voice made the girl flinch. 'You showed none for me. All you cared about were your fancy French friends. Well, I wonder what they will do for you now? Now that you are a penniless...'

'Please go away, Henry,' she said quietly, meeting his angry look. 'She is not yet dead. May we not leave the quarrelling for another day?' She was dimly aware of his hatred, but in her grief she could only wonder what she had done to arouse it. Was it only because she had rebuffed his advances?

After he had left, she sat holding her friend's hand, praying that the doctor was wrong. If only Sophia would open her eyes once more, so that she could at least tell her how much she loved her.

'You were so good to me, my dearest,' she whispered chokily. 'I don't know what I would have done without you when Mama and Papa died...'

Suddenly she became aware that she was no longer alone. Glancing round, she saw the Comte de Montpellier watching her from the doorway. Something about the look in his eyes made her lift her head proudly. She would not suffer him to feel sorry for her! He had thought to amuse himself at her expense, to see if he could make the silly little English companion fall in love with him.

'Yes, monsieur?' she asked haughtily. 'Did you wish to speak with me?

Gérard sensed her hostility and understood the reason for her anger. She had accepted his confession with dignity, but she must despise him for the way he had behaved. How could he blame her when he knew he had been wrong? Looking at her now, he saw the pride and spirit in her. She was as lovely inside as out, and he had been a fool to doubt it. More than a fool, he became aware, remembering that despicable wager with André. Yet had the wager ever been more than a jest? Was it not true that he had wanted her from the first moment he saw her? Wanted her, but known she was beyond his reach? Love was forbidden to him...

'I came to see if you needed anything, mademoiselle.'

'No, I can manage, thank you.' She spoke with dignity, showing neither anger nor pain, though she was inwardly racked by both. 'It is only a matter of time. There is nothing anyone can do!'

'I am very sorry.' He sensed the deep, tearing grief in her, wanting to cross the short distance between them and take her in his arms to comfort her, but knowing instinctively that she would reject any sign of sympathy from him. 'I shall leave you in peace, but you know that I shall be happy to assist you in any way I can?'

'Mr Greenway will do all that is necessary.' Annelise gave him a cold stare, wishing that he would leave. 'Now, I should like to be alone, if you don't mind?'

He nodded, accepting her censure as justice, and left without another word. After he had gone, Annelise covered her face with her hands as the hot tears stung her eyes. Oh, why did he have to appear so concerned for her welfare when his heart was false? She needed someone to turn to so much at this moment, but how could she trust him now, after he had admitted that his kindness had been part of a plot to seduce her? Only a selfish, careless man would behave so badly! Her heart cried out that she could never have given her love to a man who was totally worthless. What a fool she had been! Yet he had seemed so different from all the others.

'I cannot bear it,' she whispered. 'I am so alone...'

But she had to bear it, because there was no one to help her. No one but the man she had just sent away. As the long, hot afternoon wore on, a feeling of dull acceptance came over her. Her friend was dying. She must return to England and seek employment as a governess. This time there would be no one to help her; she was alone.

From somewhere deep in the heart of the city there came a sound that might have been the booming of cannon. Or perhaps it was thunder, she thought. It was hot enough for a summer storm. Unbearably hot. Feeling damp with perspiration herself, Annelise bathed the old lady's forehead in an attempt to keep her comfortable, though she knew it was doubtful that Sophia even knew she was there. Once or twice she heard shouts from outside and the clatter of running feet, but all these things were muffled by her grief. Outside her window Paris was in turmoil, the repression and suffering of years boiling over in a great tide of hatred that was to set France alight;

but to the English girl that Sunday afternoon in July 1789, there was only the deep, personal grief of losing her dearest friend.

'You cannot mean it!' Annelise stared at the sullen-faced Englishman, her cheeks blotched with the tears she had shed as Lady Sophia slipped away from them just before midnight. 'I came out here as your grandmother's companion; you cannot intend to desert me?'

Henry could not meet her intense gaze. 'I have no choice,' he muttered. 'It will cost a great deal to—to take her home, and I have scarcely enough to settle our account here. You must pay your own bills and make your own way back to England.'

'But I have no money,' she protested. 'Not a penny! How can I pay my account here?'

'That is your affair. You can expect nothing from me.' He glared at her. 'Sell some of the things she gave you. She spent enough on you!'

His accusation was unjust. Annelise had always refused the pretty trinkets her friend had offered to buy her, thinking herself fortunate to be living almost as a daughter of the family. If only she had asked for a small wage, just something to tide her over in an emergency. She was entitled to be paid for her services as a maid, if nothing else, and if she had cared to make a fuss, she believed Henry would be forced to pay at least her fare home, but pride forbade it. Her pride and her grief. She could not bear to make an unpleasant scene with Sophia lying dead in the room. She would manage somehow.

'Very well,' she said, giving him a scornful glance. 'I shall not ask a second time.' Bending to kiss Lady Sophia's cold cheek, she left the room without looking at him again. His behaviour was disgusting, and she knew that his grandmother would have been furious. Sophia would never have left her in such a predicament.

After a few hours spent in restlessly tossing from side to side in her bed without sleeping, Annelise rose and dressed in a grey silk gown tied with black ribbons. At least she had a suitable dress to wear, she thought wryly. Her face was pale as she glanced in the mirror to tie the strings of her straw bonnet. Henry had refused to pay her hotel bill so she must find the money herself, and quickly, for she could not afford to go on staying here a day longer than necessary. She had no idea how much it would be, let alone the price of her passage back to England. There was only one course open to her now; she must sell the watch her father had given her. It was the only thing of value she had.

She took it out of its velvet box, looking at it with regret, but there was no alternative. What chance did she have of finding a position as a governess in France? Even if she did, she would need money to live on in the meantime. Returning the watch to its box, she slipped it into her reticule and went downstairs.

The hotel manager was in his office at the back of the entrance hall. Lifting her chin proudly, Annelise walked towards him. He came out as he saw her, a look of concern on his face as he offered his sympathy.

'You are very kind, monsieur,' she said, sounding much calmer than she felt. 'Mr Greenway will probably be leaving later today...' She faltered and he nodded, making little clucking noises in his throat. 'I shall be staying for a little longer. I hope that is convenient?'

'Certainly, mademoiselle,' he said. 'You must tell me if I can be of service to you.'

'Thank you.' She smiled slightly. 'I—I must go now. I shall return soon.'

'But you are not going out alone?' He looked alarmed. 'The streets are not safe. Have you not heard what took place yesterday?'

Annelise frowned, recalling the disturbance she had heard in the street. 'Was there more trouble?'

*'Mon Dieu!'* He crossed himself swiftly. 'Such terrible goings on, mademoiselle. There was a riot in the streets. It seems that Monsieur Necker has been sent packing, and the people are incensed. They demonstrated against it and there was firing...'

Monsieur Necker: the people's champion. Annelise had heard him hailed as the saviour of France. She had only a hazy idea of the politics behind the recent troubles, although she had been told that successive governments had failed to resolve the country's financial difficulties. Somehow the recent formation of the Third Estate, or National Assembly as it was now styled, had accentuated the dissent between the King's party and the commons instead of healing the breach as it was meant to do. At one time Necker had seemed to stem the tide of dissatisfaction among the people, stabilising the economy, but now his dismissal would help to flame the embers of a smouldering discontent into a raging fire. She had seen the hunger in men's faces and felt their anger, but she could know nothing of all that had gone before to bring about this state of near revolution. Even now, the thought uppermost in her mind was that she must sell her watch.

'That is unfortunate,' she said, smiling a little uncertainly at the manager. 'I shall be very careful—but I simply must go out. I have no choice.'

She turned and walked away, leaving him shaking his head and clucking softly to himself. It was not that she was ungrateful for his concern, but her need was desperate. Once Henry had gone—for a moment emotion stung her throat as she thought of her friend's last journey—once she was alone, the manager's concern would naturally turn to how she intended to settle her account. Besides, she had to learn how to fend for herself now. In future there would be no carriages to ride in, no picnics in the park... Tears blinded her, but she blinked them away, refusing to indulge in self-pity. She had been fortunate to find a friend in Lady Sophia when she needed one.

Having noticed a small jeweller's shop a few streets away some days previously, she intended to make her way there as quickly as she could. She was not an imprudent fool, and only her pressing need made her go on when she stepped outside to hear the mad pealing of the tocsin from churches all over the city. At once she was aware of the charged atmosphere. Shouts and wild laughter, hurrying feet and one cry that was repeated again and again: 'Arms! Give us arms!'

Two days ago they had asked for bread, but now the mood had changed. She felt it instantly. The people were arming themselves as if for war. She could see a new determination in the faces of the men as they hurried by. Some were wearing green cockades, others a hastily concocted tricolour of red, blue and green on a white background. It seemed to be a kind of badge that was recognised by all who wore it. What was going on? Surely all this could not be happening simply because a minister of the government had been dismissed from his post! No, it was something far more serious and deep rooted.

Fortunately everyone seemed to be too intent on what they were doing to notice a girl in a simple grey gown as she hastened through the streets. Had she but known it, the mob had but one common desire. The search for weapons led first to the Hôtel-de-Ville, where only a few old firelocks were found; then on to the Garde-Meuble to disappointment and His Majesty's store of tapestries; what weapons there were in store were entirely unsuitable for the use of the rampaging citizens of Paris. At the Maison de Saint-Lazare, now a religious house of correction, the crowd were more fortunate. Here they found no arms but bulging granaries and a cellar full of wine! Enough to fuel the fires of anger against those who had hoarded such riches at a time of need.

Knowing nothing of all this, Annelise was conscious of something important going on in the city. Whatever was happening, she was sure it was not just another small bread riot. Obviously, the sooner she sold her watch and returned to the hotel, the better. At first it did not strike her that the only shop she had passed that was open was a baker. It was not until she saw the jeweller's shop was closed, its shutters firmly battened in place, that she understood. Of course! All the shops except those selling food were closed. It was as if the citizens of Paris had declared a public holiday—but a holiday with a sinister purpose!

Returning the way she had come, Annelise heard a rumpus ahead of her. Shrinking into a passage connecting two rows of houses, she watched a crowd of about twenty men, women and children chasing an unfortunate fugitive down the street. They were shouting abuse and waving their fists angrily. Some of the children threw stones plucked from the pavement at him. From what she could make out of the insults hurled after the fleeing man, his only crime was to be a shopkeeper who was considered to have charged too much. Shivering, she waited until the street was clear. The hotel manager had been right—it was too dangerous to be out. She sighed with relief as she ran the last few steps into the hotel and straight on up the stairs to her room. Paris had gone mad!

Her relief at being safely inside was short lived, however. Having tidied herself, she went to Lady Sophia's bedchamber. It was empty, save for a maid who was busily stripping the sheets. She seemed surprised to see Annelise, clearly thinking it was strange that the girl had not left with her companions.

'But the gentleman left half an hour ago, mademoiselle,' she said.

Henry had lost no time in departing! Annelise could understand why he was anxious to be on his way. While she was out she had heard talk of barricading the gates of the city, and he must be anxious to get through before it became impossible. Even so, she felt a little upset that he had not bothered to say goodbye. She would have liked to accompany Lady Sophia's body back to England, but Henry had been determined to prevent that. It was almost as if he wanted to leave her behind in France. Again she wondered at the reasoning that had led to such heartless behaviour, but she could only think that it was because she had refused his lovemaking.

Sighing, the girl realised that she must speak to the manager about her account. She could only hope that he would be reasonable. He came out of his office as she went downstairs again.

'Thank heavens you are safely returned,' he said. 'I was worried about you, mademoiselle.'

'You are very kind.' She smiled at him. 'I was foolish to venture out, but—but I had hoped to—to avail myself of funds with which to pay your account, monsieur. I am afraid I was unable to do so, but I promise to settle in full as soon as I can.'

'But it has been paid!' he cried, shaking his head in distress. 'If only you had mentioned it earlier, you need not have had a wasted journey. Your account has been taken care of until the end of the week.'

'Until the end of this week?' Annelise felt the relief wash over her. That would give her plenty of time to think about what she was going to do. 'Did Mr Greenway say anything? Did he leave me any message?'

'No...' There was a momentary bewilderment in his eyes, then he frowned. 'Monsieur Greenway did not pay your account, mademoiselle. It was a lady. She could not wait to speak to you, but said she would return this evening. She said she had something important to discuss with you.'

Annelise stared at him in surprise. For one moment she had thought that the Comte de Montpellier must have paid her bills, but now she was puzzled. Who was this mysterious woman, and why had she come to her assistance?

'I—I see.' She looked at the manager, her mind in turmoil. 'Do you know whether the Comte de Montpellier is in his room, monsieur?'

Now it was his turn to look surprised. 'But did you not know, mademoiselle? The Comte left the hotel very early this morning. I believe he had an urgent summons from his estate.'

'Oh...' Why did she have this terrible hollow feeling inside? She had refused his offer of help so coldly that it was hardly likely that he would bother to say goodbye. Yet his desertion hurt her far more than Henry's. He had said she might turn to him for help, then left without a word. Well, it showed that he was not to be relied upon, and perhaps it was for the best. 'I—I understand,' she said, her throat tight. 'Thank you, monsieur. Will you let me know when this lady arrives, please—I suppose she did not leave her name?'

'Let me think...' He wrinkled his brow in concentration. 'Ah yes, I believe it was Madame Reinhold. Yes, that was it. A friend of yours, perhaps?'

'No, I do not recall having met her.'

'Then perhaps I have made a mistake?'

'No, I expect I must have met her.' Annelise smiled at him wearily, the hours without sleep beginning to take their toll. 'I shall be in my room when she comes...' She turned and walked up the stairs, feeling suddenly drained of energy. All she wanted to do for the moment was to sleep...

It was late in the afternoon when Annelise awoke, feeling much refreshed. She washed in cold water, putting on a dark blue gown and tidying her hair. It would be as well to look presentable when Madame Reinhold called, though she had still not been able to fit a face to the name. They had met many new people these past few weeks, but she did not normally forget names. So she was not really surprised to find a stranger at her door when the summons finally came.

'Mademoiselle Pembleton, I believe?' The woman smiled at her. 'May I come in?'

'Of course.'

Annelise knew instantly that they had never met. She would not have forgotten this woman's name. Madame Reinhold was a mature lady with striking looks. Her black hair was dressed fashionably in a mass of ringlets, and her blue eyes were full of life and intelligence. She was very energetic, and it showed in the way she stripped off her silk gloves, getting down to business at once as she took a seat and looked at the wondering girl.

'Now, you are puzzled as to why I paid your account, since we do not know one another. At least, you do not know me. I have heard much of you.' Her eyes gleamed with secret laughter. 'I happened to hear that your employer had died, and I enquired what the situation was.

Learning that you had apparently been left in the lurch, I settled the outstanding account.'

'That was good of you, madame, but why should you do that for me?' Annelise stared at her intently. 'What do you ask in return?'

'Ah, I was told that you had a quick mind. I like that in those I wish to do business with. I said that we had never met—but I have seen you at the theatre with André Beaumarchais and Gérard de Montpellier, and I know you to be a girl of good character...' Madame Reinhold laughed delightedly. 'Why so surprised, my dear? You must know that everyone in Paris has been remarking on your looks. You have been quite a sensation...But I digress. I have a little problem, and I believe you may be able to help me.'

'I should be glad to—if I can,' Annelise said uncertainly, wondering what this woman had in mind.

'I am in need of a governess for a small boy.'

Relief washed over Annelise: she had been expecting something far less pleasant. 'You want a governess for your son? You are offering me a position in your household?'

'Not in my own house, but in that of a friend.' The blue eyes surveyed her assessingly, almost as if she was pleasantly surprised by what she saw. 'The boy has no mother, you understand, only a grandmother. His father thinks he needs the care of a younger woman. I have been entrusted with the task of finding a suitable person.'

'And you think I would be suitable?' Annelise regarded her doubtfully. 'But you do not know me, madame. How can you tell whether I am a fit person to have charge of a small child?'

Madame Reinhold clapped her hands, her intelligent eyes sparkling with amusement. 'If I had had any doubts, that question would have answered them. You come

highly recommended, my dear. Monsieur Beaumarchais
sings your praises to anyone who will listen. Please say
you will accept my offer? I must leave Paris early in the
morning, and I do need your help. I assure you that this
child is in an unhappy situation. It would be cruel of
you to refuse.'

'Will you be able to leave Paris?' Annelise stared at
her as she considered her offer.

'Because of the trouble, you mean?' Madame
Reinhold stood up, pulling on her gloves. 'I have heard
that others have experienced some difficulty at the barriers, but I do not think that we shall do so.' She looked
enquiringly at Annelise. 'You do mean to come with me,
I hope?'

Annelise had a sense of being rushed into a situation
she did not fully understand, yet what could she say? It
was a wonderful opportunity for her—and she was
already obliged to this woman.

'Yes, I shall be glad to help you, madame.'

'That is excellent.' Madame Reinhold reached into her
purse and took out several gold coins, handing them to
the girl. 'This will enable you to purchase anything you
may need before we leave. It is an advance on your salary,
so do not refuse it. You will be paid the same amount
each month. Now, do not bother to see me out, my dear.
I shall call for you at seven in the morning. Please try
not to keep me waiting.'

She smiled brilliantly before sweeping out of the room,
leaving Annelise feeling breathless as she looked at the
five coins in her hand. For a girl who had had no money
of her own for months, it was a small fortune. Just
looking at it gave her a sense of security. It meant that
she was truly independent for the first time in her life.
Should she not fit in at . . . wherever she was going, she

would be able to give notice at the end of the month and return to England.

As the first feeling of euphoria wore off, Annelise realised that she had not asked many of the questions a wise employee asks of her future employer. She had no idea where they were going tomorrow, or who her employer was. He was a friend of Madame Reinhold, but that meant little to her, for she did not really know anything about the woman. A niggling doubt at the back of her mind was allayed as she closed her fingers over the gold coins. It would be strange working for her living, for being Lady Sophia's companion did not count, but she would manage somehow. No, she would do more than manage. She would make a success of her life!

For a moment Annelise lay in the darkness, wondering what had woken her. Then she heard it again; a low, whimpering sound like someone in pain. It seemed to be coming from outside her door. Frowning, she got out of bed and slipped on her robe, walking bare-footed across the floor. Opening her door, she saw what at first appearance seemed to be a bundle of rags on the ground, but then the cry came again and she realised that it was a child.

Kneeling down beside the little creature, she saw that it was a girl of perhaps ten. As she reached out to touch her, the girl shrank away, obviously terrified, but not before Annelise had seen the bruises on her face and neck.

'Oh, you poor little mite!' she cried. 'Don't be afraid of me. I shan't hurt you.'

The child stared at her with wide, scared eyes, and she realised she had spoken in English. Repeating her words in French, she was pleased to see some of the fear leave the child's face.

'Will you come into my room and let me bathe your face?' she asked, offering her hand.

The girl nodded, taking her hand and trying to rise. She fell back with a moan, and Annelise bent down, scooping her up in her arms. She was so light and thin that it was easy to carry her inside. Annelise laid her gently on the bed, and fetched water and a cloth to wipe the dirt and smears of blood from the girl's face. As she gently opened her torn dress, she saw that there were hard welts all over her body, as if she had been beaten regularly.

'Who did this to you?' she asked.

'My father,' the girl whispered. 'It was because I would not lie about the Marquis de Aragonais. He—He wanted me to say that Monsieur Edmond had hurt me, but I would not. Monsieur has always been kind. It is my father who beats me.' She began to cry silently, huge tears running down her pale face. 'I ran away. He was following me, and I came in here. I knew he would not think to come here—but when I go home, he will kill me.'

Annelise bathed some of the bruises, trying not to hurt her. 'But why did your father want you to tell lies about the Marquis?'

'Because he hates him. The Marquis dismissed my father from his service for stealing, but he refused to give up my mother and me. He—He loves my mother even though he cannot marry her. I was to have gone with them when they left Paris, but my father caught me and kept me his prisoner.'

'What is your name?'

'Flore—Flore Génévois.'

'Supposing you could get out of Paris, Flore, what would you do then?'

'I should go to the Marquis's château in Etaples. If he and my mother were not there, I should follow them to England.'

'Could you go so far alone?'

'The Marquis has servants who would help me. Servants who are loyal to him.' Flore sighed deeply. 'But I cannot leave Paris. No one may leave. It is forbidden.'

'Are you willing to trust me, Flore?'

The girl studied her for a moment, then nodded her head. 'Yes, mademoiselle. I think you have a good heart.'

'I may be able to help you. I do not promise; I say only that perhaps I can get you out of Paris. Now, I am going to leave you for a moment. You need food and clothes. The manager here has a little girl; I know because I have heard her singing in the garden. I am going to ask him to sell me a dress and some food for you. I shall not be long.'

'You will not tell my father?'

Annelise shook her head. 'I promise I shall not tell anyone who you are. The manager is very kind; he will understand when I explain that you need help. Now will you promise to stay here and not run away?'

'Yes, mademoiselle.' The child smiled suddenly. 'I am very hungry. I have not eaten for three days.'

# CHAPTER FOUR

DRESSED IN a travelling gown of dark green velvet with a black cape, bonnet and gloves, Annelise was waiting in the hotel lobby when Madame Reinhold arrived. The woman's smile of approval faded as she saw the child.

'What is this, mademoiselle? Where has this child come from?' Although Flore was neatly dressed in a blue dress and cloak, purchased with one of the gold coins Annelise had received the previous evening, nothing could disguise that she was a child of the streets.

'This is Flore,' Annelise said. 'She is coming with us.'

'No, I cannot permit that.'

Annelise's fingers tightened round the child's little hand. 'I have given her my word, madame. She cannot stay here; her life is in danger.'

'I am very sorry, but I have no papers for her.'

'Then I shall not come with you,' Annelise said, her face taking on a stubborn look. 'She will be no trouble to us. After we leave Paris, she will find her own way to the Marquis de Aragonais' château. She has some money to buy food on the way.'

'She is much too young to travel alone,' Madame Reinhold said, frowning. 'We should have to send a servant with her.'

'Then you will take her?'

'It seems you leave me with no alternative.' Her frown relaxed. 'You are a very determined young woman. I like that! Very well, I shall think of something. Perhaps it may help us, providing that no one recognises her.'

'Could you not say she is your own daughter?'

'*My* daughter?' The woman arched her brows. 'The daughter of my maid, perhaps. We shall see. Jacques will see to your baggage. Is this everything?'

'Yes, madame.'

Annelise glanced at the footman, who was attempting to strap her trunks on to the back of the coach. He did not seem very expert at the task, and there was something not quite right about him that made her wrinkle her brow. However, once inside the coach, she forgot the clumsy servant, who had now taken his place on the box with the driver, as she listened attentively to Madame Reinhold's account of what had taken place in Paris during the past twenty-four hours, while keeping a firm hold of Flore's hand, and whispering that she was not to be afraid.

'Patrols of "patriots", as they call themselves, have been scouring the streets all night. They broke open the debtors' prison at La Force—and the Gardes Françaises refused to stop them. Indeed they have joined this new army. They have been stopping everyone at the barricades, and they hanged a score of their own comrades for getting drunk at Saint-Lazare!'

'Shall we be allowed to leave the city, madame?'

'Wait and see.' Madame Reinhold's eyes were lit by an inner excitement. 'One word of warning: show no surprise at anything I say, and do not contradict me. And as for you . . .' She looked hard at Flore. 'You are not to say one word, do you hear me?'

Flore nodded solemnly, her hand clinging tight to Annelise's.

'Flore will say nothing, and neither shall I.'

Looking out of the window at the almost empty streets, Annelise caught the feeling of excitement. The sun had not yet risen, and it was strangely quiet, like the calm before a storm. However, as they neared the gates to the north of the city, the noise of sheep and cattle together with upraised voices met her ears.

The sounds were less strange than the sight that accosted them as they reached the square, for it was crowded with carriages, carts and livestock. It was quite obvious that some of the richer citizens had tried to leave Paris with their possessions, and just as clear that, for the most part, they had failed. Everyone was being checked and forced to remain within the city.

Annelise glanced at her companion uncertainly. How could Madame Reinhold hope to succeed where so many others had fallen prey to the hawk-eyed guards?

'Say nothing,' the woman whispered as their coach was halted by three men wearing tricolour cockades pinned in their hats. 'You cannot speak. You are dumb, do you understand?'

Annelise nodded, her eyes wide. Her heart was hammering wildly in her breast as one of the men approached the window. His cold eyes seemed to pierce her.

'No one must leave the city,' he said. 'It is by order of the National Assembly.'

'I have permission to leave, monsieur,' Madame Reinhold said. 'I have papers signed by Mirabeau himself.'

The patriot frowned as she waved her papers under his nose. He had heard of Mirabeau—who among them had not? Mirabeau had dared to stand up to the King himself and defy his orders. He was a brave man and a champion of the people, but these aristocrats would use any lie they could think of to pass through the barricades, and he had heard a rumour that Mirabeau was ill. His eyes narrowed as he looked at the bold seal on the paper. How could he tell if it were genuine? He could neither read nor write.

'My orders are to let no one through,' he growled.

'Would you stop this poor girl from reaching her beloved uncle?' Madame Reinhold asked, her eyes flashing. 'Do you not know who she is?' She indicated Annelise with a jerk of her head.

He screwed up his face, his dark eyes suspicious as he stared at the girl. 'Who is she, then?' he demanded truculently.

'Why—only Monsieur Necker's favourite niece. He has sent for her to join him.'

'Monsieur Necker?' he asked. 'Is that true, girl?' He thrust his head in through the open window, peering at her curiously.

Annelise nodded, remembering that she was to stay silent.

'What's wrong?' he muttered. 'Lost your tongue?'

'The poor girl has never been able to utter a word. It is a terrible affliction, but she is a sweet thing—and the darling of her uncle's heart. He will be angry if she is delayed for no good reason. What is your name?'

'I am called Hubert Grosard, and I never heard as Monsieur Necker had a dumb niece...'

'Then your ears must be full of dirt, Monsieur Grosard!' A second man had joined him at the window. 'Everyone knows about the wench. She's been cursed from birth. Here, let me look at that...' He snatched the papers from Madame Reinhold and squinted at them for a moment. 'This 'ere writing means naught to me, but I've seen Mirabeau's seal once and it were just the same as this.'

Balked of his prey, Grosard frowned. 'Who's the child?'

'She is a poor child whose parents could no longer afford to keep her,' Madame Reinhold said. 'Mademoiselle Necker has taken pity on her.'

'Is that true?' The man squinted evilly at Flore.

The child opened her mouth, and a torrent of abuse that could have come only from the gutters of Paris poured from her. She called him a pig who shoved his ugly nose into a substance that was better left unmentioned and called his parentage into doubt. If Grosard had thought that this might be the child of an aristocrat, he was totally disabused. He glared at her and shrugged his shoulders, as if abandoning his cause.

The second man thrust the papers back at Madame Reinhold and jerked his head at the men guarding the gate. 'Let this one through, citizens. It's Necker's poor afflicted niece.'

His word seemed to carry some weight, for they began to move the barriers aside. Grosard walked off to examine the contents of a cart close behind, and whatever he found caused great excitement, and most of the men guarding the gates rushed to help him to pull off the sacks of flour, sides of bacon and cheeses. Food was more welcome to the fathers of hungry children than all the gold and silver in the King's palaces!

The man who had secured their safe passage remained at the barriers, impatiently waving them through and muttering curses. Annelise noticed that he was tall, and though he was undoubtedly lean and wiry, he did not look as gaunt as some others did. As they passed him in the coach, he happened to glance at her, and their eyes met for one instant before he looked away. She felt a little shock of surprise, feeling sure that she had looked into those eyes only a few days previously. Yet the face was that of a man she had never seen, brown and pockmarked, with thick busy brows.

Turning to Madame Reinhold impulsively, she was about to speak, but a whispered warning stopped her. 'Take care, Mademoiselle, we are not safely away yet.

Besides, some things are best left unspoken. When we are in safety, many others remain at risk. Those who stay behind to help them are best served by silence.' She flicked her eyes towards the child and back.

Annelise did not believe that Flore would betray anyone, but she was only a child and it was better that she did not know any more than was necessary about the people who had helped her. It was easy to understand why Madame Reinhold had been certain they would pass through the barriers, and why she had been annoyed about their extra passenger. Whoever that man who had helped them really was, he was very brave. If she had noticed tiny clues that could betray him, so might others. She dreaded to think what those patriots would do to André Beaumarchais if they guessed that an aristocrat had joined their ranks—and that Monsieur Necker's poor afflicted niece was actually an Englishwoman. They would fall on him like a pack of dogs and tear him limb from limb!

'If I did know who our friend was, I would never mention it to to anyone,' she said, when the gates of the city had been left far behind. 'You may trust me, madame.'

'That is good,' she replied, 'for we are about to lose our footman. His friends are waiting for him with horses up ahead.'

'I shall not ask his name,' Annelise said with a smile. 'I guessed before we left the hotel that he had never been used to menial work.'

'He is important, Annelise. We should not otherwise have risked your safety. That little charade at the gates was more for his benefit than ours. Had they known Jacques' true identity, he would have been held as a hostage and his life might have been in danger.'

'I understand. I am glad to have been of some small service.'

The carriage had drawn to a halt, and the footman jumped down. He came to the window, bowing elegantly to the ladies, every inch the accomplished courtier that he was.

'I owe you my life, ladies,' he said kissing the hand Madame Reinhold offered. 'One day the debt will be repaid.'

'There is no debt, monsieur. What has been done was for the honour of France and His Majesty.'

'His Majesty will also be grateful.' Jacques smiled at Annelise. 'My thanks, mademoiselle.' She blushed and shook her head, and he laughed. 'You may speak now, you know.'

'No thanks are necessary, monsieur. I am happy to have been of service.'

He touched his lips to her hand. 'I shall not forget. But now I must go; His Majesty must hear of what's afoot. The people are in an ugly mood. Something must be done to bring them to reason before it is too late.' His eyes turned to Flore, sitting quietly at Annelise's side. 'And now, child, you must come with me. I shall see you safely returned to your mother and the Marquis.'

Flore looked up at Annelise, reluctant to let go of her hand until she nodded. 'You will be quite safe with this gentleman, Flore.'

'Forgive me for the way I behaved at the gates,' Flore said, shamefaced. 'The Marquis would be very angry if he had heard me speak so rudely.'

'You helped us on our way, child,' Madame Reinhold said kindly. 'But you must mind your manners now.'

Annelise smiled and kissed her cheek. 'Go with him now, Flore.'

Jacques lifted her down, striding away with her in his arms towards the waiting horses, and soon the horsemen disappeared into the trees. She believed she had seen their clumsy footman before at Fontainebleau. If she was not mistaken, he was a very important man indeed: a prince of the blood royal. It was on the tip of her tongue to ask, now that Flore had gone, but she checked herself. Obviously he had been on a secret mission for the King, and his safety in the future might depend on the discretion of his friends.

Instead, as the carriage moved forward again, she turned to the woman beside her with a questioning look. 'Where are we going, madame?'

'Did I not tell you?' Madame Reinhold seemed surprised. 'Why, to Normandy. The château is not far from Abbeville. It is set on a rise with the forest to the back, and meadows and a pleasant stream in front. The original house was burned to the ground in the fourteenth century, when the English won the battle of Crecy. The Comte's family built the present château soon afterwards...'

'The Comte?' Annelise cried, her heart beginning to thud frantically. 'You cannot mean the Comte de Montpellier?' Even before the answer came, she knew the truth. Of course! How could she have been so foolish as not to realise it must be him?

'But yes, mademoiselle. I thought you understood, but perhaps I did not make myself perfectly clear. It is Gérard's son you are to care for.'

'The Comte's son...' Annelise murmured. Her head was spinning and she felt oddly breathless. She was going to see him again! She ought to be angry at both him and Madame Reinhold for deceiving her, for she realised that it had been a deliberate plot between them. Would she have agreed so readily to take the position if she had known that he was to be her employer? But could she be deceiving herself now? Was she not overjoyed to learn that she would see him soon? Perhaps it was foolish, but she suddenly felt alive again. 'Then it was he who asked you to settle my account?'

'Yes, of course. Gérard was most concerned when he learned that Lady Sophia had died. He could not delay to see you safely on your way, so we made this little plan together.' She smiled winningly at Annelise. 'Will you forgive me, mademoiselle? I assure you that no harm was or is intended to you. Gérard really does need a governess for his son—and he thought you might be in some difficulty.'

'I am not sure that I should forgive you, but how can I refuse?' Annelise smiled. 'After what happened at the barricades this morning, your little ruse seems unimportant.'

'Good. Gérard said that we could rely on you, and I agree. I think you will be kind to little Jean, and that is my main concern.'

'Is that my pupil's name?'

'Yes,' she nodded, sighing. 'But you must regard him more in the light of an invalid who needs your love and devotion. He is six years old, but so thin and light that you would think him younger. The poor babe has never known a mother's love, for she died soon after he was born. It was a terrible shame to keep him shut up alone in that place with only his grandmother for company— besides the servants, of course. Claude is devoted to him, but he is old, and Jean needs a woman's care. I was delighted when Gérard told me that he intended to employ you as a governess.'

'You sound as if you are fond of the boy, madame?'

'Lisette was my second cousin, and I introduced her to Gérard. Naturally I am fond of her child, though I do not see him as often as I would wish. I have other duties—at court.'

'I see . . .'

Annelise was silent, thinking of the child and his unfortunate mother. And his father. Gérard de Montpellier had lost his wife.

'How—How long had Lisette been married?'

'Just two years. It was very tragic. Gérard was almost out of his mind with grief. He shut himself away in his rooms for months and would see no one. I believe he would be there yet had it not been for André Beaumarchais. He persuaded him that his life must go on.'

'That was terrible! He must have suffered a great deal.' Annelise saw the Comte in a new light. He must have loved his wife very much to be so overcome by grief. Perhaps that was why he thought of all other women as merely playthings? Perhaps he could not bear the thought of being hurt again?

'It is never spoken of.' Madame Reinhold's eyes were very bright. 'So, mademoiselle, you see what a formidable task you have before you.'

Why was it that Annelise had the strangest feeling that she was not speaking only of the Comte's son?

The château was much larger than Annelise had imagined, and at first sight it looked rather grim with its conical towers, drawbridge and moat, but as they drew nearer she saw that the drawbridge was a permanent fixture and that the moat had been drained and grassed over. Once it had been a fortress, but now it was merely an aristocrat's home.

As the carriage clattered over the bridge, she noticed a great deal of activity going on, with servants hurrying here and there. They were laughing as they worked, the women waving and calling to each other as they carried baskets of clean linen from the laundry to hang it out in the fresh air. Almost immediately she realised that there was a vast difference between the appearance of these people and the gaunt citizens of Paris. She mentioned it to her companion, who smiled and nodded.

'Gérard is a good master,' Madame Reinhold said. 'On this estate you will find that no one is starving. The peasants all owe loyalty to their seigneur, but they are no longer bound to him. Every man or woman who works for the Comte is paid a fair wage for his work— I fear it has made him unpopular with his neighbours, who still demand all their old feudal rights.'

'I think it is admirable.'

'It is certainly expensive, but Gérard can afford it.' Madame Reinhold laughed wryly. 'He and I do not see eye to eye on all his reforms, but we agree to differ. In most things our minds are as one—except on the matter of Madame Margot Vicence. If I were he, I should have sent that one packing long ago!'

'Madame Vicence?' Annelise asked. 'Who is she?'

'Lisette's mother—but no blood relation of mine.' Madame Reinhold pulled a face. 'I was fond of Patrice, but I never did manage to like his wife. However, I may be prejudiced. All I will say is that you must stand up to her from the beginning. She will try to intimidate you, but do not allow her to do so. Gérard wishes you to care for his son, and that is all you must consider.'

It was clearly not going to be an easy position, and Annelise began to understand why the Comte was willing to be so generous. The isolation of the château was enough to deter many would-be governesses without an autocratic woman hovering in the background. Curiously, Madame Reinhold's warnings only made Annelise more determined to succeed. She was not a timid mouse to turn tail at the first obstacle! Besides, she had decided that she wanted to stay.

'Will the Comte be at home?' she asked.

'I am not sure.' Madame Reinhold seemed to evade the question. 'Gérard is a busy man. He will return as soon as he can, you may be certain.'

Since she was clearly not prepared to say any more, Annelise had to be content. The coach came to a halt in front of the main door—a stout, oak door studded with iron bolts that looked as if it could withstand any battering ram—and then servants were bustling about them; far more than seemed necessary she thought. There were at least a dozen to see to the horses and unload the baggage. An old man with white hair and a deeply lined face appeared to be in command. He bowed respectfully to Madame Reinhold as he helped her down.

'Good evening, Claude,' she said.

'Your room is ready, madame,' he replied, inclining his head. 'Everything is in order.'

'Good. Where have you put Mademoiselle Pembleton?'

'Next to the boy, madame, as the seigneur ordered.'

'Very well. See to the trunks. I shall take Annelise up myself.'

'Madame Vicence asked to be informed when you arrived. She is waiting for you, madame.'

'Then she may wait a little longer. We are tired and we need to refresh ourselves. Do not frown so, Claude; her wrath will fall on me not you.'

Madame Reinhold swept on past him, through the stone arch of the porch into a small, dark hall and on up the winding staircase, drawing Annelise in her wake. Their footsteps echoed in the stillness, reverberating from the stone walls and high ceilings. Once the upper gallery was reached, however, the echo was softened by the rich tapestries and carpets. If the entrance had seemed cold and forbidding, here there was only comfort and beauty. Gilded cabinets were set at intervals along the walls, and above them matching mirrors, their wooden frames carved with swags of fruit and flowers. At the end of the gallery was a pair of impressive doors, the panels painted white with pictures of cherubs garlanded in flowers in the centre. Madame Reinhold threw them open with a flourish, a hint of triumph in her eyes as she turned to Annelise.

'There! Some small recompense for the difficulties you may encounter, I think?'

'Oh...' Annelise breathed, enchanted by what she saw. 'It is beautiful—the most beautiful room I have ever seen.'

Madame Reinhold laughed. 'I thought you would like it. It was intended for Lisette, but she never slept here after it was finished. She preferred the west wing.'

'But this is so pretty!' Annelise moved about the room in a dream, touching the silken hangings with the tips of her fingers. Everything was done in shades of pink and cream, from the deepest damask to the palest rose. Even the ceiling was painted with clouds and angelic-looking cherubs. There were velvet padded footstools, elegant chairs with spindly legs, delicate tables, tiny gilded cabinets containing gold-topped bottles and jars; it was a room fit for a princess, comparable to anything she had seen at Fontainebleau. How could any woman refuse to sleep here? 'Are you sure all this is for me?'

'It connects through a sitting-room with the boy's apartments.' Madame Reinhold smiled at her. 'Come, let me introduce you to Jean.'

Annelise followed, her heart beating rapidly. Somehow this was all so unexpected, and she was not sure what to make of it. Was she really here as a governess, or had the Comte decided to continue his attempt to seduce her? He had said the charade was over, but had it really ended? Her head told her that she should turn round and walk out of the house at once, before she was drawn so tightly into his net that she did not want to escape, but her senses were responding to the beauty of her surroundings, and she knew she did not want to leave just yet. Then she forgot everything else as Madame Reinhold opened the far door.

'Jean—are you not pleased to see me?'

A small boy had been sitting on a velvet chair that looked far too large for his tiny frame, swinging his legs aimlessly as he stared into space. Hearing her voice, he flung himself from it and rushed to her, throwing his arms about her waist.

'Madame, you have come!' he cried excitedly. 'I wished for you to come, and now you are here.'

She bent down to gather him in her arms, smothering him with kisses. 'My sweet baby, have you missed me so much? Well, I have brought you a companion so that you will not be so lonely when I am not here. Her name is Annelise. She is very kind, so you must love her, too, and do as she tells you.' Taking his hand, she led him to Annelise. 'Say *bonjour*, Jean.'

Looking down into a pair of serious grey eyes, Annelise felt her heart jerk. Somehow she had expected to see a smaller version of the Comte, but there was nothing of the father in that little face. A face that seemed too small for the huge eyes that looked at her with such a heart-wrenching appeal.

'*Bonjour*, Jean,' she said. 'May I have a kiss, too, please?'

As the small, warm body launched itself at her, she felt her heart twist with pain. The child was starved of affection, and so desperately alone. She knelt down to hug him properly, feeling such a depth of emotion that she knew this was something worth while.

'Have you come to live here?' Jean asked, staring up at her intently. 'You won't go away again, will you?'

In that moment the Comte's motives in bringing her here no longer seemed to matter, neither did the sharp-tongued châtelaine who was waiting to meet her. Her heart went out to the child, and she knew that she was going to stay.

'Yes, Jean,' she promised. 'I shall stay as long as you want me.'

'Is that a promise?' he asked. 'A real, true promise?'

'A true promise, Jean.'

His face lit up, and he took her hand, leading her further into the room. 'Come and see my soldiers, Annelise. I have a whole army! My father brings me a new one every time he goes away.'

Judging by the rows of brightly-painted wooden soldiers lined up in battle formation on the floor, the Comte was often away. There were infantry brigades and cavalry, besides perfectly proportioned cannon and a splendid fort. It was obvious that Jean lacked for nothing that money could buy—but just as clear that he needed the things only a loving heart could supply.

'I have a present for you, Jean,' Madame Reinhold said, watching him fondly. 'I must take Annelise to meet your grandmother now, but when we return . . .'

The boy's face paled and he clung to Annelise's hand. 'You won't go away? You promised you would stay with me!'

'And I always keep my promises.' Annelise smiled at him. 'You can show me the rest of your things later. I want to see what books you have.'

'I have a bestiary,' he said proudly.

'Then perhaps we can look at it together. Do you like stories?'

'What kinds of stories?' He looked at her curiously.

'Stories about kings and queens who lived long ago.'

'Did they fight battles? I like those stories.'

'Then I shall tell you a story when you go to bed.'

'You really will stay? You won't let Grandmama frighten you away?'

'Jean! You must not say such things,' Madame Reinhold exclaimed, with a look at Annelise.

'No one will frighten me away.'

'Aren't you afraid of anyone?' His eyes were round with wonder. 'Not even Papa?'

'Certainly not,' Annelise said firmly.

'Everyone is afraid of Papa.'

'Well, they must be very foolish! I am not afraid of him.'

'I am glad to hear it, Annelise. Jean, you will have your new friend thinking I am an ogre.'

The Comte's words took everyone by surprise. Annelise felt her heart begin to race madly, finding it difficult to control her emotions as she turned to meet his mocking gaze as he stood on the threshold.

'Papa, I did not mean it,' Jean said, his head hanging. 'But Grandmama told me that I should be afraid of you. She says that you do not like me very much and that you will punish me if I am naughty.'

The Comte's face was suddenly bleak. 'Are you afraid of me, Jean? Have I done anything to make you fear me?'

'No...' Jean replied, but there was a note of uncertainty in his voice.

'Come here.' Gérard's voice was gentle but firm. Jean went to stand before him in a subdued manner, as if he thought he was to be punished, but his father swept him up, holding him so that they looked into each other's eyes. 'Never be afraid of me, Jean. No matter what other people may tell you, I shall never harm one hair on your head. Do you believe me?'

'Yes, Papa.' The child suddenly threw his arms round his neck. 'I love you.'

'Well, don't strangle me!' The Comte ruffled his hair and set him down. 'Now stay with Madame Reinhold while I take Annelise to meet your grandmother.'

'You will take her?' Madame Reinhold asked, then nodded. 'Of course. You must have ridden like the wind to get here...' She checked as his eyes gave a silent warning. 'Forgive me.' Turning to Jean, she took his hand. 'We shall go to my room and find your present.'

He held her hand but hesitated, looking at Annelise. 'You won't go away?'

'You have my promise, Jean.' She smiled as his eyes lit up, watching as he trotted obediently away.

'You have a delightful son, monsieur,' she said, glancing up at the silent man by her side.

'So...' Gérard said softly. 'You have fallen under his spell. I thought you might be very angry at the deception used to bring you here?'

'With you, I am a little angry,' she said, but already laughter was sweeping the anger away as she gazed into his challenging eyes. 'I had quite decided that I should never speak to you again, monsieur, but your son is enchanting.'

'I am glad you think so.' The dark eyes regarded her seriously. 'Jean needs love. Not the distant love of a father who is often away, but the warm, giving love of a tender-hearted woman.'

'Y-You think I have a tender heart?' Annelise asked, her pulses racing.

He took two strides towards her, his hand gently cupping her chin to tip her face towards him; then he smiled, bending his head to touch his lips to hers briefly in the lightest of kisses, while making no attempt to hold her against her will.

'I think you are beautiful,' he said huskily. 'I thought so from the first moment I saw you at Fontainebleau. Like a fool, I wanted to snatch greedily at something I can never have. Now I am content to have you here, to know that you will give your love to my son.'

'Oh . . .' she breathed, her head spinning dizzily. He sounded as though he was making a declaration of love, and yet there was a curious finality about the way he put her from him.

'Now you must meet my mother-in-law,' he said, and the bleak look was there in his eyes again. 'She is a little fierce, but I shall not let her humiliate you while I am here. When I leave, you must stand up for yourself—and Jean. I do not like her influence over the boy.'

'I am not afraid of words, monsieur.'

'Very little frightens you, I think?' An odd smile played at the corners of his mouth. 'I wonder if I was wise to bring you here? You will shed new light in our dark corners; your keen eyes will see everything, and our secrets will not be safe from you.'

'Do you have secrets, monsieur?'

'That is for you to discover.'

'I think you mock me.'

'Myself, perhaps.' His eyes darkened to the colour of night. 'Do we not all have our secret fears, Annelise?'

There was an expression in his eyes that disturbed her; it was as if he was in torment, a victim of his own doubts and fears, whatever they might be. She thought that there were many secrets a man like that might have locked away in some tiny corner of his mind.

'I was always afraid of spiders,' she said with a little smile. 'There, I have told you my dreadful secret. Now you may indeed mock me, for it is a foolish fear and one that I have vowed to conquer.'

He laughed, softly at first and then loudly, with enjoyment. 'How glad I am that you have come into my life, my little English rose! Discover what you will, then, and let your sunlight into this house. It is time. God knows, it is time!'

She looked at him curiously, but he only shook his head, refusing to be drawn further. There was mockery in his face as he bowed, ushering her before him, but she felt that his scorn was more for himself than her. He was a strange man, she thought, a creature of conflicting moods and emotions. She had seen passion in his face when he kissed her, but he controlled it rigidly, not letting it touch her, almost as if he feared the conflagration it might ignite if allowed to spread. So absorbed was she in guessing at the nature of the true man that it was a few minutes before she realised that they had entered another part of the château. The furniture here was darker and heavier, belonging to an age gone by. There were not so many tapestries on the walls, and the bare stone made it seem colder. She shivered, and he glanced at her in concern.

'I should have warned you to wear a cloak when you visit Margot. She does not feel the cold as we mere mortals. I have offered to refurbish her wing, but she prefers it this way. She had the furnishings when she was a bride and brought them with her when she moved here.'

'She is a widow, then?'

He nodded, frowning again. 'She came here when—when my wife was ill. Lisette wanted her mother, and I agreed that she should come here. Since she has no other family, I have allowed her to go on living here.'

What was it about his mother-in-law that brought such a bleak look to his eyes? Annelise looked at him as he stopped in front of a door, seeming to hesitate a moment before he knocked. In another man she would have thought it nervousness, but the Comte was unlikely to be afraid of any woman, let alone one who lived on his bounty. Yet there was a pulse beating at his temple, as if he were under strain.

His knock brought no immediate answer, but just as he was about to knock again, a voice called out that they might enter. The room was gloomy, with barely enough light for Annelise to see where she was going. She was vaguely aware of the bulky shapes of the furniture, and of a woman sitting with her back to the heavily draped window.

'Margot!' the Comte exclaimed, annoyed. 'This is nonsense. I have told you that you will ruin your eyes if you persist in sitting in the dark.' He strode to the window and pulled back the curtains. 'There, that is better.' A shaft of evening sun penetrated the gloom.

'You know the sun hurts my eyes, Gérard,' the woman complained. 'But have it your own way. It is your house, and I suppose you can do as you wish.'

In the sudden light, Annelise could see the woman clearly. She was dressed all in black, in the fashion of a decade earlier, her face unnaturally pale, as if she seldom ventured out into the sunlight. Her eyes were black slits that glittered with malice as she looked at her son-in-law, but her mouth was heavily rouged. It gave her a garish, somehow threatening appearance.

She hated the Comte! Annelise sensed it at once. No wonder he had seemed so uncomfortable a few seconds earlier. The woman hated him, yet he tolerated her as a guest in his house. Why?

Margot turned her slitted gaze on Annelise. 'So you are the new governess. Come closer; let me look at you. The last slut who came to teach my grandson was a fool and a whore. If you are no better, you may as well pack your bags at once, for I'll not have you in the house!'

'You will please not insult Mademoiselle Pembleton, Margot. I have engaged her to care for my son, and she will stay here for as long as she is needed.'

'Your son.' Margot's lips curled in a snarl. 'You've scarcely seen the boy in a month. What do you care for his welfare? As little as you did for his poor mother, I dare say! Why don't you stay away altogether and leave him to me?'

'So that you can turn him against me?' Gérard asked, his hands curling into tight fists at his sides. 'You would ruin him as you did your own child...'

She gave a scream of rage, jumping to her feet as if she would fly at him. Then she sank back into her chair, covering her face with a black-gloved hand, and groaning.

'That you should reproach me,' she moaned. 'You—who took the only joy from my life.'

'Margot, don't distress yourself.' Gérard's face was white, the veins cording in his neck as he watched her rocking back and forth. 'Forgive me, I should not have said that. It was not your fault that Lisette...'

She looked at him then, her face ugly with hatred. 'You do and say as you please. You are the master here and I am dependent on your charity. Leave me now— and take that wanton with you!'

'Margot!' The pain in his cry spurred Annelise to action.

'Madame, your insults are misplaced,' she said quietly but with a touch of hauteur. She moved closer to the chair so that the older woman was forced to look at her.

'I am neither a wanton nor a whore. I have come as a companion to Jean—and from what I have seen, he sorely needs one.'

'Indeed?' Margot glared at her. 'And who are you to judge my grandson's needs?'

'The woman his father has chosen to care for him. Madame, I respect you as the mother-in-law of my employer, but I shall not be insulted by you. As a member of the aristocracy, it behoves you to treat your servants with respect.'

'You are not a servant, Annelise,' Gérard said, but the tension had gone out of him and there was a mixture of amusement and admiration in his eyes. 'Come, we shall leave Margot to her own company.'

'No!' Madame Vicence sat up straight in her chair. 'You may go, Gérard. Leave the girl with me. She has some steel in her backbone; I wish to talk to her alone.'

'Do you wish to stay?' Gérard raised his brows at her.

'Why not?' There was a flash of fire in Annelise's emerald eyes that seemed to say that she was more than a match for her adversary. 'Please tell Jean that I shall be there to tuck him up in bed later.' She had thrown down the gauntlet and now turned to look at Margot.

'Your servant, mademoiselle.' A glint of laughter showed in Gérard's eyes. 'Margot, I shall see you again before I leave.'

She shrugged. 'Please yourself.' She pursed her lips as he left the room without another word, her sharp eyes studying Annelise intently, taking stock of what she now perceived to be a worthy opponent. 'You take much on yourself, young woman, presuming to teach me my manners. My family was one of the oldest and most respected in France.'

'Forgive me, madame. My late employer was also a great lady, but she would never have insulted one of her servants. Especially one she had just met and could not therefore know.'

'Indeed!' Margot's foot tapped on the floor. 'I will admit I appear to have judged you too hastily. I thought my son-in-law had brought one of his sluts into the house, but you have good blood in you. Why have you been reduced to the status of a governess?'

'My father lost his fortune through—unwise investments.'

'A gambler, was he? Ha! So was my late husband. I should not otherwise be forced to live in this house.' She laughed harshly. 'So we have something in common, girl. I'll tell you something: if you're imagining you've found yourself a rich husband, you're a fool. Gérard won't marry you—and if he does, you'll live to regret it. Don't let his charm deceive you. He's ruthless and cruel. He uses women and then tosses them aside—as my poor Lisette discovered to her cost. Why do you think she . . .'

'Stop this, madame!' Annelise protested. 'I do not know why you hate the Comte so much, but I shall not listen to your complaints against him. He is my employer, and I must be loyal to him.'

'Must you indeed?' The black eyes glittered beneath lowered lids. 'You're a stubborn wench. Well, you'll learn in time. Don't come crying to me when you're carrying his brat in your belly, for I'll not help you.' She thumped the arm of her chair, suddenly angry again. 'Go away now. I'm sick of the sight of you.'

'Would you like me to draw the curtains before I leave?'

'Yes. Damn you! You won't win me over so easily.'

Annelise pulled the curtains together, then turned with a smile on her lips. 'There, madame, now you can indulge your self-pity in comfort.' With that, she walked unhurriedly from the room, her head high, leaving Margot to splutter indignantly behind her.

Outside the door, the little smile of triumph faded from her lips. There was so much hatred in Lisette's mother. What terrible secret lay between her and the Comte? She had accused him of taking all the joy from her life, and his guilt had been stamped into every line of his face.

Gérard had challenged her to discover all his secrets, and already she felt that she was too close to discovering the first. Was he really a heartless womaniser as Margot claimed? Had his wife truly been unhappy because of it? No, she would not let herself believe it. The Comte could be moody at times, but his smile could set her heart fluttering like a bird in a cage. She was fascinated by him and his son, so much so that she was willing to take a risk. She suspected that her heart was more than half his already, and she knew that if she were sensible, she would leave now, before it was too late. Yet she wanted to stay. She wanted to live in the beautiful rooms that Lisette had never used, and she wanted to care for Gérard's son.

'Sometimes it is as well to take your chances when they come.'

It was as if Lady Sophia was standing by her side, smiling at her. 'You were so wise, my dearest friend,' she whispered, feeling the spirit of love so close that it seemed to enfold her. 'If I ran away now, I should never forgive myself.'

She was caught by the mystery of the château, and by the charm of its owner. She could not leave if she wanted to. Admitting it, she realised that she was happy. Suddenly her heart was lighter. She began to sing a lullaby that brought a smile to her lips as she hurried through the gathering dusk to her own apartments.

# CHAPTER FIVE

THE SOUND of a child crying woke Annelise. She lay listening to it for a moment, not quite sure where she was, then realised it must be Jean. Throwing back the bedcovers, she jumped out and reached for her wrap, thrusting her feet into soft-soled slippers, and striking a tinder to light the candle. She hurried to the boy's room, setting her chamberstick on a table beside the bed and gathering the boy into her arms. Holding him close, she rocked him gently and kissed the top of his head, enjoying the soft, clean smell of his hair and feeling tenderness stir within her.

'What is it, my love?' she asked, lifting his chin to wipe away the tears. 'Did you have a bad dream?'

He nodded, holding on to her tightly. 'He—He was chasing me through the forest. I was afraid of him.'

'Who was chasing you?'

'The ogre.' He shivered, his eyes wide with fear. 'Grandmama says he will eat me if I don't do as she tells me.'

'That is just a silly tale to frighten you into being good, Jean. Ogres are just imaginary monsters—like the fairy story I told you earlier.'

He looked at her uncertainly. 'Then why did she tell me it lived in the forest? I like to go there. I found the lurcher bitch and her puppies hidden away in a thicket. Grandmama forbade me to go near them again when I told her, and she said the ogre would get me. Why do people say things if they are not true?'

Annelise felt a surge of anger against the woman who had frightened the child. How could Madame Vicence be so cruel to her own grandson?

'Oh, I don't know—many reasons.' Annelise smiled at the child as she stroked his hair. 'I think she must have been very cross. She probably told you that silly tale because she was afraid you might get lost in the woods and she wanted to stop you going there. Perhaps you should not go there alone. It is a big place, Jean.'

'Grandmama is often cross.' Jean snuggled up to her. 'You won't be cross, will you?'

'Only if you are very naughty, and then only a little bit cross.' Annelise kissed him. 'Do you think you can sleep now? Or do you want me to stay with you?'

'Will you stay here in my bed?'

'If you want me to.'

'Madame Reinhold stayed with me once,' he said, yawning. 'They thought I was dying.'

'Close your eyes,' Annelise said. 'You think too much of unpleasant things. You are a child, and you should be happy. Now go to sleep or you will be too tired for our picnic tomorrow.'

'We always have a picnic when Madame Reinhold comes.'

'Stop talking,' Annelise whispered, but there was no reply, and she saw that he was fast asleep.

Smiling, she blew out the candle, but she did not immediately close her eyes. Instead, she lay wondering what kind of a woman would deliberately fill a child's head with stories that must give him nightmares. Her arms closed about the tiny body protectively. It seemed that she had arrived just in time!

'The Comte has gone?' Annelise looked at Madame Reinhold in surprise. 'Without saying goodbye to his son?' Or to me? she might have added as the disappointment surged in her.

'He does not like to upset his son.' The woman shrugged her shoulders. 'He looked in on the boy last night, but he has important business elsewhere and had to leave early this morning. He will return as soon as he can. He never stays away for too long, and his visits normally last longer.'

He would return when he could. That might mean anything, Annelise thought, a little annoyed. It was no wonder that his relationship with his son was difficult; if he came and went so abruptly, Jean must feel disturbed. Especially with a grandmother like Margot Vicence. She told herself that her indignation was all for Jean's sake, but a little voice in her head insisted that she was lying.

'I too must leave tomorrow,' Madame Reinhold went on. 'I am expected at Versailles. So we must make the most of today. Jean loves his picnics, and I shall show you the best places to take him.'

'Thank you, madame.'

Annelise hid her chagrin. It was stupid of her to feel let down. She knew she had no right to expect anything more from the Comte. She was after all a servant, even though he had denied it when she had said as much to his mother-in-law. Yet there was that kiss and the way he had looked at her when he said he thought her beautiful. For a moment she could have sworn that there was something deeper than passion in his eyes. Perhaps she was making too much of it. It was after all only a simple kiss. Scolding herself, she made up her mind to put all thought of him out of her mind and think only of his son. Jean was her reason for being at the château, and she was becoming very attached to him. He needed a friend, and she was determined to help him to forget all the unhappy days he had spent alone in his rooms.

Actually, it was Jean who helped her to put her own problems out of her mind. In the sunlit meadow by the stream, he was a natural, seemingly healthy child with all the energy of a normal six-year-old. He insisted on playing his favourite games of hide and seek and blind man's buff, teasing his two captive slaves unmercifully when it was their turn to don the blindfold.

After wearing them all out, he flopped down on the grass, panting, and pleading to be allowed to paddle in the shallow part of the stream. Before Annelise could give permission, Madame Reinhold shook her head and exclaimed in alarm.

'No, Jean, you know that is not possible. You catch cold so easily.'

'But it is so hot,' he complained, his mouth sulky. 'Why can I not swim as René does?'

'Who is René?'

Jean looked guilty, avoiding her eyes. 'He—He is a boy from the village. I see him in the woods sometimes.'

'Oh, Jean! You know your father does not like you to mix with the peasant children.'

Seeing the stubborn look on the boy's face, Annelise intervened. 'Surely there is no harm done, madame? He ought to have the company of boys his own age.'

'You don't understand.' Madame Reinhold frowned. 'Well, I suppose you are right. But there must be no swimming, Jean, do you hear me?'

'Yes, madame.'

Jean looked as if he were about to burst into tears. Jumping up, Annelise hunted in the grass for some flat stones and began skimming them across the surface of the stream. His interest caught by this new game, Jean found his own little store of stones and was soon laughing in triumph as his stones went further and faster than hers.

The rest of the day passed pleasantly without further incident, and soon enough Annelise was tucking a sleepy child into his bed.

'Tomorrow we must start your lessons,' she said, and he pulled a petulant face at her.

'I want to go to the forest,' he protested. 'Please say we can, Annelise?'

'Perhaps—after your lessons.' Annelise kissed him, refusing to be drawn into an argument. She saw a gleam of respect in his eyes and knew that he had been testing her. This son of Gérard's was no fool. She was willing to spoil him whenever possible, but she had been employed as a governess, and it was time he began to learn his letters and simple sums.

She had found all the materials she needed for their work in Jean's rooms. It was clear to her that provision had been made for his education, and she realised that the Comte must have been considering the idea for some time. He had actually taught the boy to write his own name, though nothing more. Perhaps he had not had the time.

Annelise decided to begin with the alphabet, and they spent the next few mornings working on two or three letters at a time. Jean was intelligent and soon began to enjoy his lessons, crowing with triumph whenever he achieved a new word. He was an excitable child, often noisy and occasionally a little wild, but she preferred it when he was happy, recalling the sad little face that had greeted her on the day of her arrival and comparing it with the laughing eyes that greeted her each morning now.

In the afternoons they went out walking, exploring the meadows and woods. Jean seemed to have no fear of the forest, at least while they were together and the sunlight flitered through the leaves, but she noticed that he held her hand tightly one evening when they had stayed out later than usual and it was growing dark before they got home. However, they saw no sign of any ogres or monsters, meeting only the charcoal-burner with his load of wood on a small handcart. He looked at them strangely, then nodded and walked in the opposite direction.

Although she had dined in the huge dining-hall while Madame Reinhold was still at the château, Annelise preferred to take her meals with Jean now that they were alone. She had soon learnt that Madame Vicence seldom dined with her son-in-law, preferring her own apartments. She was not exactly a recluse, but it was clear that she did not intend to mix with her grandson's governess any more than was necessary. Apart from the weekly reports she demanded on Jean's progress, there was no need for them to meet. When they did, Margot would nod her head in passing. It was as if she had decided to ignore Annelise.

The servants, however, were prepared to be friendly, and she often stopped to talk to them. They were predominantly male, apart from the women employed in the laundry, Madame Vicence's personal maid and a couple of girls in the kitchen.

When she asked Claude why there were not more women servants in the house, he shrugged his shoulders. 'The seigneur dismissed all his wife's women after she died. We thought it was because he could not bear to be reminded of . . . her death.'

Annelise sensed a mystery. 'How did Lisette die? Was it in childbed?'

'No . . .' He glanced uneasily over his shoulder as if to make sure that they were not overheard. 'The boy was only a few months old when it happened. She had been unwell, and she—she went up to the tower in the west wing and threw herself down.'

'You mean she killed herself?' Annelise stared at him in horror.

'Yes, mademoiselle.'

'But why would she do that?'

'We were not told.' Claude glanced over his shoulder again. 'She was a very gentle lady, easily frightened. She began acting strangely while carrying the child, and after his birth she sat alone for hours on end. The seigneur could do nothing to please her. It was as if she hated him.'

'Did she have reason to hate him?' Annelise had to ask, even though she felt the question to be a kind of betrayal.

'No. I'll swear the seigneur never glanced at another woman—that came later.' Claude looked uncomfortable. 'Forgive me, I have said too much.'

'Perhaps I asked too much. Thank you for telling me.'

After that, Claude seemed to take her under his wing. Nothing was too much trouble, and if he saw her wandering about the château, he would point out the various rooms, helping her to find her way. Once she asked him to show her Lisette's room, and after some hesitation he did so. It was in the same wing as Madame Vicence's but there was nothing remarkable about it. It was just a pleasant, sunny room, but decorated in blues and greens. There was no clue in the empty chambers as to why Gérard's wife had taken her own life. Nor why she preferred to sleep in this small room rather than in the sumptuous apartment he had prepared specially for her.

Annelise had discovered that the Comte's apartments were next to her own. There was a door that she suspected might connect them, which would be natural since

they had been designed for the master and mistress of
the house. She tried the door, but it was locked on the
other side. That made her frown for a few minutes, for
she would have liked to have the key herself, but then
she dismissed her doubts as foolish. The Comte was too
much of a gentleman to abuse the situation. At least,
she believed he was.

Only a few of the servants were allowed in to clean
Margot's rooms, and Annelise soon discovered that she
was not welcomed unless invited. She ventured to take
Madame Vicence a posy of flowers she and Jean had
picked one sunny afternoon, and was told never to do
so again unless summoned. After that, she stayed clear,
realising that the older woman did not want her com-
panionship. She wondered at the bitterness that had
soured Margot's life, then she forgot. It was no longer
important. Gérard had come home!

They had been picnicking by the stream. It was such a
hot day that Annelise had allowed Jean to paddle for a
few minutes, and had dried his feet and legs thoroughly
before putting on his stockings and shoes. Both of them
were looking decidedly crumpled as they walked back
to the house, carrying the hamper between them and
singing a nursery rhyme she had been teaching him.
Seeing the carriages drawn up in the courtyard, they
stopped and looked at one another.

A very elegant lady was getting out of one of the ve-
hicles, assisted by André Beaumarchais. Two other
gentlemen emerged from the second coach, and a stun-
ningly beautiful woman emerged from the third, helped
by the Comte himself. For a moment Annelise stood
staring in surprise, then she tugged Jean's hand, in-
tending to take him round to the side entrance, but it

was too late. Gérard had seen them, and he beckoned imperiously.

Conscious of her windblown hair and the grass-stains on her crumpled gown, Annelise was reluctant to answer the summons. Another, older woman had joined the others and they were all looking at her expectantly. Her cheeks were flushed as she approached, holding Jean's hand tightly. At the last moment he broke from her and ran to his father.

'Papa! Papa!' he cried excitedly. 'We did not know you were home.'

A smile flickered in the dark eyes, and they looked beyond him to the obviously reluctant woman. 'We can see that from your appearance, Jean. Ladies, this disreputable fellow is my son. Jean, at least show our guests that you can behave like a gentleman, even if you look like a village brat.'

Though his words were harsh, they were said with affection and Jean laughed, bowing very creditably before the ladies. 'Your pardon,' he said, with a touch of his father's hauteur. 'We have been picnicking by the stream, and Annelise let me paddle—that's why my stockings are wrinkled.'

'Indeed?' Gérard frowned, a hint of anger about his mouth, though the ladies laughed. 'I shall have something to say about that later.'

Annelise saw the glimmer of annoyance in his eyes, and her chin went up defiantly. It was ridiculous to treat Jean as an invalid, when she knew that he was perfectly healthy. He had not even had another nightmare since that first night, and she would defend her decision before Gérard's guests if he challenged her. However, he merely inclined his head stiffly.

'Madame Dubonnet; Madame St Blaise; Mademoiselle Dubonnet—this is Mademoiselle Pembleton, my son's governess.'

Three pairs of female eyes regarded her with undisguised disdain, their expressions making her very aware of her untidy appearance. Her cheeks hot, she curtsied, feeling the anger stir in her breast. Gérard need not have subjected me to this humiliation, she thought furiously, her eyes flashing. He could have let me escape into the château and change instead of forcing me to meet his guests.

She turned her angry gaze on him, letting him see that she was in no mood to be trifled with. 'If you will excuse us, monsieur, we both need to change our clothes.' Without waiting for his answer, she turned to the boy. 'Come, Jean, we must not intrude.'

He took her hand, looking from her to his father with a glint of excitement in his eyes. He glanced at her several times as they walked into the house together, as if sensing her mood.

'Are you cross, Annelise? You said you wouldn't be cross. Is it because I told Papa I'd been paddling? You said I must always tell the truth—but now you're cross.'

'Not with you.' Annelise laughed as she saw the mischief in his eyes. He had changed so much in these past few weeks. 'I expect I shall get into trouble for letting you get your feet wet, but I don't see why you shouldn't paddle when the weather is hot—though you must never do it unless I am with you.'

'I promise,' he said, the mischief leaving his eyes. 'Papa won't send you away, will he?'

'I shouldn't think so.' Annelise raised her brows. 'Who else do you think would put up with you?'

'Only you!' Jean started to giggle and threw his arms about her waist. 'I do love you, Annelise.'

'And I love you,' she said. 'Even with wrinkled stockings.'

Although she had reassured him that she would not be dismissed, Annelise felt uneasy. Madame Reinhold had stressed that Jean took cold easily, and it would be her fault if he became ill. Yet she was sure in her own mind that he was perfectly healthy. It was foolish to treat him as a delicate invalid when he ought to be playing with other children.

Just as she was preparing the child for bed, Claude entered the room with his supper tray. It was set for one person, and she anticipated the summons before he spoke.

'The seigneur requests that you dine with him and his guests, mademoiselle.'

Annelise frowned, hesitating for a moment before nodding her agreement. She was tempted to plead a headache even if it meant that she must forgo her supper, but her pride would not let her take refuge in a lie. Since the Comte had invited her to dine, she would show those haughty ladies who had accompanied him home that she was not to be sneered at.

There was one dress in her wardrobe that she had never yet worn. It was a pale green satin sewn with pearls and silk rosettes, and she had made it herself just before her mother died, anticipating the London season that had never been hers. She had taken great care over the embroidery, but it had cost a tiny fraction of the gown that Madame St Blaise had been wearing. Even so, she did not believe that anyone would guess it was her own work.

She dressed her hair in a knot at the back of her head, letting two shining ringlets fall gracefully over one shoulder, and pinned her watch to the tightly-waisted bodice of her gown where it dipped to reveal a glimpse of her breasts. Looking at her reflection in the mirror,

Annelise felt a glow of satisfaction. Tonight she did not look like a humble governess!

Her appearance in the dining-hall made quite as much of a sensation as she had hoped, all eyes turning towards her as she entered. She saw surprise and annoyance on Madame St Blaise's lips, a hint of outrage in Madame Dubonnet's face—and admiration in four pairs of male eyes. Only Marielle Dubonnet appeared indifferent.

'We have been waiting for you, Annelise,' the Comte said, a faint smile playing over his mouth.

'I dressed as quickly as I could,' she replied with a flash of defiance. 'If I had known earlier that I was required to dine...'

'You will always be needed when we have guests,' he said. 'You know André, of course. May I present Monsieur Dubonnet and Monsieur Berrard.'

She felt the pressure of his fingers on her arm, glancing up at him in surprise as he steered her towards the chair at the end of the table. 'Here?' she asked, and saw a gleam in his eyes. 'Surely Madame Du...'

'You will do as I say,' he murmured. 'Do you understand me?'

'Yes, monsieur.' She met his eyes with a challenge of her own. 'For the moment I must obey.'

'Ah, Annelise, how you tempt me,' he said softly and moved away.

She sent a look of indignation after him, but was left with nothing to say or do but be polite to his guests. This she managed easily, having André to one side of her and Monsieur Berrard to the other, both of whom were willing to be pleased with her—though she intercepted killing looks from each of the other ladies.

She wondered why the Comte had insisted on having her at his table, since it clearly offended his female guests. Surely if he needed a hostess, he could have persuaded

Madame Vicence to leave her apartments for once? Yet it was a pleasant gathering, and the widow's brooding presence would have ruined the atmosphere. Watching Gérard laughing with Madame St Blaise, she realised how much it must mean to him to have a party such as this at his home again. She knew from Claude that there had been no guests, apart from André and Madame Reinhold, since Lisette's death.

André was speaking to her now. She turned to him with a smile as he said, 'And how do you like living at the château, mademoiselle?'

'I like it well enough. Jean is a lively charge, and I am never bored in his company.'

'He is much recovered, then? I had thought him a semi-invalid.'

'I have seen no sign of it. He has more than sufficient energy, I promise you.' The look that accompanied her words made him laugh.

'I have young nephews of my own,' he said. 'Your news about Jean is excellent. Gérard will be pleased to hear your opinion. He has always worried about the boy's health, I know.'

'I believe there is no reason for anxiety.' Annelise glanced at the Comte, sensing that his eyes were on her. 'Have you come from Paris, monsieur? What is the news?'

'You heard that the Bastille was taken in July, just after you left?' As Annelise shook her head, his brows went up. 'Of course, you have so few visitors here. I thought . . . But I see I was mistaken.'

'You thought the Comte would have told me? I have not spoken to him since—since he arrived, until a moment ago. He has told me nothing.'

'I see . . .' André frowned and glanced towards his friend. 'Well, let me tell you what I can. After the fall of the Bastille, Necker was recalled—and you may imagine with what joy he has been received by the people. His progress has been almost royal. Speaking of royalty, four princes of the blood royal ran for their lives, thinking no doubt to lose them if they stayed on French soil! But His Majesty rode into Paris, braving the sullen looks of the people.'

'Surely that was dangerous? Had it not been for you, I should hardly have escaped. Oh, forgive me...' She blushed. 'I should not have said that.'

André laughed. 'I knew you had recognised me. Tell me, what gave me away?'

'It was your eyes—and your hands.'

'My hands?' He looked at them. 'What is wrong with them?'

'They are too soft to belong to a peasant, monsieur, and the nails were clean and unbroken.'

'Thank you. I shall remember that in future. It may save my life.'

'Surely you do not mean to go on risking your life?'

'There is as much danger in the country as in Paris.' André hesitated. 'I do not wish to frighten you, but many châteaux have already gone up in flames...'

'It will not happen here?' Her eyes widened in horror.

'Gérard has come back to see that it does not.' He smiled at her reassuringly. 'Tomorrow I leave for England with our friends, but I shall return to do what I can. I fear there will be many who will not escape this terrible retribution.'

'Can nothing be done to stop it? Surely the harvest has been good this year? Claude was telling me that the Comte's tenants have done remarkably well.'

'There is grain in the fields, yet the price continues to rise. In the Assembly they have abolished privilege, but words do not fill empty bellies. The people have been roused, and the fires rages over France, particularly in the Mâconnais and Beaujolais, but the whole of the south-east is in turmoil. In the north, too, barriers are being burnt, tax-gatherers put to flight and anyone who has held an official post goes in fear of his peasants' wrath.'

'We are fortunate that we live so quietly here.' Annelise shivered, her eyes straying to the Comte. 'Gérard does not intend to take his son to England?'

'No...' There was a guarded expression in André's eyes. 'I have tried to persuade him, but he will not listen. He has always treated his people fairly and he believes they will remain loyal to him. He will stay here.' He looked at her intently. 'Do you wish to return to England, mademoiselle?'

'I...' Annelise began, but was interrupted by the Comte.

'Would you take the ladies into the adjoining salon, Annelise,' he said, looking at her across the table. 'We shall join you in a moment.'

Directing an apologetic look at André, she obeyed. She was not certain what answer she might have given had the interruption not come when it did. If she stayed in France her life was at risk, yet how could she think of leaving when Jean and his father were to remain?

Sweet wine, marchpane comfits and coffee had been set out in the withdrawing chamber for the ladies. Claude served them, coming first to Annelise exactly as though she were indeed the chatêlaine, to receive her instructions. This brought her a darkling glance from Madame St Blaise.

'How long have you been Jean's governess?' she asked, her cool tones revealing what she thought of being forced to dine with underlings. 'Gérard did not tell me you would be here.'

Her manner implied that she had some claim on him. Had she been his mistress at Versailles? Her purple gown was evidence of her status. Was the Comte to be her next husband? It seemed likely that she had hopes in that direction, Annelise thought. Gérard de Montpellier was a wealthy man with a young son who needed a mother. It would naturally annoy a hopeful widow to find a young and presentable woman ensconced as a governess in the home she had planned to make her own.

'A few weeks only, madame,' Annelise replied. 'I believe you leave for England tomorrow?'

'Gérard insists on it. He is concerned for my safety.' Madame St Blaise fluttered her fan. 'I should prefer to stay with him, naturally, but he will not hear of it.'

'I shall be glad when we get to England,' Madame Dubonnet said, her cheeks flushed with annoyance. 'Fortunately, we were at Versailles when the mob ransacked our château, otherwise we might all be dead. If we escape with our jewels and our lives, we may thank God for it!'

'Calm yourself, Mama,' her daughter said. 'André will see us safely over the water.'

Annelise was glad of the diversion. Madame St Blaise had made her position clear. A woman of perhaps thirty, she had both poise and beauty. If she was his mistress, Gérard would have no need to look in his son's governess's direction.

The three ladies had begun to talk among themselves, pointedly ignoring Annelise. She bore with it for several minutes, then got to her feet startling them all to silence.

'Since I am obviously in the way, I shall bid you goodnight, ladies.'

Walking from the room without a backward glance, she was conscious of a feeling of triumph. How dared they be so rude? It was Gérard's fault, she thought angrily. He had humiliated her before them when he arrived, and they believed she was of no consequence. His belated action in seating her in the place of honour had only made things worse. They had seen it as impudence on her part. But her sense of triumph faded as she reached her own rooms. They were right to treat her as a servant, she realised, for that was all she was in this house. Any secret hopes she might have cherished of becoming more to its master were ashes now. If he was in love with Madame St Blaise... No, he could not be, her heart protested. He could not love a woman with hard eyes and a tight, ungenerous mouth...

Was she jealous? Too honest to lie to herself, Annelise acknowledged the shameful truth. She was in love with her employer. She had fallen in love with him from the moment their eyes met in the gardens of Fontainebleau. Even after he had confessed his intention to seduce her in Paris, she had continued to love him. He had made her angry, but love had taken the sting from that anger. Now she was angry with him again, but she was also jealous!

Another girl might have collapsed in tears, but Annelise undressed calmly, not even tearing her pretty gown. She put on a blue velvet wrap over her night-chemise and sat down to brush her hair, the ritual soothing her inner turmoil. She sat for a long time, staring into the mirror, waiting. Somehow she was sure he would come. He would be so angry with her for deserting his guests that he would be unable to keep his temper in check until the morning. It grew chilly as the hours passed and she sensed the stillness in the house. Everyone must have retired long since. Perhaps she had misjudged the effect her disobedience would have. He would not come now... Yet even as she stood up, about to go to bed, her door was thrust open and she saw him in the doorway, his face dark with anger.

'So...' he said coldly. 'You waited. You knew I would come?'

'You are angry.'

'I have the right. How dare you humiliate me by leaving my guests like that?'

'How dared you humiliate me before your mistress?' Her eyes flashed green fire. 'Why did you drag me in front of them as if I were some kind of prize?'

'My mistress once, but never since I first saw you,' he muttered hoarsely. He took two strides towards her, a nerve pulsing in his throat. 'My only thought was to see you and speak to you again when I saw you with the boy. You looked so beautiful with your hair blown by the wind and that wonderful, sleepy look in your eyes. I did not mean to humiliate you. I have thirsted for the mere sight of you these many days.'

'W-What do you mean?' she whispered. 'What are you saying?'

'Don't you know? How can you not feel it?' he whispered. 'It burns inside me like the fires of hell. I want— I need you so badly. Yet if I take what I desire, I am forever damned.'

She saw the tenseness in him, and shivered. 'Why should you be damned?' she whispered, a little frightened by the intensity of his gaze. What terrible thing was in his mind that he should stare at her like that? She made an involuntary move towards him, as if wanting to ease his torment.

'Annelise, no,' he groaned. 'Do not tempt me so...'

Even as he spoke, he was reaching for her. This time his kiss was no passionless thing, but a hungry yearning that demanded a response from her, setting her whole body on fire. She leaned into him, feeling the deep shudder run through him as he held her crushed against his breast. His lips moved feverishly from her lips to her throat, devouring her. She yielded to him with a sigh, knowing instinctively that this was meant to be. When desire to match his own raged inside her, how could she doubt that it was for this one moment she had been born? Now his lips were once more covering hers, thrilling her to the very core of her being. It no longer mattered what was in his mind or even that this might be part of some scheme to get her into his bed. She was swept away on a heady tide of passion, knowing only that she wanted to be with him like this, to feel herself as one with him.

'Oh, Annelise,' he murmured huskily, 'I knew it would be this way with us from the first moment I saw you. It was as if Destiny had reached out and touched me.'

'Gérard,' she whispered, her arms twining about his neck as he bent to lift her in his arms, carrying her towards the bed. He laid her down gently and bent over her, smoothing back the shimmering strands of red-gold hair from her forehead. She trembled with pleasure as he parted her robe, touching his lips to the hollow at the base of her throat. 'Oh...'

His hand moved beneath the silk of her nightgown, caressing the soft mounds of her breasts. She moaned, catching her lip between pearly teeth as her breath came faster and she arched towards him, quivering with anticipation.

'Annelise...Where are you?' The sobbing cry made her stiffen and sit up, pulling her wrap together. 'Annelise... I want you...'

'I must go to him,' she said apologetically as she heard Gérard's stifled exclamation of annoyance. 'He needs me.'

'*I* need you,' the man muttered ruefully, but he made no attempt to hold her as she slipped from the bed.

She smiled at him and shook her head. 'Perhaps he will sleep soon,' she said.

She was a little anxious as she hurried to the child's room. Was he ill? Had she been wrong to let him paddle in the stream after all?

'What is it, Jean?' she asked, pressing a cool hand to his brow. 'Are you feeling ill?'

'No.' He threw his arms about her. 'It was the dream again. He—He was chasing me through the forest...'

She looked up and saw Gérard watching them from the doorway, shaking her head at him. 'It was only a dream, Jean,' she said. 'You ate too much supper. I told you that ogres are only legends. There is nothing in the forest to harm you. We have been there many times together and we see only deer and rabbits.'

'I know.' He gazed up at her, wide-eyed. 'Will you stay with me tonight?'

Her eyes went to the man. He smiled ruefully and nodded, closing the door softly behind him.

'I shall stay if you want me to,' Annelise said, kissing the top of his head. She slipped in beside him, gathering him to her.

The wild pulsating in her blood had slowed at last, and her cheeks were warm as she remembered her willingness to abandon herself to love. Perhaps this was best, she thought. Perhaps it was better that she should have a chance to think about her situation calmly. Gérard had made no mention of love. Was she really prepared to be his mistress? Would it not be more sensible to return to England while she still could?

Feeling the warmth of the small body curled against her breast, she was aware of a great tenderness. She was tied by the bonds of love, no more able to leave the father than the child. Somehow she knew that they both needed

her—and perhaps Gérard's need was even greater than
his son's . . .

Jean was sleeping peacefully when Annelise rose and
dressed. There was a fresh, still quality about the early
morning air, a pearly light that made her fingers long
to hold a paintbrush again. She had had no time to indulge her talent since coming to the château, but now
she felt an urge to spend a little time alone. A time to
think . . .

Taking her sketchbook with her, she slipped out of
the house and into the coolness of the forest. The birds
had started their morning chorus, and she could hear
them calling from the tree-tops. A blackbird's fluty song
was answered by the shrill piping of a red-breasted robin,
while the thrush called a shy melody from somewhere
deeper in the forest. It was good to be alone for a while,
to let her thoughts wander at will. There was a precious
stillness about the woods this morning, making her feel
at peace. She found a fallen tree and sat down, opening
the little vellum-bound book and taking up a piece of
fine charcoal. The book contained many sketches she
had made in England and one or two hasty ones she had
done from memory of the gardens at Fontainebleau. It
was her habit to make several drawings of scenes that
caught her eye and then to recreate them on canvas later,
trusting to her memory for colourings and shadings. She
thought that one day she might try to paint the château
itself.

She had tried to draw Gérard's face, but failed. He
was still too much of a mystery to her, even after last
night. It was the memory of what had so nearly taken
place then that had brought her out into the woods. She
needed to be alone, to think about what had happened.
If Jean had not called out, she would have given herself

to his father. Her cheeks stung with embarrassment as she realised how wantonly she had behaved, falling into his arms so easily. What must he be thinking of her?

Hearing a rustling noise in the bushes, she looked up, her heart beating rapidly. 'Hello...' she called. 'Is someone there?'

There was no answer, but as she got to her feet, a man came through the trees towards her, and she drew a sigh of relief. It was only André. He was wearing leather breeches and a thick woollen waistcoat of a reddish brown, and carrying a gun over his shoulder. He had obviously decided to see if he could shoot a rabbit or some game birds.

'Annelise,' he said, smiling at her. 'Did I startle you? I am so sorry.'

'It does not matter,' she replied. 'It was just that I thought myself completely alone.'

He came to stand just behind her so that he could see her work. 'This is really very good,' he said. 'Have you shown your sketches to Gérard yet?'

'No, not yet. I am hoping to paint the château one day.'

'If you paint as well as you draw, he should give you a commission.' Seeing Annelise's blush, his eyes narrowed. 'Unless of course you mean to be the mistress here?'

'Monsieur Beaumarchais!'

'I did not mean to offend you. As Gérard's friend, I should be glad to see him married to a woman like you—a woman who could give him happiness instead of pain.'

'Was—Was his marriage not happy?'

André frowned. 'It was a disaster from the beginning. But if you wish to know more, you must ask Gérard.'

'If he wishes to tell me, he will do so,' she said quietly. 'I thought that perhaps you might know why he sometimes seems to be haunted by his memories.'

'Haunted?' André nodded, his face grim. 'While he allows Lisette's mother to live in the château, he will never be free of the past.' He shook his head as if to show his disapproval, then thought better of it. 'Are you ready to return? I do not think it particularly safe for a young woman to be wandering in the forest alone, especially with the mood of the peasants as it is now.'

'Jean and I often walk here,' Annelise said with a laugh. 'I am sure none of the Comte's people would harm us; they respect him too much. However, I was just about to return.'

They walked together, conversing easily, almost as if they were old friends, and parting as they reached the courtyard. Annelise ran up the stairs to her room, halting in surprise as she saw the Comte and Claude standing deep in conversation outside her door. They glanced at each other, and then Gérard came towards her, his face tight with anger.

'Where have you been?' he demanded. 'Claude has been looking everywhere for you.'

She stared at him in surprise. 'I went for a walk in the woods. Why, has something happened? Is Jean ill?'

'No, he's still asleep,' Gérard said, his eyes narrowing with suspicion. 'Why did you go to the forest? Was it to meet someone?'

'Why should you think that?' Annelise asked, raising her eyes to his. 'I was sketching...'

'Then where are your things?'

She gave a little cry, suddenly realising that she had forgotten her book. 'I laid them down when André...'

'So you did go to meet someone!'

'André happened to be passing, that's all.' She opened her hand to show him the piece of charcoal she had been using. 'I must go back and look for my book.'

'You will stay here,' he said sharply. 'The book does not matter. I'll buy you a dozen when I go to Paris.'

She felt a surge of anger. Did he imagine that he could replace something of sentimental value just by purchasing a new book? And what did he mean by accusing her of meeting another man? If he thought that she would go from his arms... The indignation rose in her and she turned away angrily. He caught her arm, swinging her round to face him.

'André is leaving this morning. Do you wish to go with him?'

'How dare you!' she cried. 'Do you think I am a wanton, to go from one man to another without a thought? If so, I shall leave this house today!'

'Annelise, no!' he cried, and his fingers bit into her flesh.

As she heard the note of pain in his voice, the anger began to drain out of her. Why was he behaving so strangely? Surely he must know how she felt about him by now.

'Why should I want to leave you?' she asked softly. 'My place is here with you and Jean—isn't it?'

A flame leapt up in his eyes. 'Yes, for as long as you wish,' he said. 'I want you to stay, Annelise, but I would not keep you here against your will.'

'Surely you cannot doubt it?'

'I thought you had run away,' he said. 'When Claude said he could not find you, I thought you had left me.'

'I would never leave without telling you I meant to go.'

She wondered at the intensity of his look. Could it really matter so much to him?

'Is that a promise?' he asked.

At that moment the resemblance between him and his son was so strong that it melted her heart with tenderness. They were both demanding and perhaps even a little selfish, but she was caught fast by the bonds of love.

'Yes,' she said, smiling. 'It's a promise.'

# CHAPTER SIX

'WHY CAN'T we have a picnic?' Jean demanded, two bright pink spots in his cheeks. 'You promised, Annelise. You promised!'

'I am sorry, Jean,' she said quietly. 'This time I cannot keep my promise.'

'Why?'

'Because your father has guests. He will want you here to say goodbye to them.'

'But I want to go to the forest. Why must we stay here?'

'Because I want you to, Jean.'

Annelise glanced over her shoulder, smiling as she saw the Comte in the doorway. He was dressed in an elegant coat and breeches of dark blue, his shirt ruffles and stock of the finest lace-trimmed linen. How handsome he was, she thought, her heart somersaulting as he smiled at her.

'Our guests are leaving in a few minutes, Jean. I want you to come with me and say goodbye to them.' Gérard held out his hand imperiously. 'And you, Annelise.'

Jean went to take his hand, but the petulant look was still there about his mouth. 'I want to go on a picnic.'

'Sometimes a gentleman has to do as he is told without question, Jean.' The Comte frowned as he looked at the boy's flushed face. 'You are indulged more than most children of your age. Please do not make me ashamed of you.'

'I'm sorry, Papa.' Jean's eyes dropped and he bit his lip.

'You should apologise to Annelise. It is not her fault that you cannot have your outing.'

'I'm sorry, Annelise.'

He looked so forlorn that she dropped a kiss on his head. 'We'll have a special picnic very soon. Perhaps your father will come with us?' Glancing up, she surprised a tender look in the Comte's eyes.

'Would you like that, Jean?'

'Yes, Papa. Will you really spend a whole day with us?'

'If it will please you,' Gérard said, ruffling his hair. 'I've been thinking that it's time you learned to ride. How would you like a pony of your own?'

Jean's eyes were so big that they almost seemed to fill his face. 'Will you teach me to ride, Papa?'

'Of course.' Gérard laughed at his eagerness. 'My father taught me when I was barely able to walk. I have waited because—because I thought you might not be well enough to enjoy physical exercise, but I think you are ready now.'

'I am never ill now—not since Annelise came.' Jean tugged at his father's hand. 'Ask her, Papa. I even paddled in the stream without catching cold.'

'Yes, so you did.' Dark mocking eyes met clear green ones above his head. 'So you did.'

Annelise blushed and shook her head at him, but would not be provoked into a reply.

Jean knew no such reserve. 'When will you get me the pony? When can I go riding? When, Papa?'

'Perhaps I shall get the pony for your birthday.'

'But that's not for two weeks! May I not have it sooner?'

Gérard smiled at him. 'We'll see. Now you must make me proud of you, Jean. No more tantrums in front of our guests.' They had almost reached the courtyard, and he turned to Annelise, offering her his arm. 'We must say goodbye to our visitors, Annelise.'

She hesitated for a moment, her heart fluttering as she looked into his eyes. Was he doing this to make up for the previous day? Did he not realise how it would seem to the others? To appear all together like this made it look as if they were a family.

'Annelise!' There was no mistaking the note of command in his voice, or the look of satisfaction in his eyes as she obeyed. 'That's better. You belong to me now, and you must obey me in all things.'

His eyes were mocking her, challenging her. She lifted her chin defiantly and heard his soft laughter. 'In all things, monsieur?'

'In all things,' he repeated firmly.

'You demand a great deal,' she whispered, her hand trembling on his arm.

'Not so very much,' he murmured. 'Trust me a little longer, and you will see how hard a taskmaster I intend to be.'

She blushed, but could not bring herself to answer. He smiled and drew her forward to the top of the steps, waving to André.

'So you are ready now? Ladies, I wish you all a safe and comfortable journey.' His hand closed possessively over Annelise's as he felt her fingers flutter on his arm. 'Perhaps we shall see you here again in happier days? We must hope that the madness that plagues our country will soon be over so that you can return to your homes in peace.'

'It is all very well,' Madame Dubonnet muttered. 'They burned our château. Think of the cost of rebuilding!'

'Oh, Mama,' her daughter sighed, 'at least we are alive.'

'And when shall I have the pleasure of seeing you in London, Gérard?' Madame St Blaise asked, pouting her rouged lips at him provocatively. 'I trust you won't keep me waiting too long?'

'I have no plans to visit London at the moment, madame.' He glanced down at Annelise, his eyes caressing her. 'I believe I shall be spending most of my time at home in future.'

The implication in his words was clear. Madame St Blaise turned away, her face angry. She gave her hand to Monsieur Dubonnet, obliging him to help her into the carriage.

'I shall return as soon as I can,' André said. 'If you meant what you said just now, Gérard, I am glad. Annelise, you have my sincere best wishes for the future. Do not let this rogue's moods disturb you; he has a good heart, believe me.'

She blushed, hardly knowing how to answer. He was speaking as if he thought she was to be Gérard's wife. 'I—I wish you a safe journey, monsieur.'

Gérard chuckled as he saw her embarrassment. 'I have not asked her yet, André, but you are right! This is the lady I intend to wed. If she will have me—and my moods.'

'Oh!' Annelise's eyes sparkled as she stared up at him. 'You are wicked to tease me, monsieur.'

'Did you think I meant to have you as my mistress, Annelise?' he asked, the dark eyes gleaming with mischief as he bent to whisper in her ear. 'And I thought you such a proper English miss...'

'Have a care, monsieur,' she muttered fiercely. 'You shall be called to account for this.'

'You see what a virago she will be, André! Yet I think I must have her, for she is the mistress of my heart.'

André laughed and clapped him on the shoulder. 'I see that I leave you in good hands, my friend. Pegasus shall be my wedding gift to you.'

'I have not earned him. In truth, the conqueror has been vanquished.'

The two men laughed together while Annelise looked on mystified, but neither was prepared to enlighten her. It did not matter. Her heart was singing and she was so happy that she could hardly breathe. Gérard wanted her as his wife! It seemed almost unbelievable.

She watched as André climbed into the coach with the others. Jean had wandered off, tired of listening to the conversation of the adults, and was playing with one of the lurcher dogs that lived in and around the stables. She smiled to see him contented, feeling her happiness overflow as she gazed up into the face of the man at her side. The troubles in Paris and the countryside seemed far away at this moment. Here, within these sunlit walls, it seemed that nothing could touch them. It was a shining moment. They stood within a circle of perfect peace, far removed from reality.

'Did you really mean it when you said you wanted to marry me?' she asked, her face glowing as she gazed up at him. 'I can scarcely believe it.'

'Can you not?' he murmured, his smile tender and yet mocking. Then his smile faded as he slowly traced the line of her cheek. 'I pray that you will never regret the decision you have made.'

'How could I? I love you.'

'But for how long, I wonder?'

Annelise felt as if a shadow had passed across the sun. Surely he could not still doubt her?

'What have I done that you should doubt my constancy?'

'I was taught a hard lesson,' he said, 'but you are right. I should not . . .'

'Papa!' Jean came running up to them, the dogs at his heels. 'Papa, will you let me ride your horse? If I am soon to have my own pony, I should begin my lessons now.'

'Impatient whelp!' Gérard smiled ruefully. 'I may as well give you your own way, for there'll be no peace until I do.' He glanced at Annelise. 'Forgive me; I shall tell you everything later. For the moment I fear I must bow to the demand of this tyrant.'

She laughed, feeling the happiness begin to swell within her as she watched them walk in the direction of the stables. How much she loved them both! And now she would have this joy for the rest of her life. It was too good to be true.

Turning to go in, she glanced up at the tower of the west wing. A face was at the window, staring down at her. A woman's face. For a moment she gasped, thinking that she had seen a ghost, then realised it was Madame Vicence, not Lisette's shade. What was Margot doing in the tower? Claude had said that no one went there since Lisette's death.

She was sure that Madame Vicence had witnessed the little scene in the courtyard and would draw her own conclusions. She had called Annelise a whore at the outset, but surely she would be pleased that Gérard had decided to marry again? Even as she tried to convince herself that this would be the case, Annelise knew she was deceiving herself. Lisette's mother did not want her son-in-law to find happiness: she hated him. Why? She had made vague accusations against Gérard, but there must be something more to cause such deep hatred! Squaring her shoulders, she went back inside, determined to ignore Margot's spying. It did not matter if she disapproved; Gérard was the master here. The château was big enough for all of them.

Annelise was singing as she ran up to her own room. Nothing must be allowed to spoil their happiness now. Gérard had at last decided to put his grief behind him and... Entering her bedchamber, she saw her sketchbook lying on the bed and ran to it with a cry of pleasure. Gérard must have sent one of the servants to look for it. How thoughtful he was! Picking it up, she opened it and felt a jolt of horror. Every single page had been slashed through with a knife.

The book dropped from her hand and she stared at it, feeling sick. Who would do such a thing? All her hard work destroyed in a single act of vengeance. And who had placed it on her bed where she would be sure to find it?

Only one person hated her that much. Yet how could Margot have come by it? She seldom left her rooms—or did she? She had certainly been spying on them from the tower, so was it possible that she had also been watching her in the woods? A shiver ran down her spine as she remembered the rustlings she had heard just before André had appeared. Could he have disturbed someone else? Feeling a surge of disgust, she picked up the book. She had to know the truth!

Why did it always strike cold in the west wing, Annelise wondered, shivering as she made her way towards Madame Vicence's rooms. Was it her imagination, or was there really an oppressive atmosphere in this part of the house?

Reaching Margot's chambers, she knocked sharply. There was silence for a moment, and then the one word, 'Enter.'

For once the curtains were open, almost as if Madame Vicence had been waiting for her. She was wearing her usual black, looking like a huge spider ready to pounce on an unsuspecting victim. Her eyes glittered with hatred.

'So you found your book!' A harsh cackle left her painted lips. 'I suppose you've come to thank me for finding it for you.'

She was not even going to deny it. Shocked, Annelise stared at her, unable to speak for the moment.

'Lost your tongue, have you?'

'No.' Annelise took a deep breath, determined not to be goaded into losing her temper. 'Why? What was the point of destroying the book?'

'It amused me. I wanted to show you what I could do if I wished.' Margot laughed bitterly. 'You are not wanted here. Until you came, I was mistress of the château. Jean no longer listens to me now, and Gérard has forgotten his debt.'

'What do you mean? What has he done that you should hate him so much?'

Margot sat forward in her chair, clutching the arm of her chair so hard that her knuckles turned white. 'If you know what's good for you, you will leave here. Now. Today! If you have no money, I'll help you.'

'I'm not afraid of you...'

'It is not me you should fear. It is the Comte you should be wary of. If you stay, he will ruin your life. He will break your heart as he broke my poor Lisette's.'

'I do not believe you,' Annelise said. 'I have nothing to fear from the Comte. He loves me.'

'Has he told you that?' Margot demanded fiercely, her fist striking the arm of her chair as Annelise nodded. 'He will not marry you. I shall not permit it! He has no right to marry again—no right to happiness.'

'Why do you say that? Why do you hate him so much?' Annelise cried. 'He has been good to you...'

'Good to me?' Margot shrilled. 'Everything he gives me is mine by right! He destroyed my life. He murdered my little girl, my baby...'

'No! No, that is a lie,' Annelise said, her throat catching. 'Lisette took her own life.'

'Because he drove her to it,' Margot shrieked. 'Ask him if you don't believe me. Ask him!'

Annelise stared at her, feeling the strength of her bitterness reach out to touch her. 'No,' she said, backing away, fighting the poison that Margot was trying to put into her mind. 'No, I do not believe you.'

As she turned and walked from the room, Margot's shrill laughter followed her, ringing in her ears.

Jean was almost asleep on his feet, yet he could not stop talking as Annelise prepared him for bed. His father had put him up on his own horse, leading him round and round the courtyard for over an hour. And he had dined with them in the big room downstairs. Now he was close to exhaustion but determined to wring the last second from his magical day.

'Everyone was watching,' he said, yawning as she tucked him in. 'Papa says I did well and he will get me the pony soon.'

'I'm sure he will.' Annelise bent to kiss his brow. 'Now it's time to go to sleep, my love.'

Jean caught her hand. 'Papa says you're going to live with us always—is it true?'

Margot's cruel taunt was echoing in her mind, but she would not allow it to haunt her. She smiled at the child. 'Would you like that, Jean?'

'Yes! I want you here for ever and ever.'

'Then I expect I shall stay. Did your father tell you why I am going to stay?'

Jean nodded, his eyes wide. 'You are going to marry him, but Papa says I'm not to tell anyone else yet. Why can't I tell anyone, Annelise?'

'Perhaps your father wants to keep it a secret for a while. Now go to sleep, Jean.'

He settled down and she sat by him for a few minutes, until she was sure he was sleeping. There was a frown on her forehead as she went into her own rooms. Why had Gérard told his son not to speak of their marriage? Did he want to keep it from Margot for the time being? Remembering her vicious accusations, Annelise could well understand that Gérard might find the prospect of telling his mother-in-law more than a little daunting. It was clear that she would make things as unpleasant as she could.

Undressing, she tried to shut out the look on the spiteful woman's face as she had shrilled her false lies. She did not—would not!—believe one word of them. Lisette took her own life... Yet why should a young woman with everything to live for wish to die? It was a mystery that she had no way of solving.

Selecting a fresh, pretty nightgown, she slipped it over her head and sat down to brush her hair. One hundred smooth strokes from root to tip, to keep it shining as it flowed over her shoulders and halfway down her back. When she was small her mother had always brushed it for her, and it was a routine she enjoyed. Satisfied with her hair at last, she put down the brush and picked up her perfume bottle, applying it liberally behind her ears, to the hollow of her throat, between her breasts and at the backs of her knees so that she was enveloped in a haze of fresh scent.

# Free Books Certificate

Dear Susan,

Please send me my 4 free Doctor Nurse Romances together with my free gifts. Please also reserve a special Reader Service subscription for me. If I decide to subscribe, I shall receive 6 superb new titles every two months for just £7.20, post and packing free. If I decide not to subscribe, I shall write to you within 10 days. The free books and gifts will be mine to keep in any case.

I understand that I am under no obligation whatsoever — I can cancel my subscription at any time simply by writing to you. I am over 18 years of age.

Your FREE
Digital Quartz
Desk Clock

Name:
(BLOCK CAPITALS PLEASE)

Address:

_____

_____ Postode_____

_____ Signature _____

10A8D

To Susan Welland
Mills & Boon Reader Service
FREEPOST
Croydon
Surrey
CR9 9EL

SEND NO MONEY NOW

NO
STAMP
NEEDED

Gérard had said nothing, and yet she was waiting, instinctively expecting him with her body and her heart, her senses heightened. Her preparations had taken a long time, but at last she was ready. She was ready and waiting to give all of herself to the man she loved, unstintingly and without reserve.

At the gentle knock on her door, Annelise stood up. She walked unhurriedly to open it, smiling a welcome as she saw him standing there, an unspoken question in his eyes. Her heart began to race and she felt a great surge of love and longing.

'Gérard,' she whispered, suddenly beginning to tremble.

'You were expecting me?' he asked softly.

The look in his eyes sent the flame running through her veins. 'I was not sure—but I hoped...' The flame touched her cheeks as she saw something in his face that made her suddenly shy. She turned away, but he caught her chin, tipping it so that she had no choice but look at him.

'No, do not look away,' he said, his voice husky with passion. 'You know I burn for you, but I shall do nothing you do not wish. I am impatient, but if you prefer to wait until we are married...'

She placed her fingertip against his lips, knowing that she wanted this as much as he. 'Do you not know my heart, Gérard?' she whispered.

'I know it.' He bent his head, brushing his lips over hers, caressing her, slowly exploring the softness of lips that parted willingly beneath his. 'My beautiful, passionate, Annelise.'

'Passionate?' she echoed, feeling the hot, trembling sensation in her stomach. 'Supposing I disappoint you? I have never...I know nothing of physical love.'

His soft laughter sent tingles running down her spine. 'You could not disappoint me, my darling.'

His strong, brown fingers smoothed her cheek and the arch of her throat, moving to push back the thin silk of her nightgown. He kissed her shoulder, his lips fluttering against her throat like the gentle caress of a bird's wing, so soft and light that they set her pulses racing. She stood quite still, savouring each moment of this new sensation, her head going back as her body arched and shivered with delight. Her nightgown slid to the floor and his eyes adored her, feasting on the sight of lovely womanhood. Skin like cream, slender yet softly curving, she was perfection, her rose-tinted nipples erect with burgeoning desire. She was breathing deeply, her lips shiny as she flicked her tongue nervously over them. His hands moved down over her breast, hips and thighs, arousing and feeding the fire that flamed between them.

'So lovely,' he murmured throatily. 'So beautiful I hardly dare to take that shining innocence.'

'I am yours, Gérard,' she whispered. 'Your woman...your own.'

He gave a hoarse cry, gathering her in his arms to carry her to the bed. His need was great, yet still his eyes continued to adore her as if he could scarcely believe that she was real. He took one slender foot between his hands, kissing it reverently, his lips travelling the length of a quivering thigh to the taught, flat stomach that jerked beneath his caressing fingers, bringing a cry from her. Stroking, advancing, his hands began a gentle assault on the warm secret centre of her womanhood, bringing her whole body to a state of sensuous acceptance. Then his clothes were swiftly shed and his lean, hard body lay close to hers. She felt and saw his throbbing manhood, her hands roaming over his strong muscled back with an age-old knowledge as her body arched to meet his.

Flesh burned flesh as they melted into one another, and she cried out with fleeting pain. Cried, and was comforted with kisses that made her take him deep inside her. His body moved in gentle rhythm, slowly, lingeringly, bringing her to a knowledge of her own passion. She moaned and writhed beneath him as little spirals of desire became shooting flames. It was pleasure, yet pain, sensation such as she had never known. Now it was almost unbearable, and her nails gouged into his shoulder as her body suddenly shook with the thrill of ecstasy that ran through her.

Their sweat mingled as they both lay spent and exhausted. Holding her to him, he rolled on to one side, one leg over her to keep her pressed against him as his lips nuzzled her ear and his teeth caught the lobe, nibbling it. She laughed, glorying in this afterplay, her hands moving freely over his firm body as she lost all shyness in the pleasure of knowing him. He was murmuring things against her ear, intimate, secret words that only lovers know and understand.

Had she ever been a timid virgin, afraid of love and concerned with her modesty? If so, he had changed her for ever. Her lips pressed against his shoulder, tasting the salt of his sweat as she kissed him.

'Is it always so good?' she asked, her fingers pushing into his dark hair.

'Patience, my little tigress,' he answered with a grin. 'Give me time, and I'll let you judge for yourself!'

'Gérard!' She jerked indignantly. 'I wasn't suggesting...'

'You disappoint me,' he murmured huskily. She was caught and held firmly against him. 'I am not so easily satisfied.'

She was to have proof of his words again and again during the long night. Not until he had taken his fill of her was she allowed to sleep, her head nestling against his shoulder.

Even then he lay wakeful, watching her sleep. He had never expected to know such happiness. She had given him so much, loving as easy and simple to her as breathing. He knew then that he would never let her go. No matter that he had vowed never to wed again. He would break that vow and take the consequences!

It was a clear, bright morning, a heat-haze shimmering over the meadow. Annelise and Gérard carried the hamper between them, Jean running on ahead with two of the dogs. The boy was excited as he called to them, hardly able to believe that his father was to spend the whole day with him.

They wrestled in the long grass, fished in the stream, wading out to find the best spot, and teased each other in a way that neither of them would have found possible before. Annelise sat on a rug beneath a shady tree, making necklaces of daisies, content to watch and supply their needs from the delicious foods in the hamper. She would have liked to sketch them together, but she knew she would carry the memory in her heart for ever.

It was almost dusk when they walked slowly back to the house. A travelling coach was drawn up in the courtyard, and they were in time to see Madame Reinhold get out. Jean gave a squeal of delight and ran to greet her, but Annelise saw that Gérard was frowning.

'What brings Hélène here?' he said. 'I trust it is not bad news from Versailles.'

Madame Reinhold kissed Jean and then came to meet them, holding his hand. She smiled in surprise as she saw Gérard decked with daisy-chains.

'At least you prosper here,' she said with a smile. 'I need not ask if you have settled in, Annelise!'

'Is the news bad from Paris?' Gérard asked.

'Oh, there are bread queues and strikes—only the pamphleteers grow rich.' She shrugged. 'A few hangings now and then, and looting. The National Guard either does not see...'

'Or does not wish to,' Gérard put in.

'As you say.' She sighed a little wearily. 'It is good to be here, my friend. At court there is nothing but gloom. The Queen sits weeping in her chambers and His Majesty's exchequer is empty. How can it be otherwise when no one works and no taxes are paid?'

'Too many taxes had been paid by some for far too long. It is the turn of those who can afford to pay. I've sent the fourth part of my yearly revenues; let others do the same.' Gérard grinned. 'But I know we shall not agree on this. Come in, Hélène, and refresh yourself.'

Seeing that they had business to discuss, Annelise led Jean into the house. She glanced up at the west tower, almost expecting to see Margot, but there was no one at the window. She scolded herself for having looked, but Hélène's arrival had shattered her feeling of peace. So far, the revolution had not touched them. The harvest had been good, and the Comte's people were well fed, sharing in their seigneur's prosperity. They might talk among themselves of the new order in France, but with food in their bellies and a good roof over their heads, most ignored the agitators from Paris.

It was Claude who had told her about the hard-eyed men who came secretly at night to make speeches and try to stir the villagers into action against the seigneur. He had assured her that the peasants listened, but sent the citizens of Paris on their way. They were staying loyal to the Montpellier family—at least for the moment.

Annelise had tried not to think about what was happening elsewhere, but now the feeling of unease she had had when André was with them returned. The whole of France had been simmering throughout the long, hot summer, anger building up in the hearts of men. Even so, it need not touch them here. So why did she have this terrible fear that her new-found happiness was threatened by events outside her control?

Annelise yawned and stretched, a feeling of lazy well-being stealing over her as she opened her eyes. She would have liked to stay in bed longer, but her room was already lit by the sun's rays, and glancing at her watch, she realised it was later than she had thought. Dressing hurriedly, she went to Jean's room, finding him playing with his toy soldiers. Madame Reinhold had brought him a fine new model cannon to add to his collection, and he showed it to Annelise proudly.

'When I am a man, I shall be a captain in the King's army and fight for him,' he said. 'I shall cut off the heads of all the peasants who insult him!'

He had been listening to more of the adults' conversation than anyone realised. How much had he heard and understood of the servants' gossip? Whenever he was not with her, she knew he liked to slip away to the stables to play with the dogs and watch the grooms. Indeed, she suspected that before she had come to the château, he had spent most of his time there.

'You are very fierce this morning,' she said. 'Don't you think that some of the peasants have a right to be angry? It is not pleasant to be hungry, Jean. You would not like it if you had nothing to eat all day, would you?'

He looked at her thoughtfully for a moment, then: 'I shall not cut off their heads if they beg His Majesty's pardon—and then I shall feed them.'

Annelise laughed, looking at him fondly. He had dressed himself; his stockings were falling down and he had buttoned his coat wrongly so that a fold stuck out in the middle.

'Come here and let me make you tidy,' she said. 'What do you want to do today after your lessons are finished?'

'Must we have lessons today?' He pulled a face at her. 'Papa said he would put me up on his horse again.'

'Then we shall work until your father comes,' Annelise said firmly. 'He has his own work to do, my love. The estate cannot run itself, and he has spent the whole of the last two days with you. Besides, I know he has business to discuss with Madame Reinhold.'

Even as she counselled Jean to patience, Annelise was conscious of an urgent desire within herself to see the man she loved. Her body still tingled from his caresses, and every now and then the memory of something he had said or done the previous night sent a thrill winging through her, making her smile to herself. How wonderful it felt to be in love. Surely she had never lived before!

She caught her breath as the door opened and looked up expectantly, but it was only Claude. Laughing at her own foolishness, she laid down the slate she had been using to show Jean how to form his letters. She was every bit as bad as the child!

'Yes, Claude? Do you want something?'

'This was delivered from Paris this morning, mademoiselle.' He held out a sealed packet. 'The messenger said it was addressed to you at the Hôtel de Boussier with a request to send it on if an address was known.'

'A letter from England?' Annelise took the little packet, staring at the wax seal with a frown. It appeared to have the mark of a firm of solicitors from London.

Who could have written to her in France? She broke it open, scanning the copperplate writing, and gasping. 'I cannot believe it! There must be some mistake...'

The servant's deeply lined face reflected his concern. 'I hope it is not bad news, mademoiselle?'

'No... A friend has done something unbelievable,' she said slowly, reading the letter again. 'I have been left a house in Bath and ten thousand pounds.'

'That is a great deal of money,' Claude said, smiling at her. 'You must be very happy, mademoiselle.'

'I—I don't know. It is such a surprise. I never dreamed that Sophia would...' She broke off as the Comte came into the room. 'Gérard, you will never guess what has happened...' She handed him the letter as Claude discreetly left them. 'Lady Sophia has bequeathed me a fortune!'

Gérard scanned the letter and handed it back. 'So, I shall be marrying an heiress,' he said with a grin. 'Thank goodness; now we shall not be ruined, after all.'

'Wretch!' she cried. 'I know it means nothing to you—but what should I do about it?'

'Apparently the lawyer awaits your instructions. A letter should suffice.'

'But how can I accept it?' Annelise asked. 'I know Henry expected to inherit everything.' She frowned as a thought struck her. 'If he guessed that his grandmother had altered her will, it might explain his attitude towards me after she died.'

'You are not thinking of renouncing your inheritance in his favour, after the way he deserted you?' Gérard's brows went up in a look of incredulity. 'Don't be foolish, Annelise! Lady Sophia was fond of you. She did this because she wanted you to have security. Besides...' There was a gleam of mischief in his eyes. 'You may need it, if I turn into a tyrant and start to beat you.'

She laughed as she saw the look in his eyes, swaying towards him to be caught in a crushing embrace. 'Be careful,' she warned. 'Jean is watching you. He understands more than you realise.'

'Let them all see and understand,' he breathed huskily. 'I want everyone to know you are mine. We shall be married at Versailles, Annelise. His Majesty has decided to give a banquet to honour his new guards, the Régiment de Flandre, and as I once held a commission in the old guards, I am requested to attend.' He smiled down at her. 'It will be an opportunity to introduce my wife at court.'

'You will take me with you?' Her eyes lit up, then she caught sight of Jean's face. 'What about Jean?' she said softly. 'Can we not take him with us?'

'To court?' Gérard was startled. 'It would not be suitable. Besides, he has never left the château.'

'All the more reason to take him with us,' Annelise said persuasively. 'You could find a little house for us and engage a nursemaid to care for him while we were out. Surely you do not mean him always to be shut up here?'

'God forbid!' he said; then a wry smile quirked his mouth as he gazed into her face. 'So...I am no longer to be the master in my own house. Must I submit to petticoat rule?'

'Wretch!' She beat against his chest playfully. 'You must be content to be the master of my heart.'

'I am more like to be your slave,' he murmured ruefully. 'Already you twist me around your little finger. Very well, Madame la Comtesse, you shall have your way. A house, a nursemaid—is there anything further you require?' His eyes sparkled teasingly, one eyebrow arched as he heard her gurgle with laughter.

'Only your love, monsieur.'

'Love? Who mentioned love?' His eyes quizzed her wickedly. 'I am marrying you for your fortune. I thought I had made that clear?'

'Indeed?' She tilted her head, looking at him defiantly. 'That is understood, monsieur—and I have accepted you only because you are the Comte de Montpellier and I have a fancy to be a comtesse.'

*'Touché!'* His eyes caressed her. 'Since it is obvious that I cannot win this game, I shall take my son to see his pony.'

'My pony!' Jean had been watching them silently, mystified by their odd behaviour, but now his eyes were shining with excitement. 'Papa, is my pony truly here?'

'We shall go and investigate,' Gérard said, laughing. 'Mademoiselle, will you honour us with your company?'

He held out his hand imperiously, and she took it, her heart beating wildly. She was almost happier than she could bear, and for a moment she was afraid. Afraid that she would wake up to discover it was all a dream.

# CHAPTER SEVEN

THE AVENUE de Versailles was impressive, some three hundred feet wide with four rows of elms; at the end, the château, with its gilded rooms and hall of mirrors, fronted parks and lakes, rose arbours, the menagerie, and the Trianons, great and small, where Queen Marie-Antoinette had spent so many happy hours.

Riding down the avenue in the Comte's splendid gilt coach, Annelise felt a little tremor in her stomach. It was the first time she had been to a royal banquet, and remembering the way she had been received by certain ladies at the assemblies she had attended with Lady Sophia, she could not help being nervous. Yet she knew she would be dressed as well as any of them this evening.

Arriving at the house Gérard had rented for them in the town, she had found a closet full of beautiful gowns; enough to fill at least three large armoires. Silks, brocades, velvets, all trimmed with the finest laces, ribbons and jewels. Made for her by Madame Reinhold's own dressmaker at Gérard's request, she learned.

She had exclaimed in surprise when he showed her the clothes. 'Surely these cannot all be for me?'

'My wife is entitled to expect only the best.' There was a hint of pride in his voice. 'The family jewels will of course be yours, but these were made for you. No other woman has ever worn them.'

Opening the large flat velvet box he gave her, Annelise had gasped with pleasure, for inside was a set of necklace, bracelets, ear-drops, brooch and ring made of dark green emeralds surrounded by diamonds. Gérard smiled as she glanced up at him in wonder, taking the ring to slip it on the third finger of her left hand.

'It fits,' he said with a look of triumph. 'The stones are not quite the colour of your eyes—but no jewel could rival such loveliness. I wanted you to have something that was yours alone, Annelise. I hope you like them?'

'They are beautiful,' she whispered, her throat tight with emotion. His thoughtfulness in giving her a new ring instead of the family heirloom—that Lisette had worn—touched her so deeply that tears misted her eyes. 'Y-You will spoil me...' was all she could say.

'If I owned the world, I would lay it at your feet,' he murmured, taking her in his arms to kiss her.

'Oh, Gérard,' she cried. 'I am so happy. I am almost afraid...'

She got no further, for his lips were on hers, and she surrendered to the pulsing of her blood as he lifted her in his arms, carrying her to the bed. There was no fear of interruption, for Jean's rooms were separate and he had his own nursemaid now to sleep near him. Letting herself respond to her lover's insistent demands, Annelise was swept away on a tide of passion, her soft cries mingling with the moans of pleasure that broke from Gérard. Away from the château with its brooding presence, she discovered a new dimension to their loving. Gérard was an instinctive lover, seeming to know how to raise her fevered body to new heights of sensual delight. It was with reluctance that they left their bed to attend His Majesty's banquet.

She had chosen a gown of pale cream silk embroidered with green to set off the exquisite jewels the Comte had given her. Its skirts were so wide that it spread out over the entire interior of the coach, leaving only a tiny space on the opposite seat for Gérard to squeeze in. He could not miss such a chance, and his comments regarding petticoats made her eyes glow with laughter.

'I like to see you laugh,' he said. 'You will be the most beautiful woman at court this evening.'

'I fear you are prejudiced, monsieur!'

She wrinkled her nose at him, but his compliments helped her through the first awkward moments in the Galerie des Glaces, a beautiful, domed apartment with long mirrors interspersed with statues in alcoves, when she felt herself under constant scrutiny. However, it soon became clear that her situation was very different now. Accompanied by the Comte de Montpellier, and wearing his ring on her finger, Annelise found herself being sought out by the very ladies who had turned their noses up at her in Paris. She was complimented on her gown several times, but when asked the name of her dressmaker, she simply shook her head and replied, 'The Comte chose it for me. He chose everything I am wearing.' It was not strictly true, since he had merely given orders that a suitable wardrobe should be prepared for her, but it amused her to see the raised eyes and know that she had succeeded in shocking the unshockable.

From the first it was evident that the mood of the court was one of gaiety and rebellion. The courtiers had had enough of the gloom forced on them by the riots in July. Although most of the guards were wearing the tricolour, some white cockades—and the infamous black!—seemed to have crept in. Perhaps an ominous sign of what was to occur later. Gérard remarked on it to Annelise in a low voice.

'I feared something like this might happen. The fools are too proud to be seen to give in to the wishes of the people. Why can they not see that they must be patient for a while? Surely it is time for a few changes?'

'Perhaps it is merely a show of bravado,' she said, squeezing his arm. The black cockades were the badge of those aristocrats who were known to take a hard line; it was they who were for turning the guns on the mob and teaching them to obey their masters. She knew that Gérard found their attitude distasteful, and she was determined to turn his mind from politics. 'Do you think that the Comte de Montpellier could be seen to dance with the lady he has chosen to marry for the sake of her fortune?'

Gérard laughed, the shadows leaving his eyes as he made her an elegant bow. 'The Comte would be honoured, Mademoiselle Pembleton.'

The music was slow and stately, the floor a sea of colour with swirling silk skirts and flashing jewels, reflected in the mirrors a thousand times. This was a night of elegance, reminiscent of Versailles at the height of its glory, when the peasants were merely faceless shadows and Majesty ruled supreme.

It was into a court bewitched by false brilliance that the Queen came later that evening, smiling and giving her hand to be kissed as she distributed her white cockades. Walking from table to table, her face sad and yet serenely beautiful, she stirred the hearts of the men who rose to kiss her hand and accept the badge of royalty. Enchanted by her beauty and by the magic of the night, cheers issued from every male throat. Who was the first to draw his sword and pledge it to Her Majesty? Who was the first to tear the tricolour from his breast and throw it to the floor, trampling it into the ground as if it were some despised thing? Once one had done it, all must follow.

Gérard did not join in the general stampede to disown the national colours, though he stood with the others as the musicians struck up their loyal theme: *'O Richard,*

*O mon Roi, l'univers t'abandonne...'* Yet his face was
grim as he watched men seemingly drunk on an excess
of loyalty go on to become truly intoxicated, their behaviour becoming wilder and wilder as the night wore
on. Finally, seeing how it must end, he took Annelise's
arm.

'I think we should go,' he whispered. 'I do not like
the look of things. Perhaps this was not the wisest time
to bring you to court.'

She laid her hand on his arm, feeling a little shocked
at the way things had turned. Some of the men were
scaling the boxes to argue with those sitting there,
shouting abuse at anyone who did not think as they did,
and generally behaving badly.

It was as they were leaving the banqueting hall that a
man blocked their path. His face was flushed from wine
and almost the colour of his puce satin coat. He swayed
slightly on his feet, leering at Annelise.

'If it isn't the Ice Maiden,' he sneered. His eyes narrowed as he looked at her, noting the jewels at her throat
and ears. 'Or perhaps the ice has melted? Should I congratulate you on your new mistress, Montpellier?'

'Be careful, Brienne,' Gérard warned coldly. 'You are
speaking to the lady who has done me the honour of
consenting to be my wife.'

'Your wife?' The Marquis's thick lips curved in a snarl
of vitriolic spite. 'Congratulations, mademoiselle! You
will be the wife of a traitor. But perhaps you are concerned only with his wealth?'

'Damn you! You'll answer to me for that!'

Brienne bowed his head, a look of insolence on his
face as he replied, 'I am at your service, monsieur. My
seconds will call on yours—if you can find anyone to
support you. Only a coward would refuse to wear the
white cockade on such a night.'

A small crowd had gathered to listen to the quarrel, and several gasps were heard as Brienne continued to insult the Comte. Gérard's face was white, his hands curled into tight fists at his side. He was tempted to strike the Marquis, barely controlling his temper as he replied.

'Perhaps a man of conscience might think his nation of equal importance to his Queen.'

There was a murmur of agreement from someone near, but also angry cries of 'Shame!'

'The National Assembly, I spit upon it!' The Marquis followed with physical action. 'If I had my way, I would take five hundred good men and teach these upstarts a lesson they would remember for many a day.'

'It is you and your kind who have brought this evil day upon us,' Gérard said, his lips white with fury. 'It will give me great pleasure to rid France of at least one parasite! Now stand aside!' Gripping Annelise's arm, he forced her past the glowering Marquis, the courtiers parting to let them through. 'It's time we left. The very air grows fetid with the stench of such filth!'

She had never seen him so angry. His dark eyes glittered with a strange fire and his mouth was tightly drawn, a pulse beating at his temple as he strode through the palace. He was hurting her arm where his fingers held her in a vice-like grip, but she dared not protest. This was not her gentle, charming lover, but a man whose temper was bordering on violence. Realising that time was the best cure for what ailed him, she was silent as they drove back to the house.

He did not speak as he handed her down from the coach, and she went upstairs alone. She had not thought him capable of such anger, and she was not sure that she liked this new side of a man she had thought she knew. It was true that he had a right to be angry, but his rage was almost ungovernable. She guessed that he had not followed her because he could not trust himself to behave calmly. Remembering Jean's tantrums, she smiled ruefully to herself. It was clear from whom he had inherited his temper. There would be storms as well as laughter in the years ahead.

The smile left her face as she suddenly realised the seriousness of Gérard's quarrel with the Marquis. He was going to fight a duel! In the middle of brushing her hair, she threw down the brush and jumped to her feet. She had been upset by Gérard's violent manner, but he was still the man she adored. It would be folly to let a stupid incident come between them. She must go to him. He might have taken her silence as being a sign that she agreed with Brienne.

As she started for the door, it was flung open and she saw Gérard standing on the threshold. His dark eyes held a look of torment, and she ran to him with a cry of welcome.

'Forgive me,' he said, catching her to him. 'I needed a moment to calm myself.'

'I understood,' she said, her arms going about him. 'I know Brienne insulted you, but why did it make you so angry? No one would believe him if he called you a coward or a traitor.'

'There are those who would believe the second, if not the first,' Gérard said wryly. 'My views are too well known. Yet though I believe in reform, I would never be disloyal to His Majesty.'

'I am sure the King knows that!'

'Perhaps—yet he is served by those who seek to use him for their own ends.' He sighed, and shook his head. 'You asked me why it made me angry, Annelise. It was not the man's words, but the man himself. There have been abuses in our system of the feudal rights of a seigneur over his peasants for centuries, and Brienne is one of the worst of his kind. No man on his estate may marry unless the girl is given up to him on her wedding night!'

'That's...barbaric!' Annelise cried.

His face was grim as he nodded. 'I know of at least two brides who took their own lives after he had finished with them. He would ride a peasant child into the ground rather than turn his horse aside. He treats his people like animals, extorting every penny from them to spend it on his vices...It is men like Brienne who have made the people hate the sight of an aristocrat. We have been enemies since the day we met, so this was bound to come, one day. I am only sorry that you had to be there to witness it.'

'I think perhaps I was the cause of it. He was determined that you should fight him. I always knew he was evil—but I am afraid for you.' She looked at him, her face pale. 'Oh, Gérard, must you fight him?'

'You think he might kill me?' A glimmer of mockery lit the dark eyes. 'That decaying, rotting bag of flesh will scarcely put me to the test! Oh, Annelise, have you no faith in your husband's skill?'

'You are not yet my husband,' she reminded him with a reproving look. 'And I had rather your skill with a sword remained untested. You have other skills that please me more.'

'Indeed? You must tell me about them.' His anger had all gone as he laughed down at her, and a new flame burned in his eyes. She saw the hunger in him and her heart began to beat wildly as she went to his arms. 'I would have killed him for daring to look at you that day I saw you running from him,' Gérard murmured throatily. 'You were mine even then. I knew it from the moment I first set eyes on you.'

There was a possessive look in his eyes, and she guessed that jealousy had played a part in his anger that evening, whether he realised it or not.

'He followed me that day,' she said. 'He tried to force me to... But I kicked him hard in the shins and ran away. In England I had been used to walking alone quite safely; it did not occur to me that he might follow me.'

He chuckled softly. 'I saw him limping, and guessed what had happened, yet I blamed you even so. I suspected you of meeting him by design.'

'You did not?' she cried indignantly. 'That—That painted bag of wind! You insult me, monsieur!'

'You were a penniless companion,' he objected, watching her eyes take fire, and smiling. 'How was I to know whether you had set yourself up to become a marquise?'

'Devil!' She pushed at him with her hands, trying to free herself. 'I shall not listen to this. Let me go at once!'

'How beautiful you are when you are angry,' he murmured, his lips nuzzling her earlobe. 'Oh, Annelise, Annelise my darling, you have bewitched me. Never leave me, for I should die.'

She could resist no longer. This clamouring of her senses was too strong for her to fight. A little cry escaped her as she pressed herself closer to him. Then she was untying the lace at his throat, her fingers impatient to touch the satin-smooth flesh beneath, tearing the fine material as it resisted her advance. Sensing a new hunger in her, he groaned deeply in his throat, bending down to sweep her up in his arms.

This time she was as impatient as he, her body meeting his with eagerness as they lay together, retracing old delights and discovering new horizons. It was as if neither could have enough of the other, their kisses growing more frenzied until they were both consumed by the fire that burned more brightly every time they loved. Exhausted, entwined as one, they slept at last.

'Annelise, I hope I do not disturb you,' a voice said from behind her. 'Your servant told me that I would find you here.'

She had been cutting a late rose in the garden, and she turned with an exclamation of delight. 'André! You are here, at Versailles! How pleased Gérard will be to see you when he returns.'

'I arrived this morning.' He came to take her basket of flowers, carrying it as she found more blooms. 'What is this I hear of a duel?'

'It is true, I fear,' she said, her smile fading. 'Gérard has gone out to make the arrangements. Two officers of the Swiss Guard are to be his seconds. They sent word this morning that they were willing to stand with him when he meets Brienne.'

'That honour should be mine,' André said, frowning. 'Would that it had been I Brienne insulted. That scoundrel deserves to be taught some manners.'

'Do you too want to kill him?' Annelise shook her head. 'You men are all the same—though in this case I cannot deny that it is a worthy cause.'

André chuckled, his eyes bright with admiration as he watched her cut another rose. She was beautiful, warm, and full of the joy of life. 'Gérard is a lucky man,' he murmured. 'When are you to be married?'

'As soon as this nonsense is over.' She arched her brow at him. 'I had thought you might have news of another wedding for us? If I am not mistaken, you heart is given to Marielle Dubonnet?'

'Unfortunately our marriage seems as far away as ever. Marielle's temper has not been improved by the change of climate.'

'Poor André.' She laid her hand on his arm, her eyes gently teasing as she looked at him.

It was thus that Gérard discovered them as he came out into the garden. For a moment he stood looking at her, watching the changing emotions on her face and the way the sunlight turned the colour of her hair to Titian red. She was so lovely that the mere sight of her was enough to start that hot churning in his loins. He could not be jealous, now he knew she was his. The memory of her warm, eager body pressed close to his was still fresh in his mind. He could almost smell her perfume and taste the sweetness of her lips. When she turned and saw him, the instant glow of her eyes set him on fire. She was his woman, and nothing could come between them. Memories of the past could not haunt him when she looked at him like that. He was born again, made whole by the uncomplicated love she offered.

She came flying to his arms and he caught her up, swinging her round in a sudden mood of exuberance. Between kisses and laughter, he turned to greet his friend, who had stood waiting patiently, a look of indulgence on his face. 'André, when did you get back?'

'From England, last night; I arrived here just an hour ago.' André frowned. 'You will allow me to support you in this duel?'

'Alas, I have settled with Montauban and Leterme,' Gérard said. 'But you will be welcome as an observer. It is set for this evening, an hour before dusk.'

Annelise turned away to arrange her flowers. The mere idea of a duel distressed her, but she knew that she must hide her feelings. Gérard was a proud man, and he would be angry if she showed fear for his safety. Neither he nor André seemed to doubt that he would be victorious, and she knew she must appear to be just as confident.

Inside, she was trembling, her stomach tying itself in knots at the thought of her lover in danger.

'Montauban has invited us to a banquet this evening,' Gérard said, glancing at her and seeing perhaps the fear that she was trying so hard to hide. 'The Flanders Regiment is repaying last night's entertainment. Do you want to go?'

'Could we not have a quiet dinner at home—the three of us?' Annelise asked. 'I am sure that you and André have much to talk about.'

'If you are sure?' Gérard smiled and she nodded, slipping an arm about her waist. 'For myself, I would much prefer it. André?'

'I shall be delighted,' he replied gallantly. 'You will excuse me for the moment; I have business elsewhere. I shall return in time to accompany you this evening.' He picked up a fallen rose and handed it to Annelise with a little bow. 'Until this evening, mademoiselle.'

She watched as he walked away, feeling Gérard's hold tighten about her waist. 'Do not be anxious, my love,' he whispered gently. 'Nothing will happen to me, I promise.'

'No, of course not,' she said, smiling at him. Yet how could she help being anxious? He had come to mean so much to her that the thought of life without him was intolerable.

The Marquis de Brienne's carriage, with its bold emblem of a serpent in flames emblazoned on the side panels, was already drawn up at the edge of the clearing when Gérard and his friends arrived on horseback. They dismounted and came to greet the gentlemen gathered in the courtyard. News of the duel had spread quickly and quite a few of the courtiers had turned out to watch the affair. The weapons were to be swords, and the duel was to go on until one or the other was unable to continue. Brienne's seconds had insisted that it was to be a duel to the death and that he would not be satisfied with a superficial wounding.

These kinds of duels were rare at court, for they were frowned upon by the King. It was more usual to consider a blood-letting sufficient for the satisfaction of honour, but the hostility between these two men had been well known for years and no one gathered at the clearing expected anything less. Brienne was an experienced duellist who had won every contest, killing or seriously wounding at least five men.

The Comte de Montpellier was an unknown quantity in the minds of most of the spectators. Not particularly popular because of his habit of speaking out against the abuse of privilege, he was thought of as a reformer, an uneasy bedmate for those who did not wish to change their way of life, yet he was also spoken of universally as an honest man. Brienne was a scoundrel, but truly one of them, and the general feeling was for him. Royalist sympathies were running high, and Montpellier did not endear himself to the excited courtiers by wearing the tricolour in his hat.

However, as the two men removed their coats, more than one observer remarked on the difference between them. Where the Marquis's bulk was clearly an excess of flesh, the Comte was all lean, honed muscle, his broad shoulders testifying to the power of the man. From the moment he flexed his sword-arm, exercising a few practice thrusts with a flick of his wrist, it was clear that this would be an equal contest.

'Messieurs,' the arbitrator called them together. 'Are you certain that this affair cannot be settled by an apology?'

'I shall accept no apology,' Brienne growled haughtily. 'This traitorous dog deserves a lesson.'

Gérard merely shook his head, his eyes glittering with anger. The sooner it was begun, the sooner he could spit this fat cockerel and go home!

'Messieurs...' The arbitrator stepped back, looking from one to the other. *'En garde... Commencez.'*

The tips of their blades touched in salute and then broke as the two men circled warily, each measuring the other. One hand on hip, they leisurely explored the possibilities, steel scraping steel exactly as if they fenced for pleasure. Indeed, from the smiles on their faces, it would seem that both relished the contest. Both were fired by a mutual dislike that would no longer be contained.

It was the Marquis who attacked first, feinting then lunging as he tried to slip beneath his opponent's guard. His attack was met by a counter-attack, surprising him so much that his foot slipped on the uneven ground and Gérard's blade ripped through the upper half of his right sleeve, drawing blood.

Immediately Gérard lowered his blade and stood back, indicating that he was satisfied. The arbitrator stepped between them, looking at the Marquis.

'The first blood is to the Comte de Montpellier,' he said. 'Are you satisfied, Monsieur de Brienne?'

'No!' Brienne snarled. 'We continue!'

Their swords touched again. This time the Marquis attacked at once, so fiercely that Gérard was forced to retreat a few steps. Rallying, he broke contact, jumping nimbly to one side and swinging round to come back at the Marquis. The ring of steel against steel echoed in the clearing, holding the watching courtiers captive by the sheer thrill of such a well balanced contest. No one could be sure which way it would go. Once the Marquis's blade pierced Gérard's shirt-sleeve, scoring the skin so that a stain of crimson spread through the lace cuffs. Again the arbitrator approached but was impatiently waved away by a panting Marquis, too intent on his prey to observe the finer points of etiquette. Thinking he saw an opportunity to end the fight, he lunged viciously at the Comte. It was at precisely at this point that the fight turned.

It seemed to observant eyes that Montpellier had decided to make an end. Now, suddenly, he was outwitting Brienne at every turn, making him look an amateur. Where they had appeared to be evenly matched, now it was clear that the Comte had merely been toying with his opponent. The look on his face was contemptuous as he parried every thrust with ease, then attacked so skilfully and with such speed that Brienne was left floundering, his cheeks turning puce with anger. Montpellier was treating him like a fool, humiliating him! He could do nothing about it, for he had used his strength in the earlier bouts and having refused his chance of leaving the fight with honour, was forced to continue or become the coward he had named his enemy. How neatly he had been trapped!

He was aware of the gasps and smirks of spectators who had transferred their allegiance to a man of such superior skill that all were forced to admire his display. Gérard de Montpellier was not so much fighting a duel as teaching the Marquis how to fence! Brienne was no longer young, and the years of excesses had taken their toll. What was this pain in his chest? Why did his vision seem misted as that mocking devil ducked and weaved, always out of reach? He was almost finished. It could be only a matter of time before the Comte's blade found its mark. Suddenly a hush fell as the onlookers awaited the inevitable. Then, almost at the same moment as

Brienne stumbled, swaying with exhaustion, a troop of men cantered into the clearing.

'Hold!' a loud, commanding voice called. 'I order you to cease fighting immediately in the name of His Majesty King Louis of France.'

Gérard had been about to deliver the *coup de grâce*, but he lowered his sword, watching with scorn as the relief flowed into Brienne's face and he fell to his knees, closing his eyes.

One of the men had dismounted. He came towards Gérard, his face stern. 'Monsieur, I am ordered to arrest you...' There were cries of 'Shame' and angry murmurs from the crowd. 'Both you and the Marquis de Brienne are to be escorted to the palace to await His Majesty's pleasure.'

Montauban stepped up to him. 'It was a fair fight, monsieur. The Comte offered to withdraw, but Brienne would not accept.'

'As a witness of the affair, your presence will also be required,' the officer said. 'This is not my affair, gentlemen. I am merely carrying out the King's orders. Now, Monsieur de Montpellier, will you come willingly, or must I place you under guard?'

Gérard inclined his head stiffly. 'If you will allow me to mount my horse, I shall accompany you now.'

'I'm going with you,' André said, directing an angry look at the Marquis, who had rejoined his cronies. 'I shall speak to His Majesty myself. This duel was not of your making, Gérard.'

'I need no defence,' he replied proudly. 'I was a willing party to it. I only wish I had finished the swine before we were interrupted!'

'Be careful,' André warned. 'Even Brienne has his friends.'

A mocking smile curved Gérard's mouth, his eyes moving scornfully to the little group who had gathered around the Marquis and were helping him to his horse. 'They too are welcome to taste my sword if they wish.'

André sighed, but refrained from saying anything more. It was useless to argue with a man as stubborn as Gérard de Montpellier.


Annelise looked at her reflection in the mirror, and frowned. She was satisfied with her appearance, but she did not really want to attend the banquet at the palace. It was the third to be held in three days! She would have preferred to spend the evening at home with friends. Her eyes sparkled as she recalled the men's high spirits on the previous evening.

Gérard had had to endure a lecture from the King on the foolishness of duelling, but he had then been released and commanded to present himself at the banquet the following night. He had come home flushed with triumph, making light of the scratch on his arm and acting as if it had all been some kind of a game. Annelise was inclined to agree with the King, feeling very grateful to him for halting the duel, though she knew Gérard was angry about his interference.

However, both he and André were in the mood for celebration, entertaining her with stories of their escapades when they were at the Sorbonne together. Gérard had been a little drunk when they went up to their room. He had kissed her and caressed her, but fallen asleep in her arms before passion could flare. Watching him, she traced the curve of his cheek with her fingertips, feeling a deep tenderness. She had been in agony, fearing the outcome of the duel, but now he was by her side and all was well.

It was as she was drifting into sleep that his cries startled her. His head began to twist restlessly as the nightmare gripped him. She struck a tinder, bending over him as the candle flamed.

'What is wrong, my love?'

'Lisette...' he muttered. 'I didn't want to hurt you. Lisette...No!'

Her face was pale as she smoothed the damp hair from his brow. It still hurt him so much. 'It's all right, my love,' she whispered. 'I am with you now.'

'Lisette!' he cried again, his body jerking violently. His eyes opened and he sat up, staring blankly into space for a moment, then he groaned and lay back on the pillows, looking at her. 'I was dreaming. What did I say?'

'Nothing. Nothing that made sense.' She smiled and bent to kiss him. 'It was just a bad dream.'

'Yes, just a dream,' he said hoarsely. 'Thank God!'

He reached out for her, pressing her down into the bed and covering her with his body. For the first time in their relationship he took her selfishly, thinking only of his own need. Missing the teasing, intimate love-play that gave her so much pleasure, Annelise accepted this need in him, realising that it was somehow connected with his dreams. She held him to her as he lay still at last, kissing his shoulder and stroking his dark head as it lay against her breast.

After a little while he looked up with an odd, almost shamed smile. 'Forgive me, I...'

'Hush, I know,' she whispered. 'I know, my darling.'

His arms tightened about her fiercely. 'Never leave me, Annelise. I don't think I could bear it!'

'I love you,' she said. 'Sleep now, Gérard. I am with you.'

The realisation of his vulnerability gave her a warm glow as she held him while he slept, curled against her breast. He was such a brave, strong man, and yet there were moments when he needed her so desperately. It made her aware of a deep well of love and strength within her, a mature love that had nothing to do with the physical pleasure he gave her. It was a bond that would hold her to him always, she thought, no matter what might come.

In the morning Gérard had made love to her again, taking great care to ensure that she was fully awakened to passion beforehand. All day he had been attentive to her comfort, as if he wished to assure her of his love, spending time with Jean to please her and seeming almost too anxious to do whatever she wished.

If only he would confide in me, she thought. It is clear that his wife's death still haunts him. He had loved her so much that it must almost have destroyed him when she took her own life. She longed to ask why it had happened, but knew she must wait until he was ready to tell her. To demand an explanation might seem as if she believed Margot's lies.

She sensed a restlessness that had not been in him a day or so before. It was as if he had to keep busy to banish the memories that could hurt him still.

'We came to Versailles so that you could wear pretty clothes and enjoy yourself,' he said, a brooding yet tender look in his eyes. 'I want everyone to see my beautiful wife.' He placed a finger against her lips as she would have protested. 'It will be tomorrow in the chapel at Versailles. The Queen has asked specially that you should be present tonight. I think she wishes to congratulate you.'

There was nothing left for Annelise to say. She could hardly refuse the honour of a special presentation to the Queen. It would be taken as an insult. She was a little apprehensive as to their reception that evening, but if anything they were more warmly received than before, and several ladies cast admiring glances at Gérard, fluttering their fans as they tried to attract his attention.

The audience with Queen Marie-Antoinette was brief but rewarding. She smiled graciously on Annelise as she curtsied gracefully, her knees trembling just a little.

'So, you are to be a bride,' the Queen said, her eyes bright. 'It will please me to be of service to you, mademoiselle. Since you have no family, you may look for my support at your wedding.'

'Your Majesty is very kind,' Annelise breathed, scarcely able to believe her ears. It was a high honour and something she could not have expected.

Marie-Antoinette turned her soulful eyes on Gérard. 'Now, monsieur, will you not accept my colours?'

What could he do? No gentleman could do less than kiss the hand extended to him so graciously. He took the white cockade with a whimsical smile. 'Willingly, madame. I shall wear the white and the tricolour combined. Should not royalty and the nation go hand in hand?'

'I am sure that no one could care more for his people than His Majesty,' she said, a trifle haughtily.

'I am sure you also have their welfare at heart, madame... yet times are hard for our people. Perhaps more could be done to alleviate their suffering?'

'What can be done is being done,' she said. 'No one is more aware of the situation than His Majesty.'

Gérard bowed his head, kissing her hand once more but making no reply. There was nothing he could say without offending her, and now was not the time for speeches.

As they moved away, Annelise glanced at him, sensing his frustration. 'I think she really believes what she says, Gérard.'

He nodded, a rueful smile flickering about his mouth. Although not a republican, he was annoyed and frustrated by a court who seemed incapable of seeing what was going on before their eyes. 'The Queen means no harm, but she is impetuous and thoughtless. France would be better served if the King had her spirit.' As Annelise looked at him curiously, he shook his head. 'Enough of politics, my love. I want to dance with the most beautiful woman at court...'

They were married early in the morning at a quiet ceremony attended by the Queen, two of her ladies, Hélène Reinhold, André and the officers of the Swiss Guard who had supported Gérard at the duel. Jean was there too, looking smart in his velvet breeches, coat and an embroidered silk waistcoat. Annelise was relieved to see that for once his stockings were straight and his hair was tidy.

After a small reception for their friends in a specially prepared pavilion, they took Jean to see the menagerie and then went home to spend the evening alone.

As they went upstairs after dinner, Annelise glanced at her husband. 'When shall we go back to the château?' she asked.

'Do you want to go back?'

She saw the doubts in his eyes and slipped her arms about him. 'It is your home, Gérard. I believe you are happier there.'

'I feel uneasy...' He shook his head as she arched her brow. 'I cannot explain. It is strange, but... I did not want to cut short this visit for your sake, but I have a feeling that I ought to return. If you do not mind?'

'Of course not. I can be happy wherever you are.'

He caught her to him, kissing her. 'You are mine now, Annelise. There is nothing anyone can do about it.'

'You are thinking about Lisette's mother, aren't you?
Why should she be against our marriage?' She waited—
would he tell her now?

His eyes were distant, as if he was thinking of something that had happened long ago. He reached out to
her, stroking her arm absently as he sought for a way
to explain. 'She will not be pleased—but I have considered her feelings enough. I have paid my debt to her
long since.' He saw the questions in Annelise's eyes, and
shook his head. 'No, do not ask. I shall tell you one
day, when the time is right.'

'I would like to share this memory that haunts you,
Gérard. Perhaps, if we talked about it, it would help?'

'I cannot!' His voice was harsh with pain. He gripped
her shoulders, looking down at her with such intentness
that she shivered. 'It does not concern you. What happened is past and gone.'

'Yet you have not forgotten?'

'No, I can never forget.'

'Then...' She faltered as she saw a flash of anger in
his eyes. 'I shall not ask again.'

'Oh, Annelise,' he caught her to him fiercely. 'Forgive
me. Remember only that I love you. If I do not tell you
all you wish to know, it is to save you pain, my love.'

Her answer was lost as his lips possessed hers. She
clung to him as he swept her up in his arms to carry her
across the threshold of their room, sensing the urgent
need in him to forget his haunting memories in her arms.
He wanted her and loved her, nothing else was important. Giving herself up to the delights of loving, she
pushed the nagging doubts to one side. Nothing could
be so terrible that she could not share it with him. Surely
he must know that?

\*    \*    \*

It was drizzling with rain as Annelise stood looking out of the small leaded window. Jean tugged at her skirt, wearied of toy soldiers and the bestiary, with its drawings of strange and wonderful animals, that he had been looking at.

'When can we go home?' he asked petulantly. 'I want to ride my pony.'

'Soon. Perhaps tomorrow. Your father has business in Paris this morning, but he will return shortly and then you may ask him yourself.' She smiled down at him, understanding his impatience. She too felt caged in this little house when the weather made it impossible to venture out. 'If the rain stops, we will go for a walk later. Why don't we...' She broke off as she heard the sound of hurrying, booted footsteps in the hall. The door was suddenly flung open, and she was startled by the Comte's appearance. 'Gérard, what's wrong? I did not expect you back so soon.'

He had come straight from the stables, his boots and breeches flecked with mud from his hard ride. She saw the grim look on his face, and caught her breath. Something was very wrong indeed!

'Paris is in turmoil! The streets are full of women, young and old, from every walk of life. Milliners, seamstresses, washer-women, every kitchen drab and lady's maid—and they are all shouting for bread. I've never seen anything quite like it.'

'Is it so much worse than before? The people have been crying for bread all summer.'

'They are marching into houses and workplaces, forcing everyone to join them. They say their menfolk have been silenced by fear and now they must speak— but they will do more than speak.'

'It is the mothers who have to listen to their children crying with the pain of hunger,' Annelise said. 'I thought the corn-boat was taking in grain twice a day? Has something happened to stop it?'

'The flour is often mixed with other substances—substances that make the intestines turn to water.' Gérard's mouth twisted. 'And even that contaminated cargo has been cut by half. Can you wonder that there are riots? Yet at Versailles there is food for banquets, one after the other. Think what they will make of that in the bread queues!'

'That is what they are saying?' Annelise glanced up at him anxiously, putting herself in the place of a mother who had been forced to listen to her children sobbing in pain. 'Of course! It must seem obscene to a woman scouring the streets for a loaf of bread to hear of banquets at the palace. One would not have been so bad— but three...'

'They are oppressed by the patrols, particularly gentlemen wearing black cockades, and threatened with violence when they protest. What do you imagine is going through the minds of those women?' He took a few paces about the room. 'I do not think that even the patrols will be able to contain them. What man in the National Guard could bring himself to fire on a woman who comes only to plead for bread?'

'I pray that no decent man would think of it!'

'I believe they will march to Versailles. It was being shouted in the streets when I left. They think there is food here; they will come to demand their share.'

Annelise stared at him, a chill running down her spine. It was hardly imaginable that a mob of women thousands strong should band together and march on Versailles. Women had homes to run, men and children to care for... Had they become so desperate that they were forced to this?

'What will happen?' she asked, her arm going protectively about Jean's shoulders. There was no telling what an angry crowd might do. 'Will there be fighting?'

'You will be safe enough here,' he said. 'I came to warn you to stay in the house, no matter what happens. Do you hear me, Annelise? I would send you back to the château, but there may be danger on the roads.'

She nodded, her face white. 'What will you do?'

'I must go to the King and try to warn him. Perhaps there is something that can be done to stop this disaster even now.'

'If food were taken to Paris?'

'I doubt if enough could be found in time, but perhaps some can be sent to help to placate them on their journey here.' He moved towards her, taking her in his arms to embrace her. 'Look after Jean, and yourself. I shall return as soon as I can. You understand that my first duty is to His Majesty now?'

'Of course.'

She let him go reluctantly, feeling a twist of fear inside her. If Gérard was right and the mob was marching to Versailles, there might be fighting and bloodshed. Her fear was not for herself, as the crowd's anger would be turned against the palace, but for Gérard. Although they had been married for such a short time, she must not be selfish. The King, the Queen and the young dauphin would be in the greatest danger. Remembering the way the courtiers had trampled on the tricolour and the Queen's unwise pleasure in their actions, she felt apprehensive. The people had a right to be angry, but to what lengths would their fury carry them? She could only wait and pray that they would stop short of taking a bloody revenge for the wrongs that had been done to them.

# CHAPTER EIGHT

THERE WAS food at Versailles, food in abundance; enough to feed them all, so the word went. They had massed in their thousands to storm the Hôtel-de-Ville, demanding to speak to the mayor, but he, craven fellow, could not be found, only Usher Maillard, a man of quick wits and quicker action. He snatched a drum, beating it so loudly that they were forced to stop shouting and listen to him.

'*Allons à Versailles!*' he cried. 'We must speak to the King. He must listen to your just demands, women of France. To Versailles, and justice!'

They shouted with glee. Maillard would lead them to Versailles. They had a leader now, a man they could follow. The mob began to move along the quayside in a slow, straggling procession, no one really knowing what was going on but driven by the common purpose. Faces peered from the upper windows of houses; if female, they were pressed to join in the glorious march.

'Join us, sisters, join us!' the marchers cried. 'We are for Versailles—there is food there. Enough for all!'

The men were joining their ranks, encouraged by the bravery of their womenfolk and ashamed to hang back now that the women had taken the lead. The mob was growing larger and larger. Where could so many people have come from?

'To Versailles!' Maillard cried, but now his voice was only one of many. The marchers were on their way, and nothing could stop them.

At Chaillot, the bakers hastened to bring out loaves and were greeted with cheers. 'Good bakers! Good friends!' The women's objective was food and justice; they were good-humoured yet. Then came bells, drums, shouting and the deafening noise of marching feet. Travellers were dragged from their coaches; fine ladies in silks and satins were made to walk in the mud beside their poorer sisters, whether they liked it or not. The women of France were out to see justice done, and they would not be denied.

Hunger could not stop them now, nor could the rain that whipped into their faces and made their clothes stick to their unwashed bodies. They had but one thought in mind: to speak to their King. *He* was the saviour of France. *He* would give them food. Blinded by the rain, suffering, enduring, they would reach Versailles before nightfall. Nothing could change that. The women had begun it, but now armed National Guards had joined the ranks; Grenadiers of the Centre, men from every district arrived bearing pikes or ancient firearms.

'Bread!' they cried. 'To the King! He will give us bread. The King is the father of the people. He will not see us starve.'

In the hall of the National Assembly, Mirabeau informed the President that the people of Paris were marching on them. 'Let them come,' Mounier replied. 'We shall soon be a republic!'

By mid-afternoon, the women had reached a hilltop overlooking Versailles. To the right lay Marly and Saint-Germain-en-Laye, to the left Rambouillet, and before them the town and the Avenue de Versailles. They had arrived!

'What do you know of this, Montpellier?' the King asked testily. He had been hunting until the urgent summons reached him, and was not at all pleased at being fetched from his favourite pastime. 'What is this nonsense about the people marching on us?'

'I was in Paris early this morning, sire,' Gérard said. 'It was beginning even then. We have since received confirmation from General Lafayette that a large crowd is headed this way.'

Louis XVI frowned, slapped one hand with a soft leather glove as he paced the floor of his sumptuous apartment—a floor covered by priceless carpets. He looked apprehensive, bewildered, as if it were all somehow too much for him to comprehend. 'Why should they come here? What can they hope to gain?'

'They are asking for bread, sire.'

'What can I do? Is it my fault that the grain prices keep on rising despite the excellent harvest? If the farmers had done their duty, this need not have happened.'

Gérard admitted that his argument was sound. Many factors had combined to push up the price. The unrest throughout the country had contributed, as had the greed of those who saw a way to line their own pockets, but there was no point in telling an angry crowd that a part at least of their troubles lay at their own door.

'They believe you can help them, sire.'

The King turned his angry gaze on him. 'Can nothing be done to stop them?'

'I am afraid it is much too late.'

'Then let the guards be called out. Let them protect their king.' He waved a hand in dismissal.

Gérard bowed and left the royal apartments. He had done what he could, but it seemed that even now the King did not realise the seriousness of the situation; if he did, he was unwilling to act.

Outside in the wide echoing hall he found André anxiously pacing up and down. He came quickly towards Gérard, his face grim. 'What had His Majesty to say?'

'He seems not to understand. Perhaps he doesn't wish to.' Gérard sighed, a surge of frustration running through him. 'Oh, the fools! Why must they insult the people by flaunting their wealth at such a time? Three banquets in three days, and nothing done to ease the plight of the starving. Then they wonder why the people are marching against them!'

'You are right, my friend, but no good will come of speaking so frankly here.' André frowned, searching for an answer but finding none. 'Could we not send some wagons with food to meet them on the way? It might stop them for a while...'

An officer's scurrying footsteps made them glance at each other. 'I think it is already too late,' Gérard said. 'Listen to that sound...'. As one, they moved to the window. '*Mon Dieu!* Have you ever heard the like?'

A sea of female faces was washing down the avenue, wave after wave of women shouting and waving their hands. They were singing something...'Henri Quatre'... and shouting '*Vive le Roi! Vivent nos parisiennes!*'

'At least they sound good-humoured enough,' André murmured in a low voice, then, shouting, 'You, sir! What news?'

The scurrying officer came over. 'A deputation of twelve women are asking to speak with His Majesty.'

'Will he see them, I wonder?' Gérard said. 'In his present mood, he is like to refuse.'

'Not if he once glances from his window.' André whistled softly. 'I think they mean business, my friend.'

'Will the guards hold, do you suppose?'

'Perhaps . . . for a while at least. But how can they fire on women? If so, the age of chivalry is long dead.'

Gérard pulled a rueful face. 'We must pray that they do not have to make the choice. Can you imagine what would happen if one of those women were killed? It could set a torch to the whole of France!'

'You should go to Annelise and the boy before it is too late,' André said, looking at him earnestly. 'Slip out through the rear gates.'

'They are in no immediate danger. I may not agree with the King all the time, André, but I am neither a traitor nor a coward. He may need the sword of every man here today.'

'The King is still popular; they call him the father of the people,' André said, frowning. 'The Queen may need us more—they would kill her gladly, given the chance.'

'Perhaps it may not come to that. All is not yet lost. If His Majesty agrees to meet the deputation, he might persuade them that he is still their friend. He has a way with the ladies!'

'Amen to that.' André smiled wryly. 'All we can do for the moment is wait . . .'

It had taken Annelise some time to settle the child, though he was sleeping now. She continued to sit by his bed, watching him just in case he should wake and cry out in fear. The noise of the crowd had upset him, and he had asked for his father several times . . . His father . . . She looked for some resemblance in his features, but could find none. He was all Lisette's child. Except for his temper. He had that from Gérard!

Getting up, she gazed out of the window. It was still drizzling. How cold and miserable those poor women must be, she thought. She was undecided whether to send some food. Of what use would a few baskets of provisions be among so many? Yet it might help some of them. A short while before she had thought she heard the sound of firing, but it had not lasted long and the women were still shouting and crying. Whatever had occurred, they had not yet attacked the palace. Why did no one do anything?

'What is it they want?' Queen Marie-Antoinette asked of her servant. 'What are they shouting?'

The servant bowed respectfully. He had spent his life in the service of royalty and was too old to change sides. He would as soon die serving his mistress as live in disgrace.

'They are asking for bread, madame. They say they are starving.'

'Have we none to give them?' She looked at him impatiently, then her eye fell on a plate of buns and she exclaimed impulsively, 'Let them eat *brioche*! She stood up, moving to gaze out of the windows, the skirts of her satin gown whispering over the marble floor. 'Are the carriages ready yet?'

'The coachmen tried to take them out, but they were driven in again, madame. Apparently orders have been given that you are not to be allowed to leave.' He looked at her sadly. 'I am very sorry.'

'So we are prisoners?' She tapped a satin-shod foot. The heels of her shoes were studded with jewels; she had jewels in her hair and at her throat, rings on her fingers, but she was still a prisoner in her own palace. 'This is intolerable! Where are our guards?'

'They have retreated inside the palace, madame. They say they will not fire on the people.'

Her face paled. She turned aside, trembling, yet determined to show no fear. She knew her duty: to be at her husband's side, no matter what. 'Very well, you may go,' she said, waving a dismissive hand. 'Stay—has the deputation left His Majesty?'

'Yes, madame.'

'Then perhaps all may yet be saved.' She raised her head proudly. 'I shall go to him.'

The deputation of twelve returned to their friends, bearing good news: His Majesty had agreed to their requests. They were charmed by his manner. He had treated them so kindly. One had been near swooning, and he had supported her in his arms.

But where was the proof of his good will? The document as a token of his good faith? Words were nothing. The women were sick of words. In the National Assembly they had words in plenty. Words would not put bread into the mouths of hungry babes! Now the cries turned against Louison Chabray—she who was held in His Majesty's arms.

*'Traîtres! A la lanterne!'*

She was saved by the royal bodyguards who rode up and snatched her from the avenging mob, but still the indignant cries went on. The women were cold, hungry, miserable but still determined. They had not come all this way for nothing!

'Send to the King again. We must have proof,' someone cried, and the shout was taken up by a thousand voices. 'Proof! We must have proof!'

Another deputation was hastily formed, although the darkness was closing in. They stood chilled to the bone, wet and hungry, their bellies rumbling for lack of food. Food had been promised hours ago, but it had still not arrived. They felt cheated and angry. How could they believe in promises?

In the exchange of shots earlier, a horse had been killed. Some of them skinned and roasted it, using wood torn from fences and gates to build their fire, but it satisfied merely a few empty stomachs. Some food had been sent by the townsfolk, but even that was nowhere near enough to satisfy the hunger of this huge crowd.

Messengers had been flying back and forth all night—to the palace, to the Assembly—but so far nothing seemed to get done. Then at eight o'clock a letter was brought from the King, agreeing to their demands. A few cheers greeted its arrival, but then others began to ask for more concessions. Could not the price of meat be fixed at six sous for a pound, and a half-quartern loaf at eight?

Usher Maillard had started on his way back to Paris with the decree concerning bread. Before him, Louison Chabray, proudly bearing His Majesty's letter. Surely they must be satisfied now? Some food was at last sent out to the weary women.

As the long, endless night wore on, news came of General Lafayette's arrival, the roll of his drums echoing in the darkness. He himself had come to offer his own life as hostage for the King's, bringing with him a list of demands from the citizens of Paris, which His Majesty was pleased to grant. His Majesty was not so pleased with a request to come and live in Paris, but what could he do but agree? At least with the arrival of Lafayette the situation seemed to have settled down.

At last there was time for sleep.

Annelise was woken by the sound of firing. What was happening? It was a dull, misty morning, hardly light. She could see nothing, but it sounded as though the mob was angry. The shouting was much louder than it had been the previous evening. She turned sharply as a knock at the door sent her hopes rising. Had Gérard come home at last?

Opening the door, she saw Jean's nursemaid. 'What is it, Marie?'

'I thought I should tell you, madame: the word is that they are storming the palace.' The girl shivered. 'Our coachman was nearly set upon in the town. Oh, madame, what shall we do if they come here?'

'It is unlikely,' Annelise said. 'But if they should try to break in, you must lock yourself in with Jean. I don't think they will harm us; they will be looking for food. I shall tell the servants to give them whatever we have.'

The maid looked alarmed as her mistress pulled her gown on over her nightdress. 'You are not going out, madame?'

'I shall be but one woman in thousands,' Annelise said, selecting a dark wool cloak and some stout shoes. 'No one will take any notice of me. I shall be quite safe.'

'Oh, madame,' Marie exclaimed, 'supposing you are set upon?'

'I am wearing nothing of value.' Annelise laughed at her horror-stricken face. 'Do not worry, Marie, I can take care of myself. I want to see what is happening.'

She went swiftly downstairs to leave instructions with the servants in case the mob began breaking in, though she believed it was unlikely, as the house was situated in a quiet cul-de-sac. Even if they started looting, they would hardly come here. Her fear was for all those inside the palace—and her husband in particular. He had not come home all night and she was anxious. She must see for herself what was going on.

It was apparent at once that some elements of the crowd had come merely to make what they could out of the confusion, and there was some evidence of looting. Hurrying through the streets in the gloom of a wet autumn morning, she saw groups of men and women straggling dismally here and there as if uncertain of what was happening. They called to one another, asking for news.

'Is it true that the palace guard fired on the people?'

'Yes, friend. They killed at least ten.'

'No, it was but one.'

'What is happening now? What is all the noise about?'

'They are for storming the Queen's apartments.'

Hearing the rumours fly from mouth to mouth, Annelise's heart was beating wildly as she made her way towards the palace. The nearer she got, the more she was jostled and pushed, but no one really looked at her. In her dark, hooded cloak, she was just one of many. Finding it impossible to get right through, she looked around for a friendly face and saw an elderly man a few paces away.

'What were the shots earlier, monsieur?'

'A bodyguard fired on someone,' he muttered, shaking his head. 'It was all to have been settled peacefully, but this is a bad day, madame, a bad day.'

'Indeed it is,' she agreed. 'Have you heard what has happened inside the palace?'

'The Queen's apartments were defended,' another man answered her. He was a big, burly fellow with a sullen look about him. 'Two guards were cut down and left for dead. God curse them!' He spat on the ground. 'They should have dragged the Austrian bitch out by her hair.'

'You insult the Queen, monsieur,' Annelise cried angrily. 'Your cause may be just, but such words are treason!'

'I'm no traitor.' He looked at her closely, noting the softness of her complexion and the good quality of the cloak she was wearing. 'What are you doing here? You're not one of us.'

'You leave her be, citizen,' the old man defended her stoutly. 'She's my grand-daughter and in service to an aristocrat. She's as entitled to her say as you. Besides, we came here for the food they promised us, not to commit murder.' He laid his wrinkled brown hand on Annelise's arm. 'Come away, child, I'm tired. We'll find somewhere to rest before we start the journey home.' His fingers curled about her wrist, forcing her through the crowd and away from the dangerous area round the palace, not speaking again until he found a quiet spot.

'You must be more careful, madame,' he said. 'You should not be out on such a day. It is not safe for someone like you.'

'Thank you,' she replied with a rueful smile. 'I spoke in haste. It was foolish of me.'

'Foolish, but honest.' He sighed deeply. 'Our family have always been loyal to the King, but times are hard. The people are desperate. In every house there is someone close to starvation...'

'I know. I wish there was something I could do to help.' She looked at him thoughtfully. 'I have a house near by. Would you walk back with me? At least I could give you food for yourself and your family.'

'You owe me nothing, madame.'

'Perhaps not, but it would please me if you would accept a small gift?'

'How can I refuse when my grandchildren are crying for food and their mother is at her wits' end.' He gave her a toothless grin, his gnarled hand patting her arm. 'Would that there were more like you, madame. Come then, I shall see you safely home.'

Hubert Grosard stiffened as he saw the woman walk away with the old man, suddenly losing interest in what was going on in the palace. He had seen that face before somewhere. No man could forget a woman as lovely as that; there was something about those eyes and that hair—something that stirred a chord in his memory. He knew it was important that he should remember. Whoever she was, she was an enemy of the people, he was sure. Grosard hated all aristocrats, especially the one he owned as master, the man he would kill if he had the courage. Every time he shouted his anger at the nobility, it was of one man in particular that he thought.

If only he could remember where he had seen the woman, he thought. He began to follow the ill-assorted couple, certain that whatever else they might be, they were not related. Keeping a safe distance behind, he trailed them through the town. Then, as they paused at the entrance to a large house, the woman stopped and glanced back. She was smiling now, and as Grosard saw the smile, he suddenly remembered. It was the woman who had pretended to be Monsieur Necker's niece! An aristocrat who had lied in order to escape from Paris.

He remembered the humiliation he had felt when he discovered he had been duped. It was that woman who had made a fool of him—that woman who had stolen the child Flore Génévois. Her father had come to the gates later that same day, asking for his beloved daughter, his description so accurate that Grosard had recognised it at once as belonging to the child who had been spirited out of the city by one of those accursed aristos. Oh, yes, he was quite sure of his facts now—but what should he do about it? How could he ensure that this woman was brought to justice?

He enquired from a passer-by the name of the residents of the house she had entered. When he was told that the Comte de Montpellier and his family were staying there, it brought a gleam of greed to his eyes. Now he knew what to do. If things went as he hoped, he might see justice done and earn a few coins for himself!

Jean was restless, bored with being in the house and constantly asking to be allowed to play in the garden. Feeling tense herself, Annelise found her patience stretched to the limit as the morning wore on, though she did her best to keep him amused. It was not Jean's fault that her nerves were on edge. She had sent one of the men-servants out to investigate the situation at about eleven, but he had returned without discovering much more than she had already seen for herself.

'The King was called out on to the balcony,' he said. 'And the Queen was called for. She showed herself, and then went inside.'

'At least they are both safe for the moment,' Annelise said thankfully, adding silently: 'I wish Gérard would come home so that I knew he too was safe.'

However, it was not until more than two hours later that she heard the tread of his footsteps in the hall. Rushing to meet him, she saw that he looked tired and there was a dark stubble on his chin.

'You have not slept all night,' she cried. 'Thank God you are back! I was so worried when I heard the shooting.'

His face was grim as he took her in his arms, holding her close for a moment. 'Some idiot fired on a few looters. Lafayette and others had negotiated a settlement and then it seemed as if all must end in disaster. At one time they stormed the palace itself.'

'I know. They attacked the Queen's apartments, did they not?'

He nodded, brushing back a lock of dark hair from his brow. 'Two men were hurt defending her rooms, but fortunately neither was killed. She escaped safely to His

Majesty's chambers...' He sighed deeply, frowning. 'Well, it is settled for the moment. The royal family have set out for Paris, hostages against the promises that have been made to the people.'

'Are they safe now?'

'Who can tell? There were those who advised His Majesty to flee to Metz. If he had succeeded, France would almost certainly have been plunged into civil war. As it is, we can only await the outcome of all this.' He smiled at her suddenly, running a hand over his unshaven chin. 'Forgive me for coming to you like this. After I have made myself respectable, we shall dine together. I have scarcely eaten since I left you yesterday. I begin to understand how those poor wretches must have felt last night.'

'You must be hungry. I'll speak to the servants while you change.' She hesitated, then said, 'Shall I tell them that we are returning home in the morning?'

'I meant to speak to you about that later.' Gérard frowned. 'I'm sending you back to the château, but I must go to Paris. André is alerting men he knows to be loyal to His Majesty. I'm afraid there may yet be civil war, Annelise.' He sighed as he saw the stubborn look in her eyes. 'It will be safer for you and Jean, my love.'

'Let me come with you,' she begged. 'Send Jean and Marie home, but take me with you.'

He trailed one finger down her cheek. 'I would if I could, but the situation is too dangerous at present. I should never know a moment's peace. You know I believe the people's cause is just, but I also have a duty to the King. There are many who would gladly see him dead. It is my intention to speak against this in the Assembly. Somehow, reason must prevail in all this madness. The King must be brought to understand that he can no longer rule in the old way. He must come to terms with the people.'

'If you take on the role of peacemaker, you will be caught in the middle,' Annelise said. 'You will have enemies at court and in the Assembly.'

'I know.' A wry smile twisted his lips. 'I have never cared much for popularity, but it will be a difficult time; that is why I must be sure that you are safe. You mean more to me than my own life. My enemies might seek to use you as a weapon against me. If I know that you are safe at home in the château, I shall be able to devote all my efforts to the cause.'

Annelise sighed, acknowledging that he was right. 'Then I must do as you say. I cannot make things even harder for you.'

He pulled her closer, kissing her tenderly. 'You mean so much to me, my darling. My life would be nothing to me now without you.'

'Nor mine without you,' she whispered. 'Please be careful; for my sake.'

His eyes sparked with laughter. 'Do not fear for me, Annelise. I have many enemies, but I also have many good friends; men who think as I do. I have spoken in the Assembly too often for my views to go unnoticed, and there are still enough right-minded men in France to demand justice for all. We must work together now to ensure the future of our country.'

He was a man of ideals; she understood that now, and she honoured him for it. 'I am proud to be your wife, Gérard,' she said, her eyes glowing as she looked up at him. 'I shall do as you ask—but now I must see to your dinner before you starve!'

*     *     *

They had been travelling for almost half an hour when Jean suddenly became restless, kicking his shoe against the side of the carriage.

'You must not do that,' Marie reproved him. 'It's not polite.'

Jean scowled and ignored her, looking at Annelise. 'Why isn't Papa coming home with us?' he demanded. 'Why does he have to go to Paris?'

'Your father has important business there.' Annelise smothered a sigh. She understood only too well how upsetting it was for the child. He had just got used to having his father's company, and now they were to be parted again. It was not to be expected that he would accept it without complaint. 'He will come home as soon as he can.' She glanced at the ring on her finger; it was hard enough for her to be parted from her husband so soon after her wedding day. 'I shall . . .' She broke off as the coachman gave a shout and the carriage lurched to a sudden halt. 'What on earth?'

Putting her head out of the window, she saw that a group of armed men were blocking the road. A sick dread clutched at her stomach, and she had to fight hard to get control of her nerves before opening the carriage door.

'Oh, do not get out, madame,' Marie cried. 'They will attack you.'

'Stay here with Jean,' Annelise ordered. 'You will be quite safe. I must find out what is going on.'

An argument was ensuing between the Comte's servants and the band of men standing in their way. Annelise heard Martin the coachman demanding that they should stand aside and let him drive through.

'This carriage belongs to the Comte de Montpellier,' he said. 'Clear the way, or it will be the worse for you!'

The coachman, groom and footman Gérard had sent with them were all carrying pistols, but so were the men blockading the road. From the stubborn looks on their faces, it was clear that the situation could rapidly turn into a bloody affair. Annelise lifted her skirts clear of the mud as she stepped down from the carriage.

'What is the trouble?' she asked. 'Why have you stopped my coach?'

There was silence for a moment as they all stared, then one of the men in the crowd pointed an accusing finger at her. 'There she is, citizens! I told you she had become the Comte's wife. She is a traitor to the people! She stole Flore Génévois from her father's care!'

There was a murmur that gradually rose to a growl from the throats of those men with burning, revengeful eyes. The cost of the dress she was wearing would feed their families for more than a year.

Annelise lifted her head proudly, recognising the man who had spoken as the one who had questioned her identity at the gates of Paris. She would never be able to forget him—and obviously he had remembered her.

'I did not steal Flore from her father,' she said quietly. 'I found her outside my door. She had been badly beaten, and she was crying. I looked after her, and she begged me to help her to escape from her father.'

'Liar!' cried another man, whom Annelise did not recognise. 'I have never beaten Flore! I was always devoted to the child—ask my neighbours. Ask anyone if I do not speak the truth!'

There was a murmur of agreement from the men around him. They did not know or care whether he had beaten his daughter—a man had rights over his own child, after all—what mattered to them was that an aristocrat had committed yet another crime against the people. A child had been taken from her father; that much was not in doubt. The woman had admitted it. These aristocrats thought that they could do whatever they liked and never suffer for it, but things were different now. The King had promised justice for all the people. This woman should be made to pay for what she had done.

'Where is my little one?' Flore's father demanded. 'What have you done with my child?'

There were more angry murmurs from the crowd, who began to move towards Annelise. For the first time she was afraid. She took a step backwards, her heart pounding wildly. They looked as if they intended to take their vengeance now!

'I'll shoot the first man who lays a hand on Madame la Comtesse!'

She heard Martin's shout and the answering cries of the mob. The tension was rising, and at any moment it could explode. If the mob went wild, they might kill everyone—including Jean. That was something she could not permit. She lifted her head, hiding the terrible fear inside her as she faced the man who had accused her.

'I'm ready to prove my innocence before a tribunal,' she said proudly. 'Let us go now, and when you send for me, I shall answer the summons. I give you my word that I shall do so.'

Grosard laughed scornfully. 'Why should we let you go? We have you now.' He leered at her. 'You cheated us once. You shall not so easily escape us this time, Mademoiselle Necker.'

Annelise felt her knees tremble as she saw the hatred in his eyes. 'Then let my servants go and I shall come with you. Do not shed the blood of innocent men, I beg you. They have committed no crimes against the people. Neither has the nursemaid nor the child.'

'Let them go,' someone said. 'We want no bloodshed; only justice. The woman is prepared to stand her trial. Let the others go.'

Now there were murmurs of agreement, and Grosard frowned. His orders were to take only the woman, and it was she who had made a fool of him. He was not sure that the righteous indignation of these citizens whom he had incited to help him to arrest a traitor would extend to the murder of servants and a child. No; better to take the woman without a fight, he thought, his eyes gleaming greedily as he remembered the gold coins he had been promised.

'Tell them to surrender their arms,' he said at last. 'Everyone is to get down from the coach, except for the driver. We shall take you and your carriage, madame. Your servants can walk home.'

It would ensure that her servants could not reach help in time to rescue her, Annelise realised. The faint hope that Gérard might follow and snatch her from these hard-faced men was stillborn. She felt sick with terror, but knew she had no choice. Raising her eyes to the watchful servants, she nodded her head.

'Do as he says. I am innocent. No harm will come to me.'

'No, madame!' Marie shrieked from inside the carriage. 'They will kill you.'

'May I speak with my servant?' Annelise looked at her accuser. 'I shall not try to run away.' Grosard inclined his head, and she moved towards the coach, speaking softly. 'You must not interfere, Marie. Tell my husband that Madame Reinhold knows the truth. He must find Flore and her mother. They will testify to my innocence.'

'Oh, madame,' Marie caught back a sob. 'How can I leave you to the mercy of those terrible men?'

'You must think of Jean,' Annelise said. 'It is our only chance.' She looked at the boy, who was white faced and clearly mystified. 'You must be very good now, dearest. Go with Marie and do exactly as she tells you.'

'I want to stay with you,' he muttered rebelliously. 'I shall kill those bad men with my sword.'

'Not this time, darling.' Marie had got down from the coach and was beckoning to him, but he ignored her, clinging on to the carriage door. Annelise caught him in her arms, and he put his arms about her neck, clinging to her desperately. She lifted him out, setting his feet on the ground. 'You must be very brave,' she said, smiling at him. 'Your father would expect it of you. He will know what to do. I shall be with you again very soon, my love.'

'One day I shall kill all the bad men,' Jean muttered, his bottom lip trembling.

Annelise knew that the tears were very close, so she only smiled and gave him a gentle push towards his nurse. Marie grabbed his hand, holding it tightly so that he could not wriggle free.

The servants had gathered at the side of the road, looking at one another uneasily. Deprived of their weapons, they suspected treachery from the mob, but fortunately the brave citizens were satisfied with their victory. Several of them got on behind the coach, others took up positions at either side of the driver. Grosard motioned to Annelise to get inside, climbing in after her.

'So, madame,' he said, grinning at her. 'Now we shall see if the Comte de Montpellier will risk everything for the woman he loves.'

Annelise suddenly realised that there was more to her arrest than she had at first thought. She stared at him, seeing the gleam of triumph in his eyes.

'Who are you? Why have you done this?'

'You are an enemy of the state, madame.'

'No...' Annelise shook her head. 'You had another reason for this, monsieur. You have set a trap for my husband. Someone has paid you to accuse me of stealing the child—you and Flore's father.'

His mouth twisted in a cruel smile. 'Your husband has many enemies, madame. Yet I have simply done my duty, like a good citizen. Neither you nor the Comte can prove otherwise.'

Annelise was about to reply when she heard something. Looking out of the window, she saw that Jean was kicking and yelling as he tried to break away from his nurse. Somehow his show of rebellion gave her strength. She smiled proudly into the eyes of her captor.

'I am innocent of any crime. My husband will have me free within hours. Whoever your master is, he has made a mistake! The Comte may have many enemies, but he also has powerful friends.'

# CHAPTER NINE

'*MON DIEU!*' Gérard exploded, his eyes furiously raking the faces of his servants. 'You dare to tell me that you allowed these men to abduct your mistress? Pray explain your cowardly conduct. You had weapons—why did you not use them?'

'It was madame's wish,' Marie said, as the men remained silent, their eyes downcast. 'She was afraid for Jean. She believed that those men might kill us all if your servants fired their weapons. Oh, monsieur, forgive me for letting her go with them. I begged her to stay in the carriage, but she would not listen. There was nothing we could do but obey her orders.'

'Marie speaks for us all,' the groom said in a low voice. 'We did not know what else to do, and madame ordered us to lay down our weapons.'

Gérard's eyes flashed fire. He took a turn about the room, his mind whirling in agitation and despair. 'Why has it taken you so long to inform me of my wife's abduction? Thirty-six hours have passed. Anything could have happened to her!' A groan broke from his lips. 'She could be dead!'

'Madame was sure she would be given a fair trial.' It was Marie who spoke again. 'She said that she was innocent of all the charges and that Madame Reinhold could tell you about the child.'

'I am aware of the details.' Gérard frowned. 'My wife saved a child's life—now it could mean the end of hers.' His steely gaze came to rest on the silent men. 'You have not yet explained why it has taken you so long to reach me.'

'They took the carriage and Martin the coachman, monsieur. We had to walk for hours before we found an inn where we could hire horses.' The groom raised his shamed eyes to the Comte's. 'The child could not go very far without a rest. And when we finally reached Paris, we were not sure where to find you...'

Gérard stared at him angrily. He wanted to vent his fury on the unfortunate groom, but he knew that he himself was to blame for what had happened to his wife. Three servants would normally have been sufficient as an escort, but the situation was far from normal. He should have sent a larger escort or gone with them himself. He was racked with guilt as he thought of Annelise at the mercy of ruthless men. If anything had happened to her he would never forgive himself!

'Have you any idea where they meant to take her?' he asked at last.

'I heard one of them speak of returning to Paris,' the footman said. 'Madame said she was innocent and would state her case before a tribunal. Surely they would not dare to harm her?'

'Tell me again just what occurred,' Gérard said. 'I want to know every word that was spoken, every tiny detail you can remember. It seems to me that they were lying in wait for you. They must have known she was in the carriage. It sounds more like an abduction than a lawful arrest, yet how could they have known exactly when my wife was returning to the château?'

'Martin did say he'd seen someone hanging about the stables earlier,' the groom spoke thoughtfully. 'I didn't take much notice at the time, because he's always so particular, but I remember he was quite put out about it.'

'Martin...' Gérard stared at him. 'They took Martin as well! Pray God he will keep his wits about him. He may be able to slip away and warn us of Annelise's whereabouts. In the meantime I shall try to trace her myself, but somehow I do not believe we shall find her in Paris.'

It was dark when Annelise opened her eyes with a start. For a few seconds she was bewildered, unable to recall what had happened to her; her neck was stiff and she had a terrible headache, as though something had struck her at the back of her neck. Gradually she became aware that she was in a carriage, and then it all came flooding back. She recalled the abduction, and her suspicions that she was not being taken to Paris to appear before a people's tribunal, and then the sharp blow to her head when she had tried to protest.

They must have been travelling for hours, she realised, but the carriage was not moving now, and she was alone inside it, but as she came fully awake, she heard the sound of voices outside. Moving cautiously, she looked out of the window. The sky was lit by a pale moon and she could see that they seemed to be in a wood. A short distance away three men were standing looking at something on the ground, and as her eyes became more accustomed to the light, she saw that they were gathered round the prone figure of a man, Martin the coachman!

'You fool!' a male voice said angrily. 'Why did you have to hit him so hard? He's dead.'

'He tricked us,' Hubert Grosard muttered. 'I hit him, and he struck his head on a stone as he fell. It was an accident.'

'Accident or not, he's dead. Now one of you imbeciles will have to drive...'

Annelise's blood ran cold as she heard the third voice. It belonged to the Marquis de Brienne! She was not being taken to prison at all: she had been abducted by a man who hated both her and her husband. The citizens' arrest had been but a clever masquerade. Gérard would be told that she had been arrested, while in reality... Where was she being taken?

All at once, she realised that she had to escape. It was a plot to lure her husband to his death, and they had already killed Martin for trying to escape. They would probably kill her, too, when she had served her purpose! Driven by desperation, she opened the carriage door and jumped out. She started to run in the opposite direction to that her unfortunate servant had taken. She had no idea where she was going, but she had to get away before her captors realised she had come to her senses. It was no more that a second or two before she heard a cry of alarm and then the sound of heavy feet coming after her.

Gathering up the hem of her long skirt, she ran as fast as she could, heedless of the cruel branches that whipped into her face or the brambles that caught at her clothes. She had to get away from the men who had tricked her! Her heart was racing madly, her breath coming in forced gasps as she ran on, sick with fear. Her pursuer was getting closer! He was gaining! Suddenly she caught the heel of her shoe in a rut and was sent flying. She put out her hands to save herself, feeling the sting of brambles on her face and arms as she fell into a bush. Giving a little cry of pain, she struggled to her feet again, only to feel herself gripped from behind. An arm went round her waist and then a man's hand entangled itself in her hair, jerking her head back.

'Be still, madame, or it will be the worse for you!'

'Let me go!' she screamed, kicking frantically. 'You tricked me into thinking I would face a tribunal. You are a liar and a murderer! It was a trap for my husband.' She tried to wrench away from him, twisting and yelling wildly.

Grosard pulled her hair again, making the tears start to her eyes. He tugged her head round so that she was forced to look into his face, and she saw the malice in his eyes.

'You are an aristocrat,' he hissed. 'I hate all your kind.'

'But you serve the Marquis de Brienne!' she accused him, wincing as his fingers tangled in her hair and she knew that he was enjoying her suffering.

'Because I must,' he muttered. 'If I do not... You are less than nothing to me, do you understand? If you try to run away again, I shall kill you. My master wants you alive, but I would break your neck without a moment's hesitation if I had my way.'

Shocked, Annelise stopped fighting him. She had no doubt that he meant every word he said, and she knew she had no choice but to obey.

A smile of triumph twisted his thin lips as he felt her go limp, her will to resist ebbing away. 'Come then, Madame la Comtesse,' he said. 'My master is waiting for you.'

She was forced back the way she had come a few seconds earlier, his fingers biting cruelly into the tender flesh of her upper arm. He knew he was hurting her. She sensed that he wanted to see her cringe and beg for mercy, but she would not give him the satisfaction, even though she was feeling ill and close to despair. Now she dared not even think of attempting another escape.

The Marquis was waiting by the carriage, his face waxen pale in the moonlight. He looked at her as she was brought back by her triumphant captor, and she saw the expression on his face turn from one of anger to spite. His mouth curved into a vengeful sneer.

'So, Madame de Montpellier, we meet again,' he said. 'What a delightful coincidence. I have looked forward to this moment for such a long time. A very long time...'

She raised her clear gaze to meet his eyes, fighting the shudder that ran through her. 'Why have you done this, Monsieur de Brienne? What can you hope to gain by it?'

'Your husband has made a fool of me for the last time. I intend to kill him, but this time there will be no duel.' Brienne's eyes glittered in the silver light, sending a little shiver of horror through her. 'I shall let him search for you for a time—just long enough for him to taste the bitterness of despair. Then I shall tell him where to find you.'

'And when he comes looking for me, you will have him murdered,' Annelise said, her face registering her contempt. 'You are a coward! My husband bested you in a fair fight and you are afraid to meet...'

'Bitch!' Brienne struck her across the face. 'You will be very sorry you dared to defy me. Very, very, sorry!' He jerked his head at Grosard. 'You know where to take her.'

'Yes, monsieur.' The man pushed her towards the carriage, and she stumbled, almost falling.

'Fool!' Brienne snarled. 'I told you I want her alive. Kill her, and I'll have you hanged.' He turned his malevolent gaze on Annelise. 'Unfortunately I have business elsewhere, madame, but when I see you again, I shall enjoy teaching you some manners. You will regret your insults, I promise you.'

As Annelise was thrust into the carriage, she saw him stride towards a tethered horse. Then Grosard's shadow blocked the doorway as he climbed in after her.

'Where are you taking me?' she asked, retreating into the corner. 'I demand to know where we are going.'

'To my master's favourite château.' He leered at her in the darkness. 'You will find it a charming home, Madame la Comtesse. My master keeps it for special visitors... They like it so much that they never leave it again.'

Annelise could not stop shivering as the chill of his words entered her mind. Gérard had told her how evil Brienne was, but she doubted that even he realised the full extent of his enemy's vileness. Just how many murders had Brienne and his henchman committed between them? she wondered. She was terribly afraid. She knew that she was going to die, and she could not even pray that Gérard would find her. If he attempted to rescue her, he would walk straight into the Marquis's trap!

'She is not in the Conciergerie,' André said as he walked into the salon of the Comte's town house. 'I have established contact with one of the warders. If she were being held secretly, he would know about it by now. He would do anything for gold, so we may be certain he is not lying.'

Gérard's hands clenched at his sides. He had been praying that Annelise had really been taken to the prison. 'It was our last hope,' he said. 'We have tried everywhere else. If her arrest had been genuine, she would have been brought back to stand trial, yet I knew it was a vain hope. Such a false charge could too easily have been disproved. No, this is the work of someone who hates us both.'

'Then it is as we feared.' André looked at him gravely. 'She must have been taken by Brienne. You have other enemies, my friend, but none who would strike at you through your wife.'

'I should have killed him when I had the chance,' Gérard cried, tormented by the thought of Annelise in the hands of a monster. Terrible pictures flashed into his mind, making his face contort with agony. 'If he has harmed her...'

André gripped his shoulder. 'We must pray that he has not. Do not despair, Gérard. We shall find her in the end; I know it.'

'Brienne would not dare to come to Paris. With the mood of the people as it is, he must be in fear of his life.' Gérard's mouth twisted with scorn. 'Already many of his kind are fleeing from France—and we are well rid of them! If nothing more comes of this unrest, that will be an end in itself!'

An exodus of nobles had taken place after the King had been forced to return to Paris as a prisoner of the people. Throughout the long, hot summer, the unrest had been fermenting in the countryside. Those aristocrats whose behaviour had done much towards creating the discontent had fled from their burning chateaux in terror of their lives. It could only be fear that had so far prevented Brienne's peasants from turning against him, Gérard realised. He represented the worst of his kind; a despotic, greedy overlord who abused his privileges. So far he had escaped retribution, but for how much longer?

Gérard suddenly stopped pacing and looked at André in triumph. 'What a fool I am! He will have taken her to his château.'

'But which one?' André said, frowning. 'He has three to my certain knowledge: Alençon, Chauvigny and...'

'He will take her to Alençon.' Gérard spoke with conviction. 'It is protected from prying eyes by the river and the forest. I have heard that his worst excesses have been committed there. For some reason he seems to enjoy torturing the people on that estate.'

Their eyes met in shared horror as they recalled stories they had heard whispered at court. Stories so terrible that no one dared to speak of them openly.

'This time you will have to kill him,' André said. 'He will never forgive you for humiliating him in that duel.'

Gérard's mouth drew into a hard line. 'If he has harmed my wife, he will beg for death!'

There was a cruel, gloating expression on the Marquis's face as he watched the young peasant boy being flogged in the courtyard of the Château Brienne. Georges Garonne, just sixteen, had been caught stealing food from the kitchens—food he desperately needed to feed his widowed mother and five small brothers and sisters.

'Forgive me,' he had pleaded on his knees when brought before Pierre de Brienne. 'My family were starving. I had to do something.'

'Whip him!' Brienne ordered his henchman. 'I should have his hands cut off, but I'm inclined to be merciful today. You are fortunate, Garonne. Thank me for my generosity.' He aimed a kick at the youth's belly, making him cry out in pain.

The punishment had been carried out immediately, and without mercy. Hubert Grosard obeyed the master he hated, knowing that unless he did exactly as he was told, his sister would suffer. Thérèse Grosard was just fifteen, beautiful, and the only person in the world Hubert cared for. The Marquis had seized her a few months back, keeping her locked away in a secret chamber as a hostage against the good behaviour of her brother; she would remain his prisoner, alive and safe, for as long as Grosard obeyed his master and kept the other peasants in order.

Hubert's whip snaked out with cruel regularity, biting into the youth's naked back and drawing blood. He neither saw the agony he was inflicting nor heard Georges' cries of pain. While the Marquis held Thérèse a prisoner, he would do whatever he had to.

'Enough!' Brienne ordered at last as the boy fainted. 'We do not want to kill him, Hubert. He is young and a strong worker in the fields. I believe he has learned his lesson. Now I have more important business.'

His eyes glittering, Brienne turned away to walk into the house. He had enjoyed watching the youth's punishment. These Garonnes were impudent dogs! No matter how often he had one of them flogged, they still dared to defy him, but he would yet teach them to show respect for their master! If they imagined he did not see their sly glances or hear their mocking laughter, they would discover their mistake soon enough. He would kill every last one of them if he had to, until there was no one left alive to whisper of the shameful secret of his own birth.

Pierre de Brienne was a bastard. Delivered to Jeanne Garonne exactly nine months after she had been raped by his father on the eve of her wedding, Pierre had been smuggled into the Marquise's bedchamber to take the place of her stillborn child. The exchange had not, however, deceived the Marquise, and she had vented her spite on her husband's bastard, telling Pierre of his peasant origins when he was five years old in a vicious tirade. The secret shame had festered inside him as he grew to manhood, turning him into the vengeful monster he now was, with a catalogue of wicked crimes to his name, including the murder of his father's wife when he was just seventeen.

His father had died when Pierre was sixteen, falling from his horse after a wild drinking-bout and breaking his neck. Once the funeral was over, he began to plot the death of the woman he hated. She was too clever to succumb to his attempts to poison her, but in the end he arranged the little 'accident' that resulted in her death. From then on he had gone from one foul deed to the next, inflicting such cruelty on his peasants that he was hated and feared by them all.

Only one man had ever succeeded in thwarting him. Only one man had ever humiliated him—and now that man's wife was in his power. He had had her safely locked up for five days now while he considered what form his revenge should take. He had not been able to choose between rape and torture. Which would hurt her and her husband the most? He would gain more pleasure from watching the woman suffer, but he believed she might suffer more if he raped her. Instinctively, he felt that she would bear physical pain bravely, and he did not want to kill her—at least, not yet. Not until Gérard de Montpellier was there to watch. A little smile played about his mouth as he considered a new thought: why not let Montpellier watch his wife's ordeal? Yes, yes, that was a much better idea. He would lure the Comte to the château, then, when he was chained to the wall like a dog, he could watch the little entertainment...

Brienne halted, changing his direction. The woman would keep a little longer. It was time to send word to Montpellier of where he could find his precious wife!

Annelise stood at the window, watching the sun sink into the trees. How long had she been a prisoner in this room, and how much longer must she stay here? It was impossible to escape. She had realised that almost at once. The window was narrow and high above the ground; even if she could somehow manage to squeeze through it, she would fall to her death. The only way out was through the door, and that was stout with bars as well as a lock. It had resisted all her attempts to open it.

So far she had seen no one but Hubert Grosard. He brought her bread, cheese and water once a day, never speaking as he put down the tray and removed the previous day's dishes.

The frustration was driving her mad, yet what could she do? She paced the floor for hours, her thoughts whirling. There was a tiny spark of hope in her mind that Gérard would rescue her, but she dared not let herself expect too much. The Marquis had set a trap for her husband, and she could only pray that he would not walk into it. Yet, if he did not come for her...

Annelise stiffened as the door opened behind her. Would it be Grosard or his master? She lived in dread of a visit from Brienne, unable to understand why she had been spared this long. Turning slowly, she saw a woman standing on the threshold, who closed the door and held a warning finger to her lips.

'Be careful, Madame de Montpellier,' she said softly. 'If anyone hears us I shall leave at once. If I were found here, it would mean my death.'

'Who are you?'

'That does not matter. I have come to warn you to be ready...'

'Ready?' Hope flared in Annelise's breast. 'Have you come to help me to escape?'

'Yes—but not tonight. It is set for tomorrow, just after dark. We cannot be ready until then.'

'What are you going to do?' Annelise stared at her, her heart beating faster. 'Why can we not leave now?'

'Because you are not the only prisoner here.' The woman smiled slightly. 'There is another girl we must rescue before we put the château to the torch. Once we have her, Grosard will not lift a finger to help his master. Indeed, I believe he will be the one to kill him.'

'Another girl?' Annelise frowned. 'Forgive me. I do not understand.'

'The Marquis has her hidden away in the château. She is Grosard's sister and betrothed to my son. Until today no one knew where she was, but I followed him after he had my Georges beaten, and I saw where he went. I know his secret. Now all we have to do is to take the key from round the Marquis's neck, where it hangs from a gold chain.'

'Then how will you get it? Surely...' Annelise broke off as she saw the woman's odd smile.

'Sometimes the Marquis summons me to his bed...he has done so tonight. I shall please him so well that he will sleep in my arms like a babe.' Her eyes glittered with hatred. 'Often I have longed to plunge a dagger into his black heart, but I am a good Catholic. Let others carry the sin of murder on their souls! Besides, he is very strong, and I might fail. Once I have done my part, the Marquis will be made to pay in full for all his crimes.'

'Supposing he wakes when you try to steal the key?'

'Then you will not see me again.' Madame Garonne pulled a wry face. 'If you wish to leave this accursed place alive, you should pray that I do not fail.'

Annelise nodded, her face pale. 'You are a brave woman, madame. I shall pray for you—and for us all...'

'What do you plan to do?' André asked as they slowed their horses to a walk. 'I still think it might have been better if you had let me bring twenty of our men. We could have stormed the château and taken Brienne by surprise.'

'It would need an army to storm that place,' Gérard said with a shake of his head. 'No, André. My only chance is to get in without being seen and trust to luck that I find Annelise before I'm discovered.'

'That's just what Brienne is hoping,' André replied, frowning. 'He's set a trap for you. You do realise that?'

'I'm sure he has it all neatly planned,' Gérard agreed, 'but he won't be expecting me just yet. He's made no attempt to contact me. No doubt he's relishing the thought of my suffering.'

'And you have suffered.' André glanced at him. 'He won't have her killed, Gérard. She is his bait to trap you. He'll wait until he has you, too. I cannot help wishing that we had brought the others.'

'No, my friend, they are needed for other work. I shall risk no one's life but my own.' Gérard grinned at him. 'You must give me your word that you will stay here with the horses, as we agreed. If I am not back by tomorrow evening, you must return to Paris.'

'And leave you to die at that swine's hands?' André exclaimed indignantly. 'If you're not here by dawn, I shall come looking for you.'

'And waste your life?' Gérard's brows rose. 'No, André you have more important things to do. The King needs you. France needs you. You cannot throw away everything we've worked for for my sake. This is something I have to do myself.'

Their eyes met and held, and then André nodded. 'You're right, as always. Unless our people can bring sanity to bear, we are all doomed. The King must not be persuaded into a mad flight; he must come to terms with the people and provide justice for all. You have been right about so many things, Gérard. Would that we had all listened to you long ago!'

They had dismounted now, and Gérard gripped his friend's shoulder. 'We have much to do, André. If I cannot carry on, I know that you will do what is right.'

André nodded grimly. 'I'll wait here for you,' he promised. 'God be with you, my friend.'

'And with you.'

Gérard had a grim smile on his lips as he strode away through the trees. He knew that André's way might have been easier, but the risk was too great. Brienne would have killed Annelise the moment he realised that he was being attacked. No, this was the only way. Somehow he had to find a way to rescue his wife without putting her life in jeopardy.

Anne Garonne raised herself cautiously on one elbow, looking down on the face of the man she hated. There was a sickness in her stomach as she remembered all the nights he had forced her to submit to him. The first time had been when she was just fourteen and he six years older; he had caught her in the barns when she was feeding the hens, and he had thrust her down in the straw, using her as if she were an animal. She had been a virgin and the pain had lived on in her memory. She had vowed then that she would one day be revenged on him, and now her chance was at hand.

The peasants of Château Brienne were ready to rise against their seigneur. For years they had endured his tyrannical rule, knowing that any disobedience would bring swift retribution, but now the time was ripe for rebellion. All over France oppressive aristocrats were being called to account for their crimes. Château Brienne would burn merrily, Anne thought with satisfaction. She had urged caution until now, unwilling to sacrifice Thérèse Grosard on the Marquis's funeral pyre. Thérèse was a sweet girl, and Georges had sworn to marry no one else. For her son's sake as well as her own, Anne knew she must not fail now.

The key to the secret room in which Thérèse was being held prisoner was dangling from a thick gold chain round the Marquis's neck. Anne had hoped he might remove it when they lay together, but he had not, and she had felt its hardness bruising her flesh, reminding her of her purpose. Gently she examined the chain, looking for a clasp that she could unfasten. There was none, no way that she could remove the key, except by taking the chain up over his head.

Hardly daring to breathe, she lifted the chain over his face so that it lay on the pillow, yet was still trapped beneath his neck. He had not moved and his breathing was as steady and regular as before. Had one eyelid flickered? She froze, fear clutching at her stomach as she imagined her punishment if he awoke. She had been beaten many times in her life, but she knew instinctively that he would not stop there this time. He had taken his hostage because he was afraid of retribution from his peasants, and he would kill anyone who tried to steal Thérèse from him. If only he had drunk more tonight! Anne had refilled his glass whenever he drank, but for some reason he had not seemed thirsty. It was almost as if he had stayed sober to spite her.

It was now or never, she realised. She slipped her hand beneath his head, lifting it carefully so that she could pull the chain free; as she did so, the Marquis suddenly opened his eyes and grinned: a cruel, mocking smile that sent shivers running through her. Gasping, she tried to jump from the bed, but he grabbed her from behind, holding her as she fought wildly. For a few seconds they struggled fiercely, then Anne was forced on to her back and the Marquis straddled her, pinning her arms to the bed.

'Steal from me, would you?' he asked, baring his teeth. 'Or was it the key you wanted?' He laughed, letting go of one of her wrists to hit her across the face. 'You peasants are so stupid! Do you imagine that I don't know the way your minds work? I saw you watching me earlier. I knew you had discovered my secret, and that you would try to steal the key.' His laughter stung her like the lash of a whip. 'I made it easy for you, Anne. How you amused me with your efforts to make me drunk—and you were so willing to please me. That in itself gave you away. You are not clever enough to deceive me.'

'Mock me as much as you like.' Anne suddenly spat in his face. 'My mother and yours were sisters. You are a bast—— Ahhh!' She screamed as he began to beat her, slapping her across the face again and again. Then he dragged her from the bed, pushing her to the floor and snatching up a thin cane from the top of a chest to strike her on her bare buttocks.

'No! No...' she screamed, wriggling and trying to crawl away from him. 'No...'

'I'll teach you to respect me, you bitch!' he yelled, beside himself with fury. 'I'll teach you a lesson you'll never forget.'

Gérard heard a woman screaming somewhere on the floor above. It had taken him a while to find a window wide enough to allow him to squeeze through once he had broken the glass, but he had managed at last to make his way through a small anteroom and several magnificent salons to the main hall. Now, as he heard the screams of agony coming from the next floor, his face twisted with fear. Was that Annelise? His sword at the ready, he took the stairs two at a time. Pray God that the woman who was suffering so terribly was not his wife!

Pausing momentarily at the top of the stairs, he realised that the screaming was coming from a room to his right. Candles were still flaring in the branches of silver candelabra set at intervals on tables along the hall as he strode purposefully towards the source of the screams. A vein was cording at his right temple and the blood was hammering against his brain. If that monster had laid one finger on Annelise... Reaching a door at the end of the passage, he grasped the handle and threw it open, staring in horror at the sight that met his eyes.

'In the name of God, stop what you are doing this instant, Monsieur de Brienne! You will kill her.'

Brienne's arm froze in a raised position. He turned, his face a mask of shock, anger and, now, faint apprehension.

'You?' he said foolishly, becoming aware of his nakedness. 'How dare you intrude on my privacy, Monsieur de Montpellier? You will pay for this!'

Anne was sobbing. Lying at his feet, she trembled, too terrified even to try to cover herself.

'Please dress yourself, madame,' Gérard said. 'I should advise you to leave as quickly as you can.' He made a threatening gesture with his sword as the Marquis stretched a hand towards her. 'It would be unwise to try and stop her, Brienne.'

Anne's flesh was stinging from the blows she had received, but she realised that the stranger had come in time to save her from crippling injury. Gathering her clothes, she saw the gold chain lying on the pillow and snatched it up before Brienne could stop her, fleeing past the stranger to the doorway. The Marquis realised too late what she had done and gave a shout of rage, but another flick of Gérard's sword kept him at bay, preventing him from following.

'God bless you, Monsieur de Montpellier,' Anne cried. 'Kill him now, and I will bring your wife to you.' She was standing just behind him, hastily pulling on her plain black wool dress.

'You know where she is?' Gérard asked without turning his head. 'Has she been harmed?'

'I do not think so, monsieur,' she said. 'I shall go to set her free now.'

'Take her downstairs,' Gérard replied, his eyes still on the Marquis. 'I have a score to settle here.' His mouth twisted with scorn. 'I should kill you where you stand like the dog you are, Brienne, but I shall give you the chance to die like a man. Put your breeches on.'

Brienne reached for his clothes, his hands shaking as he began to dress. 'How did you know where to find her? How did you know I would be here? Did Grosard betray me?'

'A wolf always returns to its lair. No one betrayed you but yourself. The tales of your excesses here have reached the court, Brienne. After I tell His Majesty what I saw here tonight, you would not be welcomed into his presence again, or that of any decent man. That is, if I intended to let you live. You are a coward and a bully, monsieur, and I shall kill you!'

Brienne paused in the act of fastening his shirt. 'You will allow me the death of a gentleman?'

'You do not deserve it, but I am not a murderer. We shall continue the fight we began at Versailles, but it will be here and now. You must do without your seconds, Brienne.'

'As you wish.' The Marquis inclined his head. 'Since I have no sword here, I must ask you to accompany me to the hall. It is more suitable for our purpose.'

'Lead, and I shall follow.' Gérard's eyes narrowed to menacing slits. 'Should you try to summon help from your servants, you should know that I am carrying a loaded pistol. I shall use it if necessary.'

'It seems that you have the advantage for the moment.' Brienne managed a slight smile. 'If I must die, it is fitting that it should be at your hands, Montpellier. You are an excellent swordsman. I respect that—if not your republican sentiments.'

'I have no wish to see the King deposed,' Gérard replied firmly. 'I simply believe that it is time the old ways were ended. The people have suffered enough; they should be free to make a decent life for themselves and their families. We have no right to treat them like animals.'

Brienne's lips curled in a sneer of derision. 'I have heard of your reforms, Montpellier. You pay your peasants to work on your land. I suppose you treat them as equals? Do they also dine at your table?' They were walking along the passage now, the Marquis just a few steps ahead of Gérard. Brienne glanced back mockingly. 'You may sheathe your sword for the moment, monsieur. I shall not try to run away. I too have looked forward to this moment of reckoning.'

'I prefer to remain armed,' Gérard replied, unperturbed by his scorn. 'Strange as it may seem, I dare say your servants might try to save their master out of a misguided sense of loyalty.'

Brienne's right eyelid flickered. He knew that of all the servants in his house only one would raise a finger to help him; and that only if Grosard's sister had not been released. There was a sickness in his stomach, and he knew it was fear—the kind of fear he had so often instilled in others. Yet as they reached the hall, he turned with a smile on his thin lips.

'Then we shall fight to the death, Montpellier. One of us must die before this night is ended.'

As he stared into the Comte's hard eyes, it was as if he looked into the mouth of hell itself. He saw a series of pictures like flashes before his eyes as the memories passed through his mind and were gone. Had there ever been a time when he had not been hated and reviled by all those who knew him? Had there ever been a moment when he had known true love? He knew there had not, and felt the emptiness of his wasted life like a great pit within him. In that moment, Pierre de Brienne knew that he was about to die.

# CHAPTER TEN

ANNELISE SAT hunched up on the narrow bed, staring aimlessly into the corner of the room. Grosard had allowed her one miserly candle, but she had not lit it, preferring the faint glimmer of moonlight through her window. She was unable to sleep. She had been restless ever since the woman in the black dress had visited her earlier, her mind locked in frustration as she wondered what was happening. Would she succeed in stealing the key? So much depended on it! She felt a great wave of longing to be free, to see her loved ones again.

Suddenly there came a sound from within the château, yet distant and muffled so that she could not distinguish it. Jumping to her feet, she ran to the door, pressing her ear against it as she strained to hear more clearly. What had she heard? Could it have been screaming? The noise came again, and now she was almost certain that it was the cry of a woman in agony. The Marquis must have woken as the key was taken from round his throat and was punishing that woman!

A wave of despair swept over Annelise, and she began to pace about the small room, her hands clenched into tight fists at her sides. The desperate attempt had failed, of that she felt quite certain, and she wondered what would happen now. Would the peasants attack the château anyway? Would she die in the flames, or would she simply be left alone in this room until the Marquis was ready to vent his spite on her? She was cold, hungry and frightened, her courage ebbing as she faced the prospect of a painful death.

'Oh, please God, help me,' she whispered, near to breaking-point. 'Please don't let me die like this...'

Several minutes had passed since the screaming stopped. Annelise shivered as she wondered what had happened to that poor woman. The Marquis was a wicked, evil man, she thought, anger bringing a renewal of her strength. He deserved to be burnt in his château, even if it meant that she must die with him.

'I hope they do put you to the torch,' she said, suddenly angry. 'I hope you suffer as that poor woman suffered...'

She stiffened as she heard a new sound. Someone was running. She could hear the clatter of wooden sabots on the stone floor, and now a key was turning in the lock. She faced the door, her nerves jerking as it swung open.

'Madame de Montpellier!' Anne Garonne beckoned to her urgently. 'You must come now; there is no time to be lost.'

Annelise started eagerly towards her. 'Then you succeeded...' She gasped in horror as she saw the cuts and bruises on her face. 'Oh, he has hurt you terribly. What happened?'

'He woke when I tried to steal the key. He was beating me, but then your husband came, and...'

'Gérard is here?' Annelise cried, relief surging through her. 'Where? What is happening? You must tell me!'

'I came to release you,' Anne said. 'I shall take you downstairs; then I must find Thérèse and take her to safety.'

She turned, and Annelise followed her from the room, having to walk swiftly to keep up as she led the way. They were some distance from the main section of the house, and they had only the light from Anne Garonne's candle until they reached the rooms used by the master of the house. Annelise's mind was whirling in confusion as she hurried to keep up with her guide. At last Anne stopped and glanced back.

'From here you will find it is well lit,' she said. 'The Marquis insists that lights burn all through the night— I think he is afraid of his own dreams. Go on to the end of this hall and then turn to your right. You will see the main staircase. Your husband will be somewhere in the hall below waiting for you. Forgive me for deserting you, madame, but it is important that I find Thérèse.'

'Yes, I understand,' Annelise said. 'I can manage now. Thank you for helping me, madame. I am very grateful.'

'My name is Anne Garonne, and I was glad to help you.' Her smile was unexpectedly sweet at that moment. 'I know what it is to suffer at the Marquis's hands. Besides, your husband saved my life. It was a blessing for us that you were brought here.' She smiled again and turned away. 'You cannot miss your way, Madame de Montpellier.'

Annelise acknowledged her words with a wave of her hand. Her heart was thumping as she walked swiftly in the direction that had been pointed out to her. Excitement was beginning to course through her, lending speed to her feet. Gérard was here, waiting for her. Oh, how she longed to be with him again, to feel his arms about her and know the sweetness of his kiss. As she hurried along the corridor, scarcely aware of the magnificence of the furnishings, she wondered why Gérard had not come to release her himself. Then, as she paused at the head of the stairs, she understood.

There were candles blazing everywhere, illuminating the large room below. It was a huge, long room, empty in the centre but with six impressive walnut cabinets set at either end and along the walls. In between the cabinets were tall iron candlestands, and at either side of the open fireplace were two brass-bound chests with heavy locks. On the walls hung swords, shields and silken banners with the Marquis's coat of arms embroidered in silver on a crimson ground.

It was not the splendour of the room that drew Annelise's fascinated gaze, however, but the two men in the centre. Dressed only in their shirts, boots and breeches, they were facing each other with drawn swords, and it was obvious that the duel had already begun. A stool lay on its side near the fireplace, overturned in flurry of fast blows, and the Marquis's sleeve was torn, as though Gérard's blade had ripped it. Poised at the top of the wide stairway, Annelise drew a sharp breath, holding back her cry of alarm for fear of distracting her husband's attention and giving the Marquis an advantage.

'Gérard...' she whispered, fear clutching at her heart as she watched the deadly contest. 'Oh, my love...'

The clash of steel against steel rang in her ears, making her dig her nails into the palms of her hands. She wanted to scream or shout for help, anything to make them stop, but she knew she must stay silent. Any sudden noise from her might put Gérard off his stroke, and that could be fatal. The Marquis was fighting for his life, and he was a skilled swordsman. She was forced to watch their contest, though it made her feel faint with fear for her loved one. Yet how could she turn her eyes away when at any moment a thrust of the Marquis's sword might end it all? It seemed to her inexperienced eyes that the men were equally matched. The Marquis might not be as fast as Gérard, but he was very strong, and several times he forced his opponent to retreat. She caught her breath as Gérard almost stumbled, hardly daring to watch until he recovered and began to attack once more. Their swords crossed, feinted, cut and thrust with such speed that she could hardly keep up with the fight. First

Gérard attacked, driving the Marquis back down the long room; then the Comte was forced to retreat in his turn. It was as much as Annelise could do to stop herself crying out. If the Marquis should win... She could not bear to think about that. He must not win!

'Oh, please God, let Gérard be safe,' she whispered. 'I love him so much...so much...'

Engrossed in the fight, Annelise was not aware of approaching danger. She did not hear the soft footsteps behind her, and when a hand suddenly closed over her mouth, she was taken by surprise. Realising she was being attacked, she twisted violently, kicking and struggling as she was grabbed round the waist.

'Be still, Madame de Montpellier,' Grosard hissed. 'One sound out of you, and I'll break your neck!'

She could not let him capture her again! Once she was at his mercy, Gérard would be forced to lay down his weapon—and then they would both be killed! Her teeth clamped down hard on the fleshy side of her attacker's hand, biting him with a savagery that surprised him. He gave a cry of pain, letting go of her for an instant. Annelise twisted away sharply, catching the heel of her shoe in her hem, and stumbling. For a moment she tottered unsteadily, a scream issuing from her lips as she felt herself falling, and then she went tumbling down the long stairway, rolling down and down and hitting her head as she landed at the bottom.

There was a sudden sharp pain, and then blackness as she passed into unconsciousness.

Gérard heard the cry. His blade faltered for a moment, then he brought it up swiftly in a clever, intricate movement that sent the Marquis's sword flying from his hand. For a moment he hesitated, and then, hearing a shout, he turned to look towards the stairs, his bewildered eyes struggling to take in the scene. A man was halfway down the stairs, pointing a pistol in his direction—and a woman was lying at their foot. In another second he realised that it was his wife.

'Annelise!'

As the hoarse cry left Gérard's lips, several things happened at once. Two women appeared on the landing. One them screamed a man's name and began to run towards Grosard. He saw her; his expression stunned and then turning to one of incredulous delight. Almost in the same instant as Gérard started towards the stairs, the pistol fired—but not at him. From behind there was a scream of pain, and glancing around, he saw blood streaming from the Marquis's arm. 'Hubert, no!' a girl's voice cried as the man with the pistol prepared to fire again. The Marquis seemed to sway on his feet for a moment, his face a ghastly shade of white; then he swung round, half running and half staggering towards the front door.

Gérard saw these things as a blur, his mind concentrated only on the prone figure of his wife. She was lying so still! He threw down his weapon and hurried to her side. Kneeling on the ground, he lifted her head gently, supporting her neck as he felt for signs of injury. Thank God her neck was not broken! There was a sticky patch at her temple, however, and when he looked, he saw blood on his fingertips.

'No!' he choked. 'No! Don't let her be dead.' Tears ran down his cheeks as he stroked her pale face. 'Annelise... No...'

'Is she badly hurt?' Anne Garonne asked as she knelt at his side. She felt for the girl's pulse, relief flowing through her as she found it was beating strongly. 'She lives, monsieur. She lives!'

Gérard looked up, anger burning in his eyes as he saw the man who had caused Annelise's fall. 'If she dies, I shall kill you,' he said, and there was murder in his eyes. 'You pushed her. You tried to kill her!'

Grosard turned pale. 'No, Monsieur de Montpellier,' he muttered hoarsely. 'We struggled and she fell; it was an accident. I swear that it was not intentional.'

The girl behind him came forward, her thin, pale face tight with emotion. 'Oh, the poor lady,' she whispered, tears starting to her eyes. 'Forgive my brother, monsieur, I beg you. He has suffered so terribly since the Marquis made me his prisoner.'

'You were his prisoner, too?' Gérard frowned as he lifted Annelise's limp body gently in his arms. 'Where can I take my wife? She must have attention at once.'

'This way,' Anne Garonne said, beckoning to him. 'You must lay her on the sofa in here while we bathe her head. Someone will fetch a physician later.' Her gaze rested briefly on Grosard. 'You have work to finish, man. Do it now for all our sakes.'

He nodded, understanding the message in her eyes. 'Stay here, Thérèse,' he ordered. 'Stay with Anne and Madame la Comtesse.'

Gérard's face was grim as he followed Anne into one of the salons he had passed through earlier. Annelise was alive, but she had suffered a severe blow to the head, and could still die. The thought tortured him. He could lose her even now. He was aware that Grosard intended murder, but nothing mattered to him now except Annelise. He doubted he could have prevented what was about to happen if he had tried. Yet why should he even consider saving the life of a monster? If Annelise died, it would be because of what Brienne had done—but she must not die! A tiny pulse was throbbing in his neck as he fought to hold his emotions in check. She must not die! He could not live with himself if she were to die like this.

Laying her down on a daybed covered in crimson velvet, he knelt by her side again. He kissed her eyelids, her cheek, her lips, pleading with her not to leave him, hardly aware that Anne Garonne had fetched water and clean linen until she spoke to him.

'The cut is not so bad, monsieur,' she said as she washed away the blood. 'She will be herself again in no time.'

'How can you be sure?' Gérard grated, his eyes raking her face angrily. 'Why did you leave her alone? I told you to stay with her.'

'Forgive me. I had to rescue Thérèse. She has been a prisoner so long—and I thought to avoid trouble from Hubert...'

'Thérèse—the girl who was also a prisoner?' He frowned, looking around. 'Where is she?'

Thérèse moved forward so that he could see her, her pallid but pretty face wearing an anxious frown. 'Whatever my brother has done, it was for my sake,' she said, in a quiet, musical voice. 'The Marquis locked me in a secret room three months ago, when he realised that Hubert had joined in the rebellion in Paris. He was terribly angry; he began to be afraid that the people here would turn against him, and so he made me his hostage. Hubert had to obey him, or—or he would have let me starve to death.'

'He threatened that?' Gérard looked at her in horror.

'Yes, monsieur. Whenever he went away, he left me enough food and water to last until he returned.' A tear ran down the girl's face as she recalled her suffering. 'But the bread became so hard that I had to soak it in water before I could swallow it, and the cheese went mouldy. Sometimes I was so hungry I thought I should starve, but he always came back just in time.'

'I'm sorry for your suffering,' Gérard said, pity making him speak gently. 'But if my wife dies...'

'Gérard...' The faint whisper brought his head swinging back to Annelise. 'Gérard... What happened?'

Her eyes were open, though her face was still terribly pale. He knelt on the floor by her side, bending over to stroke the damp wisps of hair from her forehead. She gave a little cry of pain as she tried to lift her head, sinking back against the cushions weakly.

'My head hurts...' She frowned, trying to remember. 'He—He was trying to capture me so that you would have to surrender. I twisted away, then I caught my heel and fell.'

'Are you sure you fell?' Gérard questioned. 'Or were you pushed by Brienne's servant?'

'I fell, Gérard.' She managed a faint smile for him, despite the pain at her temple. 'Please, can we go home now?'

'Yes, my darling. I'm going to take you home just as soon as I can. First I must make sure that there will be no more trouble from the Marquis.' He turned to Madame Garonne. 'My wife cannot ride a horse in this state. You will please have a carriage made ready for us.'

'Yes, monsieur. My son knows where to find your own carriage and horses.' She glanced at Thérèse. 'You stay here with Madame la Comtesse, child.'

As she was about to walk away, Grosard came into the room. His face had a wild, excited look, and his eyes were glittering with a fierce triumph.

'They caught the Marquis as he ran,' he cried, a note of exultation in his voice. 'There were a dozen of them round him when I reached him. They've killed him, and now they mean to burn the house! You must all leave at once. They are thirsty for revenge...'

Even as he spoke there was the sound of shouting and yelling, together with a great crashing noise as men and women poured into the house. Gérard got to his feet, tensing as the first of them came into the room. It was clear from their wild looks and angry cries that they would allow nothing to stand in their way. His hand reached for his pistol, but Anne laid a warning finger on his arm.

'Leave this to me, monsieur.' She walked forward, holding up her hand for silence. As a hush fell over them, she smiled proudly. 'You wish to burn the château of your master,' she said. 'It is a just revenge for the wrongs that have been done to you...'

'Yes, we've killed him. We've killed the monster! Now we'll burn this accursed house.'

'First you must let these people go their way un-harmed,' she went on, a note of command in her voice. 'They too have suffered at the Marquis's hand, and without Monsieur le Comte's help, we could not have released Thérèse.'

Gérard bent to lift Annelise in his arms, and she smiled as she slipped an arm round his neck. He walked towards the little group of sullen-faced peasants and they parted to let him through, though he saw resentment in their faces. They had listened to Madame Garonne out of re-spect for her, but they had been taught to hate all ar-istocrats. Had it not been for Anne, they would have fallen on him like a pack of dogs.

Anne and Thérèse followed him outside, Grosard re-maining behind. As they emerged into the fresh air, they could hear his voice directing the others to ransack the house and take everything of value before putting it to the torch.

'We have worked for nothing for long enough, my friends,' he cried. 'The Marquis sucked our blood, draining us of life and liberty. It is our right to take what we can from him now.'

Outside in the courtyard there was another group of peasants standing watching with anxious faces and frightened eyes. They knew the Marquis was dead, but rebellion brought retribution from authority, and someone would come to punish them as surely as the sun rose in the morning. Anne's son was standing with them. He came quickly to embrace Thérèse, and then turned to his mother with a grave face.

'They have gone mad, Maman!'

'I know. Let them have their way, Georges.' She sighed deeply, knowing that the evil must be cleansed with fire. Only then would there be a chance for peace. 'Find Monsieur le Comte's carriage. You will drive him wherever he wants to go.'

As the youth hurried away, Gérard set his precious burden down on a stone bench, sitting with his arm about Annelise as she rested her head against his shoulder. She smiled at him despite the throbbing at her temples.

'We must do something for Madame Garonne and her family,' she murmured faintly.

'Yes, my love.' He looked at the peasant woman. 'On my estate the people are free, madame. Each has a small plot of land, and I pay them fair wages to work for me. If you and your family decide you would like to start a new life, you would be welcome there. I would provide you with a cottage and anything else you might need.'

Anne Garonne stared at him suspiciously for a moment, then she realised that he was offering her true freedom—the right to make what she would of her own life. Now that Brienne was dead, there was no master here, but he had a distant cousin who would in time come to claim the land. Who knew what kind of a master he would be?

'When my son returns, we shall pack all our belongings and make the journey to your estate.'

'I shall send a wagon so that you may travel in comfort.'

'Thank you, monsieur.' She smiled at him warmly. 'Ah, here comes my son with your carriage—and just in time, by the looks of it.'

Even as she spoke, there was a terrible crackling sound behind them. Turning, Gérard saw flames shooting through the roof of one wing of the château. Now he could hear screaming and shouting as men and women ran from the burning house, clutching vases, paintings, candlesticks and whatever else they had managed to snatch before they were driven back by the smoke and flames.

'The fools,' Anne Garonne said scornfully. 'They have destroyed everything in their impatience! They are burning a fortune—money that could have been used to buy food for their families in the winter.'

'Vengeance is a fearful thing,' Gérard said. He slipped his arm beneath Annelise's legs, smiling tenderly at her as he lifted her again. 'André is waiting in the woods; he will be anxious when he sees the flames.'

Annelise nodded, lifting her hand in a weak wave of farewell. 'Thank you, madame,' she whispered as her husband carried her away. 'We shall see you again.'

Gérard set her in the carriage, placing cushions and rugs about her before going to speak to Georges. Then, in a few seconds, he was by her side, slipping his arm about her to steady her as the carriage moved off. She gave a little moan as a wave of faintness washed over her, and he looked at her in concern.

'Does you head hurt very badly, Annelise?

She opened her eyes, trying to reassure him, though the pain was almost as much as she could bear. 'I shall be better soon,' she said. 'I'm sorry to be so much trouble. It was such a foolish thing to do, falling like that.'

'*You* are sorry?' He drew a harsh breath. 'I am to blame for it all. I should have foreseen that Brienne might try to take his revenge for that duel. I can never forgive myself for my carelessness.'

She laid a gentle hand on his arm. 'Do not blame yourself so much, Gérard. You could not have guessed what would happen. I myself believed it was a genuine arrest until I realised that someone had set a trap for you. Even then I did not know it was Brienne. Not until I heard them talking after they had killed Martin did I realise exactly what was happening.'

'God rest his soul!' Gérard frowned. 'Who killed him?'

'I think it was Hubert Grosard—but he said it was an accident.' Annelise shivered. 'That man frightens me. He hates all aristocrats because of what the Marquis did to him and his family.'

'I should have killed him!'

'Please do not talk like that,' she begged. 'It is over now. I should just like to forget it.' A little shiver went through her as she recalled various moments of her ordeal.

Gérard's face was stern, a little nerve jerking in his throat. 'Brienne is dead. He cannot harm you any more.'

Annelise glanced at his profile, wondering why he looked so angry. Did he blame her for giving in to Grosard in the first place? Did he think she should have ordered the servants to fire on the crowd? He looked so strange that she felt uneasy. A single tear ran from the corner of her eye, but she brushed it away.

'Are we going to Paris or the château?' she asked. 'Jean will be fretting for me by now.'

'I'm taking you to the château,' Gérard said, not looking at her. 'Then, when you are well enough, I shall send you and my son to England for safety. I must remain here in France for the time being.'

Annelise closed her eyes. He was sending her away from him! Her head was hurting her so terribly and she felt sick. She wanted to protest; to make him understand that she would not be sent away as if she were a mistress he had discarded, but she could not find the strength to argue. She would tell him what was in her mind another day. All she wanted to do for the moment was to sleep...

For the first time in a week, Annelise woke without a headache. She stretched and sighed, listening to the gentle sound of rain in the trees outside her room. After a few minutes, she decided that she was well enough to get up, and pushed back the bedcovers. Once she was out of bed and standing on the cool, tiled floor, she found that she felt really well again. There was no more pain and that terrible listlessness that had hung over her for a week had finally gone. She bathed her face and hands, in cool water, pulling on a warm red velvet robe and running a brush through her hair before going into Jean's room.

He was sitting on a chair, swinging his legs and staring aimlessly in front of him, but when he saw her, his face lit up and he scrambled down, rushing towards her. She caught him up in an enveloping hug, and he smothered her in kisses.

'Are you better, Annelise?' he asked, excitement in his voice. 'Are you truly better at last?'

'Yes.' She smiled and hugged him again. 'I'm better, my love. I've missed you so much. Have you missed me?'

He had made one appearance at her bedside, looking pale and frightened as he stood at his father's side.

'I wanted to be with you and tell you stories,' he said, 'but Papa said I must not disturb you. I've tried to be quiet. Have I been quiet, Annelise?'

'Like a little mouse,' she laughed. 'If you wait while I dress, we'll go and look for your father. Do you know where he is?'

'I expect he's in the library,' Jean said. 'He sits there all the time—except when he's in your room. I asked him to take me riding, but he just frowned and told me to go away.' He raised troubled eyes to hers. 'Why is Papa so cross all the time? Have I been wicked, Annelise? Is Papa angry with me because I let those bad men take you away?'

'Of course not!' she cried, her throat catching with emotion as she sensed his hurt. He must not be allowed to feel guilt for what had happened! 'It wasn't your fault, Jean. You were a very brave boy, and you did exactly what I wanted. I expect your father is worried, that's all. He has been anxious about me, and the times are very difficult just now. He has a great deal on his mind. He thinks he is needed in Paris, and I've kept him here.'

Jean nodded. 'Grand-mère said something like that. She said Papa was upset about you and that I mustn't mind if he was cross, because he didn't mean to be.'

'Your grandmother said that?' Annelise was surprised that Margot had shown so much understanding.

'Yes.' Jean wrinkled his brow in thought. 'She has been different since you were ill. She keeps asking Papa how you are—and I saw her crying after he told her she was not to visit you. She kisses me all the time now!' There was an indignant note in his voice that made Annelise laugh.

'You don't complain when I kiss you!'

'That's not the same; you've always kissed me. You love me—Grand-mère is very strange. She keeps muttering things and asking me to forgive her.'

Annelise knelt down, looking into his eyes. 'Your grandmother has been very unhappy since your mother died, Jean. Perhaps she has at last realised that she does love you very much, and she wants to be friends.'

He nodded wisely. 'I expect it's because of you. Everything has changed since you came. Papa smiles only when you are there. I'm glad that he rescued you from the bad men, Annelise. I hope he killed them all with his sword!'

She got to her feet, feeling a surge of happiness as she moved her fingers in his tousled hair. 'Yes, my darling. Your papa always kills the bad men, and so will you when you are old enough. Now I must get dressed...'

She paused on the library threshold, her heart catching with pain as she saw the expression on Gérard's face. He looked like a man suffering all the torment of hellfire. Then he turned and saw her standing there, and his eyes seemed to leap with an inner flame. He got to his feet at once and came towards her.

'Why are you out of bed?' he demanded harshly. 'The doctor said you were to have complete rest.'

'I have rested,' she replied calmly, smiling at him. 'I'm quite well now.'

His eyes searched her face with a feverish intensity, as if he could not believe it. 'You are sure? You have no more pain?'

'None at all. I feel wonderful.' She laughed and slipped her arm through his. 'The rain has stopped and it's a beautiful day, Gérard. Would you give Jean a riding-lesson? I'll come and watch. I should enjoy a walk in the fresh air.'

Gérard glanced at the small, silent boy at her side, feeling a pang of regret as he knew himself guilty of neglecting his son. He smiled and nodded at his wife, feeling some of the tension of the past few days drain away. She was not going to die. He had been spared, this time.

'Yes, if that's what you both want,' he said. 'We'll go now, shall we?'

Jean looked at him anxiously. 'You won't be cross any more, will you? Annelise is better. I don't have to be quiet now—she said so.'

'If I've been unkind to you these past few days, Jean, I apologise.' Gérard looked down at his son. 'I ask humbly for your forgiveness.'

Jean shyly offered his hand. 'I forgive you, Papa. I love Annelise, too.'

Emotion caught at the man's throat. 'From the mouth of a child,' he murmured. 'What a fool I am!'

Annelise squeezed his arm, her eyes saying more than words. Outside in the courtyard a little breeze was drying the flagstones and a warm autumn sun had taken the chill from the day. Wrapped in a thick cloak of blue velvet, her husband's arm about her, she felt secure, safe and happy. Servants going about their business stopped to smile and wish her well, their faces reflecting the pleasure felt by all at the château in her recovery.

Jean's pony was brought out, and she watched the father and son together, enjoying the sound of their laughter. That terrible haunted look had at last gone from Gérard's face, she noticed, wondering at his suffering. It was strange that he should have been so distraught over her accident. She had been unconscious for only a few minutes, and though she had felt ill for several days, her life had not been in danger. So why was he so upset?

It was because of Lisette's death, of course. His first wife had died after falling from the tower, and it must have brought it all back. A shadow seemed to pass across her mind, dimming her feeling of happiness as she understood the true cause of that look she had seen in his eyes earlier—he was still tortured by his memories of Lisette. She experienced a sharp pain about her heart as she realised that he was probably still grieving for his first wife. He wanted her, Annelise, but she could never replace Lisette in his heart. Was it because he had realised that that he wanted to send her back to England? Tears stung her eyes, but she blinked them away. She would not give way to self-pity. He did care for her, and that must be enough, because she loved him.

'Why so sad?'

Annelise turned in surprise to see André standing just behind her. She smiled at him, walking to take his outstretched hand. 'I thought you were in Paris?'

'I have just arrived,' André said, taking her hand. 'You look better. I am so glad. Gérard was almost out of his mind with worry.'

She nodded, biting her lip. 'I expect it brought the memory of Lisette's death back to him.'

'He cares for you very deeply,' André said with a little frown. 'If he is haunted by Lisette's death, you must understand that he blamed himself. He feels guilty, Annelise, but it does not mean that he is still in love with her. In fact, I do not believe that theirs was ever a very happy marriage.' He looked at Gérard and then at her. 'Walk up to the house with me. I think it is time you understood what happened.'

'I'm just taking André to the house,' she called, waving at her husband. 'I'll see you both later.'

Slipping her arm through André's, she gazed up at his serious face anxiously, waiting for him to speak. It was a moment or two before he did so.

'Lisette was very young when they married,' he said at last. 'She knew nothing of life—or the ways of men. When she discovered what being a wife meant, she was horrified. Gérard told me that she wept bitterly on her wedding night.'

'So that was why she never used those beautiful rooms he had prepared for her,' Annelise said. 'She preferred to be further away from him.'

André nodded. 'She was never a true wife to Gérard. He was very patient with her, Annelise, and he tried to show her that love between a man and woman can be a beautiful thing. As time passed, she became resigned to what she saw as her duty, but she never really wanted her husband's love.. Then, when she discovered she was carrying a child, she became hysterical. She cried for days on end, and Gérard was obliged to ask her mother to come and live with them.'

'He said that Lisette wanted her mother here...'

'She was a child, Annelise. Her mother had told her nothing before her marriage and it was Margot who pushed her into an early wedding—because of Gérard's wealth, of course.' André frowned again. 'Before they were married, Lisette was enchanted by the idea of being a countess and having lots of pretty jewels. It was being a wife that she did not like.'

'Poor Gérard,' Annelise whispered, her throat tight. 'How he must have suffered.'

'Yes. All through her pregnancy, Lisette was weepy and miserable. She used her sickness as an excuse to keep Gérard away and she blamed him for it all...' André stopped and looked at Annelise. 'He did not go to another woman in all that time. I know it for a fact, yet both Margot and Lisette accused him of unfaithfulness. Gérard bore with it all patiently, waiting for several months after Jean was born before he tried to resume marital relations...' André drew a deep breath. 'I do not know quite what happened, for he has never spoken of it to me, but I know they quarrelled over something. Gérard rode off to Paris and took a mistress. It was while he was there that the accident happened. On his return, Margot turned on him and called him a murderer. She said that he had broken his wife's heart and that Lisette had taken her own life because of it.'

'But that's unfair!' Annelise cried. 'If Lisette refused to be a true wife to her husband, she could not complain if he left her to find happiness elsewhere.'

'How glad I am that Gérard and I made that foolish wager at Fontainebleau,' André said. 'You have given him such happiness, my dear.'

'A wager?' Annelise's brows went up.

'It was all my doing. Gérard was taken with you from the start, but I knew that he had vowed never to marry again. I provoked him into trying to seduce you for a wager, hoping that once he got to know you, he would fall in love. And I was right!'

She turned her bright, sparkling eyes on him. 'Do you believe that he loves me, André? You do not think that he is still in love with Lisette?'

'How could any man hanker after that poor, foolish little child when he has a woman like you?' André shook his head. 'No, my dear, you need have no fear on that score.'

'Then why does he want to send me back to England?'

'Because he is afraid for your safety,' André said. 'He could not live with himself if anything happened to you.'

'Because he loves me so much?' she whispered, her throat catching with emotion. 'Oh, thank you, my dear friend—thank you so very much for telling me that...'

André smiled and patted her hand. 'I wanted to be sure you understood,' he said.

## CHAPTER ELEVEN

THEY HAD reached the house by now. Annelise stopped and looked up at her companion, her smile bright and free of doubt. 'I have something I must do, André, so will you excuse me for a while? I know Claude will have everything ready for you.'

'You're going to see Margot, aren't you?'

'Yes.' Annelise nodded, her face determined. 'I'm sure that she has the key to this mystery. If Gérard is ever to be truly happy, he must know the reason for Lisette's death. I do not believe she killed herself because she was unhappy, and I mean to discover the truth.'

'If anyone can, it will be you,' André said. 'I wish you success, my dear.'

She smiled again, turning away in the direction of Margot's rooms. Lisette had never been a loving wife to Gérard, and he was such a sensual man. It must have been a miserable time for both husband and wife, she thought, but knowing Gérard as she did, she could not believe that he had been so unkind to Lisette that she was driven to take her own life. No, there must be something else: something that Margot was hiding. She knocked at her door, surprised when it was opened by a smiling Madame Vicence.

'Come in, Annelise,' she said, standing back. 'I hoped you would come and see me. I would have visited you, but—but Gérard said you were too ill to want visitors.'

The alteration in her manner was so marked that Annelise would have been suspicious had Jean not already told her that his grandmother's nature had changed.

'I'm much better now, madame,' she said carefully. 'I hope you do not mind that I come to see you without an invitation?'

'It is my hope that you will do so as often as you wish in future—and that you will invite me to dine with you sometimes?'

'Of course. We should all be delighted if you will join us this evening,' Annelise replied. 'I'm sure Gérard does not wish you to shut yourself away as you have.'

Margot looked down at her hands. 'You have a very forgiving nature, Annelise.'

'I see no point in living with bitterness,' Annelise said, looking at her directly. 'Do you not think that you could bring yourself to forgive Gérard, Margot?'

'I—I have nothing to forgive,' Margot choked, the words forced out of her painfully. 'It is he who will have to try and forgive me—if he can. I have been bitter and cruel, and I have suffered for it. Believe me, I have suffered the torment of the damned!'

'What do you mean?'

'I accused Gérard of driving my daughter to her death.' Margot lifted her eyes to meet Annelise's piercing gaze. 'It was a lie. I knew it was a lie—but it was the only way I could face life. I was afraid to admit the truth, even to myself. You see, I was the cause of Lisette's death.'

'You . . .' Annelise had not expected this. 'But how could you have killed Lisette? You loved her!'

'Yes, I loved her, but I did not realise how much until she was dead.' Margot's face was agonised. 'I knew she was still such a child—and a timid one. She was afraid of so many things. I pushed her into marrying the Comte because I wanted her to be rich—and because I was desperately in need of money. Gérard was very generous to me from the start. I should have told Lisette what it would mean to be a wife, but I did not. I told her only that she would have pretty clothes and jewels to wear...'

'But that is not so terrible,' Annelise said. 'She had time to learn to become a wife. I do not believe that it was because of that that she died.'

'No, it was not.' Margot smiled oddly. 'When you last visited me, you made me realise that I could not go on deceiving myself. You made me face the truth. Gérard was not to blame for Lisette's death; I was.'

'But how? I do not understand.'

'She was very fond of going up to the battlements near the west tower,' Margot said, a bleak look in her eyes. 'I was forever warning her that it was dangerous, telling her that she must not go there. This particular day I happened to see her in the tower. I went after her—but when I got there she was leaning out, looking at something on the ground. I shouted at her, and—and she fell...' Margot choked, tears beginning to run down her cheeks. 'She was startled, and she fell. She did not jump...she fell.'

'Then it was an accident,' Annelise said in a gentle voice. 'You must not blame yourself, Margot. You did not mean it to happen.'

'I should have remembered how easily she was startled,' Margot said, her face working with grief. 'I should not have shouted, but I was angry with her. I was angry because her foolishness had driven her husband away. I thought that he might be less generous to us if she refused to be a wife to him.'

Annelise nodded, understanding the way her mind had worked after the accident. She was racked by her guilt, and the only way she could live with what had happened was by blaming Gérard for it all. 'How you must have

suffered!' she said, feeling only pity. 'But someone else
has suffered terribly, too. You must tell Gérard the truth.
You know that, don't you?'

Margot gazed up at her appealingly. 'Would you tell
him for me? Please?'

'Yes, if you wish.' Annelise sighed. 'I hope he will
believe me. If only there were some proof...'

Margot stood up and took something from a wooden
box on the table. 'Give him this. It should set his mind
at rest.'

Annelise looked at the little book. 'What is it?'

'It is Lisette's journal,' Margot said. 'Read it yourself
before you give it to him. It will explain many things.'

'Thank you.' Annelise moved to kiss her cheek. 'You
have suffered enough, Margot. It is time to forgive
yourself—time to live again. You have a beautiful
grandson, and he will love you if you let him.'

Margot sniffed, reaching for her kerchief. 'Please go
away now,' she whispered. 'I may see you this evening
at dinner.'

Annelise closed the journal, a tear trickling from beneath her lashes. It was all there, faithfully recorded day
by day: everything that Lisette had thought, said or done
from her wedding night to the morning of her death.
Gérard would find it painful to read, but it was necessary that he should do so. It told the story of a young
girl's struggle to find herself—and of her determination
to try and be a better wife to her husband when he returned from Paris. It was not the journal of a woman
who had been driven to take her own life. It had been
an accident, just as Margot said.

She must give this record of Lisette's thoughts to
Gérard at once. Or would it be better to wait until later?
she thought, hesitating. First she must talk to him; she

must make him see that they should always be together,
no matter what the dangers. Yes, she would give him
the journal in the morning...

Annelise took her time preparing for bed, brushing her
long hair until it shone like silk and rubbing perfume
into her skin at all the pulse spots so that she was enveloped in a cloud of fragrance. She had put on the
sheerest nightgown in her wardrobe; pale green, it set
off the glory of her flame-like hair as it tumbled over
her shoulders. Glancing at herself in the mirror, she gave
a little smile of satisfaction.

Gérard had kissed her hand when she said goodnight
downstairs, murmuring in a soft voice that he would not
disturb her. She knew he meant her to rest, but she was
perfectly well and she wanted to feel the warmth of her
husband's arms. She had heard him moving about when
he came up a little while earlier, and she thought that
he would probably be in his bed by now. A little smile
curved her lips as she imagined the look on his face when
she walked in. Having made sure of easy access to his
room by pocketing the key that afternoon, she inserted
it in the lock now, her heart beginning to beat rapidly.
His dressing-room was empty, his clothes scattered carelessly as if he had undressed slowly, dropping each
garment where he stood. She smiled to herself, drawing
a deep breath as she pushed open the bedroom door.

There was one small candle burning by the bed. Gérard
was lying staring at the ceiling, his hands folded beneath
his head. As he heard her soft footsteps, he turned to
look at her, his expression one of such surprise that she
laughed.

'Annelise,' he said. 'Are you ill? I did not look in
because I thought you might be sleeping.'

'I am not ill,' she said, a hint of laughter in her voice. 'I have never felt better in my life.'

'Then why?' He stared at her, a flame starting to leap in his eyes. 'Annelise...'

She moved towards the bed, smiling at him. 'Aren't you going to invite me into your bed?' she whispered huskily. 'It isn't very polite to keep me standing here.'

'Annelise,' he murmured huskily, drawing back the covers, 'I thought you would be too tired...' His words were smothered beneath her lips as she kissed him, and became a groan as his arms went round her. 'Are you sure?' he asked, when she allowed him to speak. 'I did not want to impose on you...'

'Be quiet, you foolish man,' she said with a low gurgle of laughter. 'I want to be with you like this always. I was so lonely without you, my darling. Kiss me, Gérard. Make love to me. I need your love so much.'

'Annelise, my love,' he croaked, 'You'll never know how much I adore you.'

He needed no further urging and soon his kisses were setting her flesh on fire. She trembled as his fingers untied the laces at her throat, his hand slipping beneath the silk of her nightgown to caress her breasts. His touch made her moan with pleasure and she arched towards him as the desire spiralled through her. They clung to one another hungrily as though suddenly aware of their deep need for each other.

'I've longed for you so much,' he murmured, his lips exploring the slender arch of her throat, kissing the delicate hollow at its base and sending her wild with delight. 'I nearly died when I thought I had lost you.'

Carried away on the surging tide of his passion, she clung to him, sensing his torment. Later she would make him understand that he must not be so afraid for her, but for now nothing mattered but this pulsing in her

blood and the need to be one with him. There was a
sweetness in the meeting of their bodies, a feeling of
homecoming and rightness as they reached the heights
of pleasure in each other's arms.

And afterwards, when he had done, and she lay with
her head nestled against his satin-hard shoulder, nuzzling
its wetness with her lips, she was too exhausted to think
of anything but her utter content. Satiated, complete,
she slept at her husband's side.

Gérard supported himself on his elbow as he looked into
the face of the woman he loved, his eyes feasting on the
sight he had feared never to see again. He had been so
terrified that she would die, and he knew he could not
face life without her now. She was so beautiful with her
dark red hair spread out on the pillow, her face high-
lighted by candlelight and the glow of love.

She opened her eyes, looking up at him. 'I love you,'
she said, as he bent his head to brush his lips over hers.
'Don't send me away, Gérard. I want to be with you
always. I should be miserable apart from you.'

An anxious expression came over his face. 'You and
Jean would be safer in England as things are, my love.'

'No!' She caught his hand and held it to her cheek,
turning it so that she could kiss the palm. 'Send Jean
and Marie if you must, but let me stay with you. My
place is beside you, no matter what.'

She sat up, her long hair falling like a silk curtain over
her breast. He looked at her and drew a long, shud-
dering breath, entranced by her beauty and by the look
of love he saw in her eyes.

'Do you imagine I want to be parted from you for a
day or even an hour?' he asked, his voice husky with
passion. 'You are more than my life to me, Annelise,
but if you were to die because of my carelessness...'

She placed a finger against his lips. 'I am not a fragile figurine that will break if you drop me,' she said. 'I am a woman, Gérard. I love you very much, but you are not responsible for my life. It is mine to use as I will. If I choose to stay at your side, knowing that there may be danger, that is my responsibility and mine alone.'

'Annelise...' he began, but she shook her head at him.

'You blame yourself for Lisette's death,' she said. 'It was not your fault...'

'You know nothing of that!' His face twisted with pain. 'I killed her—I drove her to take her own life. You don't understand.'

'I understand more than you think. Lisette was unhappy because she did not enjoy physical love. You believe that something you said—or did—before you went to Paris made her so miserable that she threw herself from the tower, don't you?'

'Yes...' His eyes had that haunted look again. 'I had been patient with her so long, but I was still a young man and I wanted my wife to be loving and warm. I went to her room that last night and tried to make love to her. When she lay stiff and cold in my arms, I grew angry. I told her she was not natural. I said cruel things, and even threatened to send her to a convent. I told her that if she had not decided to be fully my wife when I returned from Paris, I would send her away. Of course I would never have been so harsh—but she believed me.'

'Yes, I think perhaps she did,' Annelise said gently. 'But it did not drive her to take her life. Instead, it made her consider and decide to try and be a better wife.'

'How do you know all this?' Gérard stared at her.

'Margot gave me Lisette's journal. I have read it, and I shall give it to you in the morning. It will hurt you to read it, Gérard, but you will realise that you are not a murderer.'

'Lisette kept a journal?'

'From the eve of her wedding until the morning of her death.' Annelise reached up and stroked his cheek. 'She went up to the tower because she liked it there, and Margot followed to tell her to be careful. She shouted at Lisette as she was looking over the edge of the battlements and startled her. Lisette fell. It was an accident. Margot was so torn by grief that she blamed you for it. It was the only way she could face her life.'

'My God!' He let out a sharp whistle. 'You are telling me that Margot was there when she fell—that she has known it was an accident all this time?

'Yes. Don't be angry,' Annelise begged as she saw his jaw harden. 'She asked me to tell you because she was afraid of what you would do. I think you must forgive her, Gérard. She has suffered enough.'

'*She* has suffered!' he ejaculated, jumping out of bed and beginning to pace the room like a caged beast. 'She let me believe that I had driven Lisette to her death all this time—and now you ask me to forgive her? She leaves this house in the morning!'

Annelise pulled on her nightgown and got out of bed, going to him. She gazed up at him urgently, her eyes pleading with him to listen.

'Don't be bitter Gérard,' she begged. 'I know how angry you must be, but don't you see that she has paid for what she did? Living almost as a recluse, knowing that she was the one responsible for her daughter's death. You had a good friend in André. You learned to live with your grief and take your place in the world. She stayed in her rooms, brooding over her guilt. She has suffered as much as you. Be kind to her, Gérard. It is the only way to put the past behind you. There has been enough bitterness.'

'You make a good advocate,' he said wryly. 'Why do I feel as if I am being out-manoeuvred?'

'If you want her to leave, she will leave,' Annelise said, her face serious. 'I am only asking for your understanding. The decision must, of course, be your own.'

'Witch!' Gérard chided her, amusement sparking in his eyes. 'How can I deny you anything? How can I deny the woman who has stolen my heart?'

'Then let me stay,' she said. 'Send Margot with Jean to safety if you will, but never send me away from you.'

'Annelise,' he murmured, groaning as she moved towards him, her arms going up around his neck. 'How I ached for you when you were not by my side. I am only happy when you are with me.'

His kiss was light and sweet at first, but then it deepened. His lips moved over her throat, sliding down to the rosy tip of one breast, then travelling on down over her navel with a hungry yearning. Suddenly he swooped down and caught her behind the knees, carrying her to the bed.

He grinned at her wickedly. 'If you want me to let you stay, you must convince me that it will be worth my while.'

She gurgled with laughter. The look in his eyes was setting the blood singing in her veins. She pressed her lips to the silky flesh on his shoulder, sinking her teeth into him. He gave a cry, half pain, half pleasure, catching her to him and growling with a fierce surge of passion. She arched towards him, meeting his need with one as urgent of her own, her hands stroking the smooth skin on his back, moulding the corded muscles as he covered her with his body, pressing her deep into the mattress. He felt her teeth nibbling at his shoulder and heard her groan and he laughed, glorying in the wild abandon of her love. There were no barriers between them, nothing to keep them apart. She was not a timid child but a wild, free, passionate woman with a mind of her own and the spirit to reach out for what she wanted. He would never need to be afraid for her.

She was entirely his now; his wonderful, beautiful wife. Her soft cries roused him to fever pitch as he moved inside her, and it was as if the earth stood still before exploding within him. He had never felt this way with any woman before. It was beyond anything he had ever experienced, and afterwards he lay against her, one leg curled over her possessively, holding her even in sleep. And his sleep was free of the nightmares that had haunted him for so long. He lay in her arms, content and free at last.

'Uncle André has been teaching me to fence,' Jean cried as Annelise came downstairs. 'Look at my sword! Isn't it fine? One day I shall have real one just like Papa's.'

The wooden sword he was waving was a present from André, and she smiled as she saw his pleasure. 'It is a magnificent sword, Jean.' She kissed the top of his head. He ran off to play with one of the dogs who had wandered into the house, and she looked at André. 'I thought you would like to know that Lisette's death was an accident,' she said. 'Margot startled her, and she fell.'

'You are sure?' André frowned as she quickly related the story. 'You've told Gérard, of course?'

'Yes. He knows the truth now.' Her smile was so confident that he laughed.

'Gérard is a fortunate man.'

'And why is that?' Gérard asked, coming down the stairs towards them, a spark of mischief in his eyes. 'It is fortunate that I am not a jealous man! My wife and my best friend in close conversation...'

'Wretch!' Annelise said. 'You know that André is desperately in love with Marielle.'

'I had a letter from her the other day,' André said. 'I shall be going to London to visit her, so if you wish for an escort, Annelise?'

'Annelise will not be going to England,' Gérard said, a glint in his eyes. 'She is quite determined.'

Jean came up at that moment, catching at André's sleeve. 'Come with me,' he demanded. 'One of the bitches has some puppies. I want you to see them.'

'Puppies? We must go at once,' André said. 'Excuse me, Annelise, this is important.'

'Of course.' She laughed as he was dragged off by the impatient Jean. 'Poor André! He will be glad to get to England and find some peace.'

Gérard tipped her chin towards him. 'You are sure you don't wish to go with him?'

'You know my answer to that.'

'Then so be it.' He sighed. 'I have read what Lisette wrote. As you said, it was not the journal of a woman who intended to kill herself.'

'Then you are satisfied at last?

'Yes.' He smiled wryly. 'I shall tell Margot that she can stay here if she wishes.'

'I'm glad. It will be company for Jean when we are in Paris.' She saw him frown, and shook her head. 'Together always, Gérard.'

'We'll see...' he began, breaking off as he heard voices from outside. 'Hélène!' he said, surprised as a woman entered. 'What brings you here?'

'I am on my way to England, Gérard. I was denounced in the Assembly as a traitor and managed to leave Paris only just before they came to arrest me. I believe it is time to leave France. I wanted to warn you that you should go to England as soon as you can.'

'You must certainly go with André,' Gérard said. 'But I do not believe we are in danger here. There was some trouble in the summer with agitators, but it seems to have passed now.'

'We are quite safe here,' Annelise said. 'But you must be tired after your journey, Hélène. Would you like to rest for a while?'

'Thank you.' Hélène smiled gratefully at her. 'I should like to lie down for an hour or so before I see Jean. How is he?'

'He is very well—as impatient as ever.' Annelise glanced at her husband. 'I shall take Hélène to her room.' She tucked her arm through Madame Reinhold's. 'Now, do you know where you will be staying in England? I have a house in Bath you are welcome to use until you find something of your own...'

Annelise sat before the fire, brushing her long hair until it shone. Her face was thoughtful as she stared into the flames. She had not yet had time to speak to Gérard alone since he had heard all Hélène's news, and she did not know how he felt about the situation now. If she had decided to leave France, things must be getting worse in Paris...

'You should not have waited up.' The door had opened without her realising it. Gérard came to her, taking the brush from her hand and stroking it through the shining tresses. 'André kept me talking.'

'You must have a great deal to discuss.' She smiled at him in the mirror as he smoothed her hair with his hand. 'This is nice. It's a long time since anyone brushed my hair for me.'

He bent to kiss her neck. 'Thank you for giving me Lisette's journal. I shall keep it in case Jean ever asks me what happened.'

'You will be at peace now.' She reached out to touch his hand. 'I'm sorry if some of what you read hurt you.'

'I always knew that Lisette was not in love with me.' He smiled ruefully. 'I was young and she was pretty. It hurt me when she rejected my lovemaking, but my feeling for her was really only infatuation. It could not compare with my love for you, Annelise.' He pulled her gently to her feet and into his arms, holding her so that he could look into her eyes. 'I knew when I first saw you that my life would never be complete without you, my darling. I love you more than I can ever tell.'

She slid her arms up about his neck. 'We have so much, Gérard. Sometimes it frightens me.'

'You are thinking about what Hélène said.' He stroked her mouth with his thumb, then ran his hand beneath her hair, caressing the back of her neck. 'If you want to go to England, we shall.'

'No.' She shook her head. 'You love France. The château is our home and Jean's heritage. If we ran away now, it could be burnt to the ground. No, we shall not let them drive us away.'

'You are so brave,' he murmured, 'but perhaps you should consider more carefully. The situation is Paris is getting worse all the time.'

'Is that what is worrying you?' She pulled at his shirt. 'Tell me, Gérard. Tell me what you fear.'

'I don't know,' he replied truthfully. 'I sense that France is about to change for ever. I fear there will be much bloodshed before we are one nation again.'

'There is more,' she said. 'You are thinking of going to Paris, aren't you?'

'Perhaps.' He sighed deeply. 'I don't want to leave you, but I feel it is my duty to speak in the Assembly— to try to stop this madness before it is too late. Yet how can I leave you? No, it is impossible!'

'You won't have to. I shall come with you.'

'It is too dangerous...'

She pressed her lips to his, stopping his protest with a kiss. 'Jean will stay here with Marie and his grandmother for the moment. We can always send them to England if you feel it necessary. It will give them a chance to become friends now that she is no longer bitter. I am your wife, Gérard, and I have the right to be with you—at least until I am with child.'

The dark eyes glowed with laughter as he gazed down at her, feeling her love reach out to him. 'Was ever a man plagued with such a woman? If I went without you, I suppose you would follow?'

Gladly she gave herself up to the wild singing in her blood, forgetting everything but this wondrous feeling between them. It seemed that each time they loved, it grew stronger and stronger, bonding them more tightly. Of late it had become not just a physical experience, but also a spiritual one. They were as one in heart, mind and body, so close that they could anticipate each other's thoughts and desires without needing to speak. It was a union that would give them both the strength to go on, no matter what lay ahead.

Afterwards, when Gérard lay at peace against her breast, Annelise lay staring into the darkness. Like her husband, she believed that the troubles had only just begun. France would run with blood before the madness had passed, but they would survive it together.

She touched her lips to the dark head on the pillow beside her, murmuring a prayer. 'May God protect you always, my love,' she whispered. 'Whatever the future brings, I shall always be beside you...'

# CHAPTER TWELVE

ANNELISE BUNDLED her embroidery beneath a cushion as she heard her husband's voice in the hall. She did not want him to see the tiny garment she was making. She had not told him that she was with child, because she knew that he would insist that she return to the château immediately.

They had been in Paris this time for only a few days, but the past two and a half years or so had been spent travelling backwards and forwards to the capital. After the King's return to Paris in October 1789, the situation had quietened considerably. It was still a very tense time, with patrols of citizens in the streets and new regulations almost weekly from the Commune, but life had been bearable for those who really wished to see a new constitution.

Gérard spoke often in the Assembly, and Annelise knew that he had made many enemies on both sides of the house by his outspokenness. When the King had tried to escape in June of 1791, getting only as far as Varennes, because of a series of mishaps, Gérard had condemned the flight as foolishness, yet he had fought against the republican movement. He had been one of those who persuaded His Majesty to apologise for his action, at the same time pointing out to his fellow members of the Assembly that dethronement would invite foreign attack and destroy the new constitution, towards which they had all been working for many months.

'When I think of all he has thrown away!' Gérard exclaimed to Annelise when the King was brought back to Paris, a prisoner once more. 'If only he had been patient for a few more months. I'm sure we were winning...'

The atmosphere in the capital over a period of thirty-six hours had been fraught with tension, as the people of Paris awaited an attack from foreign invaders. With the news of the King's capture, fear gave way to resentment. A rumour that His Majesty had been kidnapped was accepted by both the Assembly and the Commune. Only Robespierre of the Jacobin Club was heard to challenge it. It was decreed that the royal family must be better protected, but the people murmured among themselves that this was the third time in two years that Louis had returned to Paris as a prisoner.

Still more instances of the King's betrayal were found in a letter he had left in trust as an address to the people of France. In it, he criticised the constitution to which he had earlier professed loyalty; he complained of his imprisonment; he defended his flight, saying that it was natural for the King to put himself in a place of safety. He also said that it had never been his intention to leave French soil, but only to seek a refuge for his family and a base to oppose any attempt at invasion.

Rumours and counter-rumours abounded. It seemed as if war with the Austrians was imminent, and general opinion was that the King had planned to cross the frontier and return at the head of an Austrian army. To safeguard France, it was decided that the King must be made even more of a prisoner, and that he should not be dethroned—an act that would guarantee an invasion. Yet the denunciation of Louis' conduct was almost universal among all but the most staunch royalists.

Annelise had heard Gérard and André arguing about it fiercely. André had supported the King's flight, insisting that a full restoration of Louis' power was the only way to a return of peace. Gérard, however, while not wishing to see a dethronement, was certain that the King's only option was to come to terms with the people and accept the new constitution.

'If Louis is not careful, he will lose everything,' Annelise had heard him say again and again. 'I tell you, André, there are times when I fear for his life.'

They had argued again, and Gérard's face had been sober when he joined his wife. Annelise knew better than to question him at such moments; he was under a great strain, his personal loyalties conflicting with what he saw to be right.

In July of that year there were demonstrations in favour of republicanism, together with celebrations for the anniversary of the fall of the Bastille, held at the Champ-de-Mars, leading at the end of the day to a massacre of defenceless citizens. The Queen wrote a letter to the leaders of those who had marched on the holiday crowd, telling of her delight in the way they had upheld the monarchy. During the following days, citizens were arrested for insulting remarks against Lafayette and the National Guard. Many leading figures of the revolution were denounced and arrested in the name of the public good.

In August, a counter-revolutionary army led by royalist nobles wearing white cockades met near Nîmes and swore to reinstate His Majesty, and there were risings up and down the country. Gérard suspected that his best friend had been among those nobles. He said very little, but Annelise knew it had worried him deeply.

'Can they not see that we must go forward, not back?' he asked, his face grey with tiredness as he paced the room. 'Do they really want civil war? And André... How could he have been such a fool as to join them? He said he believed in the new constitution.'

Annelise merely nodded, feeling hurt by this dissent between the two men. André felt, as many other nobles, that things had gone too far; he was not able to accept much that Gérard saw as right and fair. The strain was affecting their friendship, pushing them further and further apart—and it was hurting Gérard.

In September of 1791 the King had finally approved the constitution without amendments, but it was too late to stop the spread of distrust and discontent. A new Legislative Assembly had been formed, and the new age had begun. Yet nothing had really changed. There were still plots and counter-plots as the autumn turned to winter, and the year ended much as it had begun. By the beginning of the new year there was a new menace.

'I can only describe it as war-fever,' Gérard said to his wife. 'As much as I hate to agree with Robespierre and his friends, I can only say I think it madness.'

'Yet if, as André says, the King believes it necessary...' Annelise ventured.

Gérard's mouth hardened. 'You should not listen to André. He is too much influenced by royalist views.'

Robespierre had declared that the idea of war as put forward by the royalist party was not a war of liberation but a war waged by a despot against foreigners, priests and émigrés. It was a means of restoring the old order. Others were sure that once the French army crossed the Rhine, they would be acclaimed by the oppressed subjects of western Germany as deliverers.

Annelise neither knew nor cared which view was right. It was obvious that her husband was caught up in a struggle he could not win. His principles were too high; his sense of justice too strong to find approval on either side. To the royalists, he was a reformer who had betrayed his own class; to those extremists who wished to see Louis dethroned, he was an enemy. His voice was one of reason in the midst of madness. He would need to be silenced.

André had warned her of the growing danger in which he stood. 'You should make him go home,' he said, when she asked for his advice. 'Make him stay at the château, or, better still, go to England for a while.'

'You know he would never desert his duty, André.' She looked at him anxiously. 'Do you really believe he may be in danger?'

He hesitated for a moment before replying, then said, 'Yes, Annelise, I do. For your sake and his, I'm warning you. Make him leave Paris.'

It was of course impossible. Gérard had fought too hard and too long to give up the struggle. She had not even put the suggestion to him. Now it was spring and she knew that a declaration of war was imminent—a war against which Gérard had fought with all his strength.

Looking up as her husband came into the room now, Annelise smiled lovingly. 'How good it is to have you home early,' she said, her heart missing a beat as she saw the look on his face. She got to her feet and moved quickly towards him. 'What is wrong, Gérard?'

'It is the end, Annelise,' he said, sighing. 'You may order your maids to pack. We shall return to the château in the morning.'

'War has been declared,' she cried. 'Oh, Gérard, after all your work!'

He took her in his arms, stroking her cheek with his fingertips. 'If that were all, I could accept defeat, but I fear the consequences. The King has refused to listen to those who advised him against this war, and in doing so he has sealed his own fate. It will, I believe, lead to his downfall.'

'Is there nothing more you can do?'

'His Majesty has been pleased to say that he will see me no more. Indeed, he is so closely guarded now that it is almost impossible to gain entrance to the royal apartments.' He frowned. 'France is now in the hands of extremists on both sides. I think it is time for us to leave, my love.'

'Leave France?' She looked at him in surprise. 'Are you sure? Perhaps you are just tired?'

'No. I have been thinking of you, Annelise. What kind of a life is this for you?' He smiled as he touched her lips with his own. 'In England, we could live comfortably again. You could entertain, and forget politics.'

'Do not desert your principles for my sake, Gérard.'

'I have fought honourably,' he said with a wry smile. 'Now I honestly feel that I can do no more. Besides, it is better that you should have peace when our child is born.'

'So you knew?' She laughed a little self-consciously. 'I was afraid you would send me back to the château.'

He shook his head, bending to kiss her. 'You are my strength and my love. I could not bear to be parted from you now. We shall go to England together.'

'I'll tell the servants to be ready to leave first thing in the morning.'

'No. I must make one last speech in the Assembly. I shall return at noon, and we shall leave immediately.'

Annelise nodded, feeling a surge of happiness. 'As you wish, Gérard. A few hours can make little difference...'

'That small box will go in the carriage with me. It is a present for Jean...' In the midst of the confusion of packing, Annelise looked up as a visitor was shown into the salon. She smiled as she saw him. 'Forgive all this confusion, André. We are returning to the château today.'

'Not before time.' André's face was grave, sending a little chill down her spine. 'I came to warn Gérard that he must leave Paris at once.'

'What is wrong?' She stared at him in concern. 'He is making his farewell speech at the Assembly...'

'He is there now?' André's eyes narrowed. 'Then I must go immediately—his life is in danger. I have been warned that he is to be assassinated!'

Annelise drew a sharp breath, her hand flying to her mouth. 'No! Who told you this?'

'Do you remember Hubert Grosard?' he asked, nodding as she frowned. 'These days he is a prominent member of the Jacobin Club. He told me that Gérard is considered too dangerous. He is to be set upon and killed as he leaves the Assembly. It will be made to appear the work of cut-throats and thieves, but it is really his political enemies who have planned the attack.'

'Why should that man help us?'

'He considered it his duty because Gérard helped Thérèse. Your husband's life is most certainly in danger.'

'You must warn him,' Annelise begged. 'Please, André, go at once!'

'You must leave Paris now,' André said. 'You too may be in danger, for there are those who would not hesitate to use you if their first plan failed. You have a small army of servants. Make sure they are well armed and that they do not hesitate to fight if need be.'

'I cannot desert Gérard...' she began, but he silenced her with a look.

I have friends who will see that no harm comes to him. You must do as I say, Annelise. Gérard will not leave Paris unless he knows you are safe. If you stay, you will be putting his life at risk.'

'Then I must do as you say.'

André smiled at her. 'Trust me, Annelise. Gérard and I may have had our differences of late, but he is still my friend.'

'Of course I trust you,' she said. 'It's just that I love him so very much.'

'I know. And because you love him, you must leave Paris now. Leave what is not packed. Go now, while you still can!'

Gérard bowed to the silent Assembly. He had delivered a last stinging speech, denouncing the war. Now he let his eyes travel slowly round the room, lingering on the faces of the men he knew so well. Some were friends who thought much as he did, though they might not say so openly; others were enemies who hated everything he stood for. Soon, he believed, these men would rule in France. It was time to leave now, before the destruction began.

'And so, messieurs, I bid you farewell,' he said. 'Make of France what you will—and history will make what it will of you . . .'

He felt their eyes stabbing him as he left his seat and walked unhurriedly down the aisle towards the door. The silence was broken now by a few whispers and some coughing. Just before he reached the exit, he paused, raising his gaze to the gallery where Robespierre sat. For one moment their eyes met and held; then Robespierre inclined his head in silent acknowledgement.

Moving on, out into the fresh air, Gérard drew a deep breath. He felt suddenly free of a tremendous burden. His duty was done. He had done everything in his power for his country; for the moment there was nothing more he could do. It was time to devote himself to his beloved wife, who had stood by him so steadfastly these past years. Perhaps, one day, he would be able to return...

He walked unhurriedly towards the hostelry where he had left his horse, relaxing as he felt the warmth of the spring sunshine on his face. It was good to be alive!

Suddenly he became aware of danger. Turning swiftly, he saw four men closing in on him. From the menace in their faces, he knew immediately that their business was murder. Drawing his sword, he held it at the ready.

'Come then, messieurs,' he cried, his eyes glinting. 'The odds are fair enough...'

They rushed at him all at once, but he brought his sword round in a swift circle, making each one draw back as his blade skimmed their stomachs. Looking at one another, they hesitated, none of them prepared to be the first to die.

'Shame, my brave citizens,' he goaded. 'Have none of you the courage to face me?'

One of them made a flurry at him, but Gérard's blade crossed, flicked and twisted, disarming the impetuous assassin easily. Then, as the others made a rush forward, a troop of some ten horsemen galloped into the street. They rode towards the assassins, sending them fleeing, and he sheathed his sword, grinning as the leader dismounted and came to meet him.

'What, would you spoil my fun?' he cried. 'Ten of you—against so few? I fear you are not a sportsman, my friend.'

André laughed. 'I should have known you were more than a match for them, Gérard, yet there may be another attempt if you tarry. I have sent Annelise on ahead. I shall ride with you myself—if you will have me?'

'If, André?' Gérard questioned with a lift of his brows. 'Our hearts are not so far apart that you need ask, are they?'

'No.' André smiled, and offered his hand. 'If I have offended you by my loyalty to His Majesty, I ask you to understand, Gérard. I know he is often weak—and even foolish—but I love him dearly. Right or wrong, I shall always defend him. I have put his cause above my love for Marielle. If I were wise I would go with you now to England and marry her.'

'Will you not do so?'

'While Louis lives, I must remain. I admit it is foolish, but I have vowed never to desert him.'

'Then I can only wish you good fortune, my friend.' Gérard clasped his hand. 'Ride with me to the château. It may be some time before we meet again...'

Annelise stood looking at the receding shores of France, feeling a deep sadness at leaving the country that had become home to her. She sighed, then turned her head and smiled as her husband put his arms about her, leaning his cheek against her.

'Shall we ever be able to return?' she asked.

'Perhaps.' He moved his lips against her hair. 'It may be that I shall have to.'

'What do you mean?' She turned in his arms to look at him. 'You would not go without me?'

'Only if André's life were in danger.' He gazed down at her, a little smile playing about his mouth. 'Do you remember the day you left Paris with Hélène?'

'Yes.' She was puzzled. 'Why?'

'Your keen eyes pierced André's disguise at the barriers. I remember he was quite piqued because you did not also recognise me...'

'*You?*' Annelise stared at him. 'Were you there?'

Gérard grinned, his eyes bright with mischief. 'Had you no pity for the poor old man who drove the food-cart that followed you?'

'That was...' She opened her eyes wide with astonishment. 'You were a member of André's band?'

'It was I who thought of it.' Gérard nodded as a look of incredulity dawned in her eyes, to be replaced by sudden understanding. 'The man you helped to save was worthy of the risk. There are still honest, decent men in Paris, Annelise. I have no quarrel with them. Although I believe their cause is lost, I honour them for fighting on. The King is misguided and weak, but I would not see him harmed—nor many who have been my friends. It is my intention to form a small group of like-minded men who are willing to follow when I call. If ever there is a need, we shall return to help those in danger.'

Annelise suppressed a tiny shiver of fear as she looked up into the face of her beloved husband. 'You will do what you must, Gérard,' she whispered. 'I shall pray that you will never again be called upon to risk your life as you did that day at the barriers.'

'Sometimes it is necessary to risk all for the sake of love and liberty,' he said, touching her cheek. 'I knew my life was worth nothing if I stayed in France now, but the fight will go on. One day France will be a country to be proud of again, and if I can do more by working in secret, then I must learn to change my ways.'

'Oh, Gérard,' she choked, her throat tight with emotion. 'I should have guessed. I should have known that you would never give in...'

Suddenly she was laughing through her tears. Her husband was a good, brave man and she was proud of him. No matter what the future held for them, she would never be afraid.

Gérard kissed her tenderly. 'Let's join Jean and the others below,' he said with a smile. 'I think there may be a storm coming...'

# This Christmas Temptation Is Irresistible

Our scintillating selection makes an ideal Christmas gift. These four new novels by popular authors are only available in this gift pack. They're tempting, sensual romances created especially to satisfy the desires of today's woman and at this fantastic price you can even treat yourself!

CARDINAL RULES — *Barbara Delinsky*
A WEDDING GIFT — *Kristin James*
SUMMER WINE — *Ethel Paquin*
HOME FIRES — *Candace Schuler*

Give in to Temptation this Christmas.
Available November 1988 Price: £5.00

# A WORLD WHERE PASSION AND DESIRE ARE FUSED

CRYSTAL FLAME — *Jayne Ann Krentz*  £2.95
He was fire — she was ice — together their passion was a crystal flame. An exceptional story entwining romance with the excitement of fantasy.

PINECONES AND ORCHIDS — *Suzanne Ellison*  £2.50
Tension and emotion lie just below the surface in this outstanding novel of love and loyalty.

BY ANY OTHER NAME — *Jeanne Triner*  £2.50
Money, charm, sophistication, Whitney had it all, so why return to her past? The mystery that surrounds her is revealed in this moving romance.

These three new titles will be out in bookshops from October 1988.

## W●RLDWIDE